YOGA
A Love Story

Douglas W. Davis is a writer, father, husband and a constant spiritual seeker. He has a passion for Eastern and Western religions, particularly in learning how they are intertwined. He currently resides in Los Angeles, California, with his family and two poodles. His lifelong goal is to unite all religious and spiritual seekers by revealing how they all stem from the same tree.

YOGA
A Love Story

DOUGLAS W. DAVIS

RUPA

Published by
Rupa Publications India Pvt. Ltd 2021
7/16, Ansari Road, Daryaganj
New Delhi 110002

Sales centres:
Allahabad Bengaluru Chennai
Hyderabad Jaipur Kathmandu
Kolkata Mumbai

This is a work of fiction. Names, characters, places and incidents are either the
product of the author's imagination or are used fictitiously and any resemblance
to any actual person, living or dead, events or locales is entirely coincidental.

ISBN: 978-93-90260-20-1

First impression 2021

10 9 8 7 6 5 4 3 2 1

The moral right of the author has been asserted.

Printed at Thomson Press India Ltd, Faridabad

This book is dedicated to my father, George, and my mother, Shirlee,
for igniting the flame within me.
And also to my wife, Alexis, and son, Nathaniel,
for stoking it further.
Alexis, you are my real-life Aanya—soulmate and
partner of many lifetimes.
Nathaniel, you are my solar guide,
pushing me constantly to new vistas and challenges.

Contents

Prologue

This is my story in all its nakedness. It is the truth as much as I remember it. I tell you this because it's been many years since it occurred and sometimes, even I don't believe that it happened. Yet, it did. All of the mystical, magical details are true. I either experienced them directly or witnessed them with my own eyes. They include things I never imagined were possible and are based upon that one true thing I know in my heart is always possible... LOVE. Love conquers all. It beats evil. It beats selfishness and it rules our universe and beyond. I implore all of you—from the atheists to the agnostics to the recalcitrant adherents—open your hearts. Whether you believe in the being that many call God or not, it is real. Its principles of ever expansion and love permeate the earth. The quicker you accept it, the sooner your life will be enriched in ways beyond measure. I was compelled to tell my story for all those like me. All Resonance Seekers out there, who are longing for that ineffable something to make their lives complete—it does exist. Some call it God, others call it Allah, Jehovah, Brahma, Vishnu, Shiva, the Universal truth... I prefer to call it simply 'The One'. It is the vivifying source underlying all sentient beings and all existence. It is Atman. Please reach out for this source. The call is always answered. You will find, as I did, that this energy is within you and without. It is ubiquitous. As I said, this is my story and it is to be enjoyed even if not believed...

1

Beginnings

I am a shoot from the blessed tree. The three previous generations of Asanga men, including my father, were born with signs that portended greatness—moments such as 7.00 a.m. on the seventh day of the seventh month. Devas and other creatures of the heavenly realm flitted and flirted about to celebrate their entrance into this world. Yet, unlike my forefathers, I, John Yogacara Asanga, had an inauspicious birth. I was born on Sunday, 13 September 1970, in Kokomo, Indiana, at the Grissom Air Force Base. My mother, Carrie, did not have a particularly long or difficult labour. Her water broke at eleven in the morning and I arrived at 7.00 p.m. on the dot in a typical Air Force hospital. The nuns wrapped me in a green flannel blanket and gave me to my proud father to hold—just like any other military dependent. My dad, Harry, as was the custom among the officers, showed up at the hospital right before the birth, hugged his wife, held his newborn son and quickly returned to duty. Yes, my birth was not propitious, but I knew that someday, like the lotus, I would emerge from my muddy origins and blossom into a brilliant flower that was truly something to behold.

My father was an aviator and weather scientist for the Air Force. If he had his way, he would have flown as close to the stars as humanly possible. My mother was his wife, yet his first and truest love was the sky. As part of his job, he tracked hurricanes, tornadoes, cyclones and just about any other crazy weather scenario imaginable. He would fly right into the eye of a hurricane to better understand the forces of nature. 'Grace under pressure,' he once advised me. 'Men of consequence know that life comes down to those who flourish when the pressure is the greatest.'

My mom was a woman for her time. She played down her superior intelligence and preferred to conduct things behind the scenes. She argued toe to toe with my father about many things, including politics, philosophy, current events and how I should be raised—culturally and with regard to my education. However, she never contradicted him in public. She supported her man. She loved her man. She bravely chose to marry outside of her race at a time when it was rare and she wore the pride of her decision with her at all times. She stood about 5'3" and weighed 110 lb. She was naturally vivacious and simply beautiful with her olive skin, auburn hair and hazel eyes. She believed strongly in the Catholic Church and would try to drag me to church with her every Sunday, but after a few masses, I decided that I would rather watch corn sweat than take my place in a pew for an hour, standing, sitting and kneeling on cue. In reality, Catholics scared me. The Gregorian chants sounded more like the background score of Vincent Price movies to me; I kept waiting for Dracula to appear. The sullen-faced priests mumbled incomprehensible Latin phrases designed rather to conjure the dead, than invigorate the living. I convinced my father to save me, and Sunday mornings became our time. He would take me out on his crop-dusting plane, and we would have fun buzzing the cornfields and riling up bulls.

Those Sunday mornings became indelible memories. Dad would break all the normal rules of flight. Only fighter jets are equipped to do complete verticals, but he figured out how to gain sufficient speed in our rickety crop duster to fly at about 80 degree without the plane stalling. Once we reached this peak angle, he would ease up on the throttle and let the plane waft gently down until we were skimming the very tops of the pines. It was exhilarating—my heartbeat oscillated between my throat and the pit of my stomach with each undulation.

'John, I'm not doing this just to make you sick,' he'd announce. 'I want you to understand that life is all about tests. You are only alive when you are closest to death. When that moment comes, what will you do? Will you recoil in fear or will you risk death to truly feel alive?'

Sunday, 11 September 1977. It was two days before my seventh birthday. We went out for an hour-long flight, just before sunset. The sky was a haze of burnt orange and seemed to spread out forever beyond the windscreen. I loved looking down at the chequerboard fields and the lazy cows grazing far below. Dad came alive behind the throttle of a plane. He held the throttle firmly with his right hand. He flipped the other instruments deftly with his left. He didn't fly with a bomber jacket on—too clichéd. He wore an old weather-beaten brown leather jacket instead—one of the few remnants from India that he kept. I can still see his strong, handsome face with coffee-and-cream coloured skin, a long aquiline nose, high cheek bones and deep dark eyes, which seemed to hold within the mysteries of the skies and the seas. I peered into those eyes and could see the key to the universe. I lose myself in his eyes, even to this day.

Dad was a methodical pilot. He started the plane the same way each time—'First Step, seatbelts on.' 'Check,' I responded. 'Second, Fuel Indicator.' 'Fuel is full,' I chimed. 'Third, Circuit Breakers.' 'BCN Pitot, Strobe Lights, Flap, Instruments LTS, Nav Dome, Radios one and two, Check, check, check, check,

check, check, check and check,' I responded dutifully. He would never take off unless I responded to all of his enquiries. He proceeded down the runway gathering speed. We went from zero to sixty-three mph in about five seconds. As we hit sixty mph, the plane began to separate from the ground. I could not see the instruments, but I knew our sound progression just before take-off. *Varooom, roomm*, then a higher pitched *varoom, rooomm, rooomm, clunk, clunk* as the wheels folded in right as we left the ground and then the engine calmed to a tiger's chuff of *gggaaah*, a constant *gggaaah* so long as we maintained that altitude. The feeling when one reaches the clouds in a prop plane is akin to being at the top of a rollercoaster ride. You know you are defying gravity, but you feel as if at any moment you could come barrelling back to the ground.

Suddenly, a little while after take-off, he gathered speed and pulled us up to a crazy vertical angle that must have been almost 90 degree. We turned over and began a steep descent. Our speed increased with every second and the whirring of the engine grew steadily louder as we plunged towards the ground.

Dad turned to me and yelled in a booming yet preternaturally calm voice, 'Son, we have thirty seconds before crashing unless you can pull the throttle up. Do it now!'

I pulled it as hard as I could, yet we still headed downwards. 'Dad, I can't do it!' He continued to face forwards, unmoving. 'Twenty seconds left. Figure it out or prepare to die,' was his only response.

I held the throttle forward, almost breaking it, but kept it there using all my strength. 'Fifteen seconds.' The picturesque chequerboard fields blurred into a noxious blur of hues that I imagined would be our grave until, at 1,000 feet, the plane finally started pulling out of its descent. Shaking with fear, sick with adrenaline, my pressure on the throttle was finally causing the plane to change its angle, but would we pull out soon enough to avoid crashing? At about 50 feet, Dad said, 'This is it. Don't quit. Don't quit!' I kept my hand on the throttle fighting against the pressure. It took all the strength my tiny arm could muster, but I did it. I held strong at 40 feet...30 feet...20 feet—undaunted until magically, we began to complete our angle shift, buzzing the cornfield with all of the 15 feet to spare.

Neither of us spoke for some time. 'Now you know,' Dad finally said, 'you stood up to the moment. People place too much importance on living and dying. If we had died without fear, we would still have lived a glorious life. In my life, I have faced innumerable storms. I am a storm chaser: that's my job. It never gets easier. Each one brings unique challenges, because each storm is its own story. Some are huge with voracious winds. Some are small but carry life-threatening whirlwinds. But inside every eye, you can feel the steadiness of God and you ask yourself how something so beautiful, so calm and so still could wreak such havoc. Life is a mystery, constantly unfolding. Never run from the storm, son. Always go towards it. The truth is in the eye of every storm.'

I sat there, shaking and sweating. Swallowing, I confessed, 'Dad, I'm not quite seven yet, I'm not so brave.' I looked down, red with shame, at my knees. 'I think I peed my pants.'

He laughed and clasped me by the shoulder. 'Being aware of your fear is not the same as succumbing to it. I know that you will live a life, resplendent, chasing many storms.'

Climbing down from the plane, I realized that I had never appreciated setting foot on land as much as I did at that moment. Dad was right. There is something about the imminence of death that is clarifying. I had witnessed my father from an angle I never thought possible, and I now saw myself as different, confident and capable of withstanding any challenge. Not quite seven, but already almost a man.

2

Primary Lessons

My early years were typically Indianan. Hot summers, cold winters and rubbing shoulders with the salt-of-the-earth locals. However, I felt they didn't really accept me—they merely tolerated me. I was always the 'half-Indian' boy, not just another one of the kids.

My schoolmates and the Kokomoans, or the townsfolk as my dad called them, were not quite so placid. They, for the most part, weren't bad people; in fact, many were quite welcoming. Yet, despite their good intentions, I never felt like a part of the community. There was always a distance between us that could not be encroached. The simple fact of the matter was that I did not look like the others. I was dark-skinned, like some of the black kids, but my hair was straighter than the white kids. I was singled out in class frequently as an example of someone 'different'.

It seemed like every year, some new kid would bring up the fact that I was the kind of Indian that played a flute and lured snakes out of a basket, not the 'woo woo' kind of Indian who fought cowboys. The moniker 'Turban boy' was the inevitable end point of the screed, usually with great yucks from the others. *Turban boy, Turban boy, da da da da da*, I heard as they ran around an imaginary pot with flutes in hand, waiting fruitlessly for the snakes to rise. When we read *The Jungle Book*, everyone wanted to know if I had a pet tiger. I fervently wished that I did, so that

I could set it loose on the boys who frequently referred to me as 'Punjab diaper head'.

Grammar school was alternatively bucolic and restive. Although I enjoyed the beautiful countryside of Indiana, I still longed for the company of those more like me. Walking to school on warm fall days, I would pretend to follow the yellow brick road, the carpet of leaves of lush colours burnished from deep red to bold magenta, dusky orange to cobalt blue black, and burnt amber to chocolate brown.

I particularly remember the clouds. On bright summer days, I could easily lose hours simply lying on my back at the playground looking up at the beautiful heavens, imagining that the gigantic cumulonimbus clouds were the living quarters of the gods. Zeus's house was large and sturdy in the middle, but with a soft pillow, where he slept on the far side. The cloud of the angels was equally large, but had wings on both sides and a landing strip in the middle so they could take off and land with ease. One cloud looked exactly like the strong face in profile of my mom's dad, Papa, his regal nose angled towards the horizon. He had told me that he would always watch over me after he was gone. This cloud seemed to me to be living proof of his promise.

I knew that I was different, and that people would tease me for that reason. I think what really bothered me most was the lack of love. When teachers and other adults in my community looked at me, they exuded a benign yet shallow tolerance of my being. Love is projected at a much deeper level, an immanent outpouring of emotion that can't be faked. You can give alms to the poor and make grand statements about all the right causes, yet still hold them at arm's length. Love is what you give with your entire soul: a heartfelt hug, a knowing smile, a quick straightening of the tie.

Perhaps, my difficulty in making friends was not based on the colour of my skin, but on the contents of my brain. I was smart. When we lined up in maths class to recite our tables, I was the fastest draw around, glibly retorting with the correct answer before my opponent could even begin to respond. Soon, the other smart kids recognized that I was one of their own. There was a black boy named Stewart whose father was a Colonel; he never let us forget that. There were three white kids, Lucy, Charles and James; Lucy was so pretty with her azure blue eyes and sandy blonde hair, while Charles was very proper, and James was the son of a minister. I think he may have been English. I believe Teddy was Italian—his hair was dark black, his eyes deep-set and his skin a creamy light brown. Maggie's dad was white, but her mom was Panamanian. I was the only Indian boy in Indiana.

3

Ladakh

I didn't know my father's full story until the age of twelve, when I spent six glorious weeks during the summer holidays in Ladakh, India. Known as the land of high passes, Ladakh borders the Himalayas and lies at the northern tip of India between Pakistan, Afghanistan, Tibet and China. Historically, it was a site for international trade, with many caravanserais strategically located along the Silk Road. My ancestors had been mystics who attended to the needs of weary travellers as they travelled from Africa and Europe to China. Many believe that the Zoroastrians of the Indus Valley spread the concept of a monotheistic universe; in their turn, the Asanga peoples propagated Yogacaran principles— the seeds of what would become Mahayana Buddhism—to the steady stream of international visitors who came to the caravanserais scattered throughout Ladakh.

We hiked to see some of the old trade roads, the meandering vistas far below us framed by the beautiful Himalayas. I envisioned varied travellers seeking respite from their arduous journeys, wealthy African merchants and European noblemen alike seated around fires with their Indian hosts, drinking strong coffee and even stronger whiskey, regaling each other with tales of glory and dissecting the eternal existential questions of the nature of men, religion and science. In my imagination, the campsites consisted of billowing white tents, lined with colourful Kashmir silk rugs, the air redolent with perfumed incense and a hint of sage, frankincense and myrrh.

My paternal uncle, Justa, whose name matched his fiery personality, was my guide to all things Ladakh and my father, Gandahara Lama Asanga, whose 'Anglo' name was Harry. I listened enthralled as he told me that Gandahara was born precisely at 7.00 a.m. on 7 July 1943, at the best hospital in Purushapura, in what would later become Pakistan in 1947. The Asangas had left Pakistan in 1946, before the Partition, as the elders knew change was coming. There were already signs that intellectuals, Buddhists and Hindus would no longer be looked upon with favour in the new land of Pakistan. Our family first moved to Jammu, an Indian Hindu stronghold just across the border, and then to Ladakh. Here, we prospered, immediately accepted as part of the Buddhist community due to our noble birth and heritage as direct descendants of the eponymous saint Asanga.

When Gandahara was born, it was deemed to be a wondrous gift. His birth was heralded as the coming of a *tulku*—the reincarnation of the bodhisattva Asanga. It was obvious that he was destined for greatness, and although his father, grandfather and great grandfather had all been yogis of major significance, Gandahara was expected to surpass them. However, he wanted no part of the destiny bestowed upon him. He respected Buddhism and was a dutiful adherent of the faith, yet math and engineering were his foremost loves, and science his only god.

As we paused in the shade of a rocky crag, I asked Uncle Justa to tell me more about my father's religious significance in Buddhism. Looking away from me, out over the valley, he confessed, 'Gandahara is very special. He sees things that others simply cannot. He has what you might call a direct line to the heavenly realm of Naha and Maitreya.' I listened closely, hanging on to every word, captivated as Uncle Justa described the many miracles performed by my father.

'During one of the worst monsoons in years, Gandahara saw a man drowning in the turbulent waters of the Chenab. He walked through the flooding waters that reached his neck. Upon reaching the man who was flailing in the water, Gandahara grabbed his hand and said, "Look into my eyes. The same father that lives in me, that same vivifying source lives in you, too. Hold my hand, rise and let's walk together out of this morass." The man held on to Gandahara's hand with a death grip. They walked out of the water, together, to safety.

'Once, Gandahara came upon a very sick man. His body was covered in sores. Flies ate at his oozing skin. Gandahara clasped the man's hand with both of his and told him, "Rise and fulfil the destiny for which you were born, for this is not it."

'The leper was healed with a simple touch of Gandahara's hand.' Justa exclaimed.

'Once, he had climbed one of the Himalayas barefoot and fasted at the peak of the mountain for a week without food or water.' Uncle Justa claimed he had returned home on a cloud, accompanied by the bodhisattva Natha. It was shortly after this incident that Gandahara was decreed the embodiment of Maitreya, the future Buddha who will achieve enlightenment and bring dharma to the world.

I didn't necessarily believe Uncle Justa's story of Dad descending from the clouds, but I still enjoyed it. People always think that when someone gives you the bare bones of a story, they are telling you the truth. However, all they can really give you is their particular perspective, their vision of the world. I have always been far more interested in the embellishments, the lies and the phantasmagoric. When people share their fantasies, their hearts sing. They reveal their Akashic memories from hundreds of lifetimes ago, back before modern civilization, to the unfettered creativity that abounded in the times of Atlantis, Olympus, Chiron, chimeras and heretics who flew too close to the sun. God deemed that men could not handle these powers and wiped them out in the Great Flood so man could start anew.

'Unfortunately,' Uncle Justa went on, his dusty forehead wrinkling in disappointment, 'there was one incident that changed Gandahara, I think forever. Gandahara had always been smart, excelling at everything, including his lessons. Our father brought in an Englishman to tutor us, believing as he did that, as Brahmin's children, we deserved only the best. However, the teacher was good, but not great, and Gandahara quickly outgrew him intellectually.'

The tutor convinced my grandfather to send Gandahara to a nearby university to challenge the young man. But it was more than a challenge; the English could not abide an Indian knowing more than the instructors, and Gandahara was regularly humiliated. I listened, horrified, as Uncle Justa described my father being taunted, called 'Punjab' and forced to live with the untouchables near the campus. 'They told him that no Indian could ever outshine an Englishman,' he informed me, with echoes of long-remembered pain evident in his voice.

Soon after this, Gandahara left school and rejected anything Indian or Hindu. He changed his name to Harry and submerged himself in his studies, with the goal of attending Oxford and proving his intellectual superiority to the British once and for all. It was at Oxford that he met a beautiful American woman with whom he fell in love. She calmed his fury with her grace and loved him for who he was, making no requirements that he be a proper Englishman. At this, I smiled, thinking of my kind and beautiful mother, the American cowgirl who had saved my father. After obtaining a doctorate in astrophysics, Gandahara taught at Harvard and became an esteemed member of the United States Air Force. 'He means well, but the rest of them are probably developing bombs that will kill half the world's population, those bastards,' Uncle Justa spat, twisting his face in disgust.

Fortunately, we changed the subject and the rest of our hike passed in pleasant conversation. At the end of the trail, Uncle Justa led me into a gleaming red-and-gold temple with walls covered in rare and precious gems. Inside, it was dim and cool, a quiet peaceful haven from the blazing sun. Here, he taught me the art of meditation. 'Just be,' he said. 'Block everything else out of your mind and just live in the present. You will find that God is there waiting for you, outside of time, an entity of pure existence, unqualified and still. He has been inside of you, all along. Once you learn to still your mind, all things will be revealed. You will discover that we are all one interconnected being. We are all simply love.'

4

Fidelity

Always part of the same social circle in grade school, Lucy, James and I quickly became best friends. James was like no one either Lucy or I had ever met before—passionate and somewhat single-minded in his faith. On the first day of junior high, all three of us were sent to the principal's office. James was there because he had demanded a clarification regarding the Pledge of Allegiance. He reminded everyone that he was the only son of a minister, and therefore, refused to recite the pledge with everyone else until he knew which god they were praying to. In front of the class, he yelled that he would not be damned by praying to a false god. Our homeroom teacher, a battle-hardened veteran of innumerable seventh-grade classes—known as Mrs Haversham, was not buying that sort of stunt on the first day of class. In her experience, she knew that any mustangs in her herd must be gelded right away if they showed signs of threatening her absolute authority. To a wave of restrained amusement and some quietly sardonic neighing, she announced to us all that 'wild horses are not welcome in my class until they learn appropriate behaviour'.

The last year of middle school had not curbed Lucy and I, nor our talent for irking those in authority. In our literature class, Mrs Haversham began by giving us a short lecture on the book we would be studying in our first semester, *Le Morte d'Arthur* by Sir Thomas Malory. It was a collection of tales concerning

King Arthur and the Knights of the Round Table. However, Mrs Haversham soon irritated Lucy's preternaturally keen sense of justice when she ruled that Princess Guinevere's lack of fidelity had been the supervening event that led to King Arthur's tragic death. Upon hearing this, Lucy angrily rebutted, 'Yeah, right, it's always the woman, isn't it?' This earned her a one-way ticket to see Principal McMullen. I, in turn, quickly followed after an existential outburst in which I rambled about the meaning of fidelity and objective truth; after all, Guinevere and Sir Lancelot were simply living their own truths. However, in hindsight, it was perhaps my somewhat crude statement 'I'm not surprised Guinevere threw down for Lancelot after he unlocked those ridiculous metal panties she was forced to wear,' that resulted in Mrs Haversham personally frog-marching me to McMullen's office.

No strangers to the principal's office, the three of us sat uncomfortably in a row of cheap plastic chairs outside McMullen's door. It was almost lunch period before the great man himself finally deigned to let us in. On par with his self-important temperament, his office was designed to intimidate, with a giant dark oak desk placed front and centre in the room, behind which he sat enthroned in a large black leather chair, exuding the smell of authority. The many plaques affixed to the wall behind the desk seemed to evidence a lifetime of learning and the aura of power. However, on closer inspection, the plaques from Michigan, Harvard and yet another from Stanford were, I thought, probably from seminars. None looked like actual diplomas.

There was a moment of silence in which we three students stood awkwardly in front of the desk while McMullen examined us. 'So, I see that you three are this year's triumvirate of teen troublemakers,' he finally stated, the alliteration rolling off his tongue, his eyes sliding from one to the next in disdain. We continued to stand there in silence. 'Every year,' he continued, 'there are a few students who think they can bend this school to their will.' Suddenly, he smacked his fist down hard on the wooden surface of the desk, causing us all to jump in surprise. '*Veritate et Justitia*... Truth and Justice! That is my motto. It's right there on that wall. So, let me tell you this.' His face had turned a mottled shade of purple and I could see that several hairs on his head were plastered to his forehead with what could only be sweat, despite the crisp, cool fall weather. 'The Truth is we don't have the time or patience to deal with your bullshit, and we won't! Those who don't fall in line at this school will thus be subject to my Justice. Get out, and don't grace my presence again.' With that, he looked each of us hard in the eye, gave an impresario-like wave of his hand towards the door, and bellowed, 'LEAVE!'

As there was no point in us returning to class before lunch, Lucy, James and I slowly made our way to the cafeteria. Away from the ominous atmosphere of the principal's office, we were inclined to view the whole episode as a joke. I told the other two what had happened in the classroom after they had left and we were soon falling over ourselves laughing, repeating 'What is fidelity?' in increasingly hysterical tones, first in the voice of Mrs Haversham and then in Latin, with our best attempts at McMullen-esque pomposity. James was the first to declare that he liked the moniker 'the Triumvirate'. Lucy and I agreed, nodding our heads as we found a table and put down our trays. As we prodded with some misgivings at the mashed potatoes the lunch lady had given us, James went on, waving his hands a little wildly for emphasis, 'Hey, I say that if we have to stand for something, let it be fidelity in its truest sense.' He affirmed that one day he would have his own church, and that he would always lead his flock with Truth, the word of God. At this, Lucy laughed and stated she would never be a part of any sexist church that tried to control women with an archaic set of rules. Having decided to change my name to something more exotic and less pedestrian over the summer, I told them, 'Listen, you're going to hear teachers calling me "John". *Fidem!* I'm Carey!' They looked at me, somewhat bemused, but agreed to respect my new moniker.

After school, all three of us stopped by the blue caves on our way home. One of the great things about growing up on an Air Force base is that there are always plenty of abandoned places ripe for exploration. Located about a quarter-mile into the forest that surrounded the flight line, the blue caves were made of agate stone and were rumoured to have been dug out by the Kokomo, the legendary Miami Indian tribe after whom the town was named. Chief Kokomo, in particular, held a special place in my heart. The legends claimed he was a rebel who had been kicked out of the tribe because he refused to follow anyone else's rules. He was also known to have been a huge man and, in light of this fact, I firmly believed that he had dug out the caves' six-foot-high ceilings himself. Over the last few weeks, after my recent trip to India, the caves had become my private meditation spot. Not wanting to appear weird, however, I kept this fact from both of my friends.

In the cool, dim shadowy recesses of the caves, I looked around once again at the gorgeous azure-coloured walls of the caves. I realized with a small electric jolt in the pit of my stomach that they matched Lucy's eyes perfectly. Together, the three of us journeyed further into the network of tunnels, only sitting down once we were in near-complete darkness. It was at that point that my life changed forever. In a solemn whisper, Lucy instructed us to think about what fidelity meant. Her voice echoed around the walls of the cave, reverberating in the gloom, 'I don't mean the truth deemed by society, but how you really want to be. This is our moment of rebirth.' Respectfully, I closed my eyes and then it happened. I head a rustle, a short sharp intake of breath, and then a movement, as Lucy leaned forward and kissed me. Her lips were soft, her breath was sweet, and I was instantly in love.

5

The Furies

The next morning, I was awake and in the shower by 7.20. Mom knocked and asked if everything was okay. I laughed at her tone of voice, which was clearly bemused, even through the door. It was understandable. Normally, I would get up as close to 8.00 a.m. as possible and rush through a military-style shower, taking all of two minutes. I did as Dad had taught me. 'Water and time are two things a man cannot waste. You get in, soap yourself up, rinse and then get out.' But this morning, I had gotten up early and taken my time in the shower. I was determined to make an extra effort to be clean and smell good. My face curved into an uncontrollable grin under the spray as I thought of Lucy. Now, more than ever, I wanted her to know that I was clean, smooth and smart. A man must be clean to show he is organized. Smooth to reveal he is calm through any situation and smart, well, because... I *was* smart.

As I walked to school, I had an extra skip to my stride and the whole world seemed imbued with a beatific glow. Everything was different now. The one thing that I had felt was missing had been found. I was not just accepted, I was loved, and by beautiful Lucy, of all people! I loved this country. I loved Indiana. As I neared the schoolyard, though, my spirits flagged a little. I considered the Triumvirate to be family, and had no idea how James would take the news. None of us had said much to the other after leaving the caves that previous evening, all three of us parting ways in silence once we reached the main street. In noble fashion, I knew that I needed to break it to him myself before he saw Lucy and me together. I was aware that he, much as I did, thought Lucy was a special girl. As his best friend, I had the responsibility of letting him down easy and not gloating in my victory.

'Listen, James,' I practised out loud, pacing back and forth in front of the school fence. 'You need to know the truth. Rest assured, we will always *have* love for you, but Lucy and I are actually *in* love with each other.' No, that was too much, I needed to be subtler. Still nervous and unsure of how I would break the news, I made my way into the school building. Shortly afterwards, I ran into James outside of our lockers around 8.25 a.m., just before the bell rang. At once, I noticed that he looked unusually well-groomed. His jeans had been ironed, and his shirt was neatly tucked in. He looked nothing like the normal James I knew. Nonplussed, I hesitated. Before I could say anything, he came forwards, grabbed me by the shoulder and said, 'Listen, I wanted you to be the first to know that Lucy and I are together. But, don't worry, this won't change anything. We still love you and I don't want you to feel left out.' My heart pounded in my ears as I stood there, completely bewildered. Finally, I managed to find my voice, and gabbling slightly, managed to stammer out, 'What on earth are you talking about, James, and…is that *cologne*?' His face struggling to remain composed, dancing between glee and an attempt to be respectful of my feelings, he went on, 'Lucy and I shared the most marvellous kiss at the cave yesterday, so it's official. We're a thing!'

I couldn't believe what I was hearing. Looking at him with dismay, I exclaimed, 'Have you lost your mind? She kissed *me* at the cave yesterday. *We're* a thing!' The next few seconds were incredibly tense as we both stared at each other in confusion, with the rapidly dawning realization that the other was not lying. Before either of us could regain our wits, Lucy appeared before us smiling, more angelic-looking than ever before, and put her arms around us both. 'Good morning, guys, and how are we today?' Embarrassed beyond belief, we quickly muttered, 'Fine, just fine.' Thankfully, at that excruciating moment, the bell rang, and we quickly made our way to class. As I sat at my desk, completely unaware of what the teacher was saying or even what class I was in, I pondered what had happened. Somehow, Lucy had duped us and managed to kiss us both. Yet, I was sure that James's kiss must have been just a peck on the cheek, not a real kiss like the one she and I had shared. There was no way she could have kissed me like that if she didn't love me... Could she? But if there was going to be a contest for Lucy's affections, it was one I would surely win. I was cleaner, smoother and, of course, smarter than James. Everything indeed was different now.

This was my very first lesson in love. Rule number one: women are always in control and men are merely helpless pawns. From that moment on, my motivation behind every action was to impress Lucy. Would she like these clothes? Did I sound smart when I answered that question? Was it clear that I, and not James, was the alpha male? Lucy, for her part, played the coquette. She'd insist in one breath that she loved us both and that there was no contest and, in the next, inform us airily that the man she'd marry would be charming, athletic, smart and able to provide for their family. Predictably, the game was on. James and I competed on the football field, in the classroom and for sartorial supremacy. Ironically, it actually ended up making us far more attractive to other girls, who began to take notice. 'Cute haircut, Carey', 'Great shoes, James', 'You're so smart!' we'd hear in passing as they tried to stop us in the corridor. But we paid no attention to their flattery as the accolades piled up. We were the top athletes, lead scholars (although Stewart and Maggie might beg to differ), and very popular...all to impress Lucy.

In the end, unbeknownst to me, I failed to make Lucy's cut because of one major flaw. My parents, mostly at my dad's insistence, were not very religious. We believed in a universal force, but due to his Buddhist background, the word 'God' was rarely spoken in our home. In some sense, my dad was still running away from the destiny he had left behind in Jammu as the 'Chosen One'. In contrast, James was a man of God and religion was at the forefront of his life. He never failed to remind us of his destiny as a minister, with the world as his flock. I remember vividly the feeling of my heart cracking and breaking into a million pieces the day Lucy informed me, her blue eyes blinking innocently, that while she loved me and my *joie de vivre*, she loved the stability of James's future career choice even more. My life was definitely going to be more exciting, but she needed to think about building a family. I was not a family guy.

Although I was devastated, in public I pretended to be fine with James and Lucy dating. Even in private, I told myself that she had done me a favour, that I had been freed from the constraints of normalcy. I consoled myself with the thought that I was destined to lead a swashbuckling life on the high seas, adventure my only calling card. With such bitterly romantic thoughts, I masked my inner loneliness with false bravado. Love was for fools. I would play the field and never be tied down. No boring family life for me.

First love is an enthralling, all-encompassing feeling. When requited, it is innervating; on the other hand, unrequited love is the diametric opposite. It takes one to unspeakable depths from which it can take years to recover, if ever. Some never recover and lead bitter, disconnected lives, allowing the protective façade they have created to thicken their skins. For my part, I vowed to never let anyone get that close to me again. There would be no thousand cuts here. Triage. I would stem the bleeding.

As high school continued, I had more than my fair share of relationships. Lucy, James and I remained good friends over the years and, surprisingly, I began to fit in better with my classmates. I intentionally cultivated my image as the exotic, sexy, naïve foreigner all the adventurous girls wanted to date to drive their fathers mad and their future husbands crazy. Still, both they and I knew that these were only fleeting, fun, quick-lived affairs with no real love. Regardless, I managed to get a crazy amount of action, at least by the relatively modest standards of a small town in Indiana in the 1980s. Had I but known of President Clinton's definition of sex back then, life would definitely have been a hell of a lot more interesting.

◈

6

In Transit

Dear Mom,

I'm on a Greyhound bus heading west as I write this. I apologize for not saying goodbye in person, but it would have been too much. It's time for me to move on. Right now, I can't really articulate the reasons why I need to leave. There's an immanent stirring within me that's telling me: 'Time to go, time to meet new challenges, time to stretch and test yourself in the real world.' So, I am off to explore, to grow and evolve into the man you and Dad raised me to be.

Please know that my love for you is always and forever. You have been and are a great mother. My leaving has nothing to do with you. Our family dynamics has changed, and I think it best I give you the space to grow without worrying about me. I need to find myself, and that may entail diving into subterranean areas and doing things that a mom should not see her son doing.

Be happy, Mom. You deserve to be happy. Don't fret about me, I will be fine. You'll see me again sooner than you might think. I hope that when we meet again, I will be a fully formed man. Someone with a wealth of experiences, both good and bad. Someone, perhaps, with a moustache. Someone that will make you proud.

Love, John

Putting my pen down, I carefully folded the letter—one of the most difficult and emotionally wrenching I had ever written—and tucked it safely into its envelope. I would post it after I'd arrived. I glanced out through the bus window next to my seat, staring past my pensive ghostly reflection in the glass. A drive through the countryside can be immensely cathartic. It soothes the mind to see the ever-changing landscape flash past you, especially as a passenger. In the old Western movies I had loved to watch as a kid, they always played the best music as the wagons set out for new vistas. The songs were bold and full of hope and promising new adventures just over the horizon.

But, such songs never told the full story. Maybe a man leaves to start a new life because he came home early and found his wife in bed with his boss. Or even worse, found that his entire family had died in a tragic fire while he was out drinking. Dark thoughts, sad stories that would never sell—but probably closer to the truth than the notion of someone leaving behind everything they've ever known solely for the sake of adventure. People don't just pick up and leave to start new lives; the universe generally nudges them in that direction, sometimes gently, often forcefully, either willingly or unwillingly setting them on their new path.

I was no different. It was time for me to leave the pastoral confines of Indiana. The reasons for my hasty departure were still so incomprehensible, so painful, so mind-numbing, that I couldn't yet articulate them to myself, but I knew without a doubt that I had to go. My life had changed irrevocably, and I couldn't go back. The people that I thought had loved me were no longer there. For the entirety of my brief almost eighteen-year-old existence, I had been taught that family comes first. If your family is with you, any challenge can be weathered. My family, for reasons that my mind skittered away from and refused to acknowledge, was no longer there for me. It was time to move on to new challenges that I would have to face alone.

Psychologists say that the mind is like any other organ of the body; when it comes to loss, it just shuts down. I remembered a friend who, when he was about fourteen, would play with his buddies on a railroad track near their houses. They would cavalierly run in front of the trains as they approached. Once the trains reached a 300-yard gap, they would dive off of the tracks in the very last few seconds before being run over. They thought this form of entertainment wildly exhilarating. They invited me to come, but I'd been there, done that. Cheating death in a rickety crop duster at 3,000 feet made jumping off of train tracks seem tame. 'Your loss,' he told me. The next day, though, it was his. He slipped on gravel at the last possible second while running on the tracks. The train screamed through, unstoppable, and severed his right leg just below the thigh. Later that week, at the hospital, I asked him how it had felt in those excruciating moments. He told me that he had felt nothing. The human body shuts down when the pain is too severe. So too does the mind.

Chicago was the nearest big city to Indiana, just a bus journey away. I decided I would lose myself there. Hopefully, I would regain my balance and remember what it felt like to have two legs.

$$\sim\!\!\times\!\!\sim$$

7

Arrival

The bus pulled into the 95th Street Greyhound station, its tyres screeching slightly on the tarmac, at around 11.00 a.m. on 8 June 1988 in South Side, Chicago. This stop marked the culmination of my uncomfortable three-and-a-half-hour journey from Indiana. I had done enough research about Chicago, which was to be my new home, to know that I should avoid arriving at night at all costs. Nevertheless, my late-morning arrival was still foreboding. Looking through the grimy bus windows smeared with condensation, there was no waiting plethora of smiling faces like there was at home. Not to say that the people outside appeared particularly mean or nasty; instead, their faces were distant, drawn, preoccupied with their own issues. Just individuals in the crowd going about their daily grind, trying to survive and make it through the day, or week, but without thought of looking any further ahead.

Standing up from my seat, I geared myself up to leave the relative safety of the bus, prepared for a war zone. Nervously, I recalled my father's advice—always face the storm, never run from it. Stepping down from the bus, I saw a few young-looking guys helping several passengers to retrieve their bags from the undercarriage. It was a hot, muggy day and their courtesy was much appreciated, especially by the women and older patrons. *But wait*, I thought, *this is the jungle. This is Chicago!* Panicking, I pushed my way to the front of the crowd to try and grab my own bag, fearful that some unscrupulous opportunist would take advantage of the confusion to steal belongings from a busload of naïve newcomers. However, once I had my hands tightly around the straps of my duffel bag, I forced myself to relax. With deep breaths, I reminded myself that this was just a city, and not the cesspool I was making it out to be.

I turned around, slightly taken aback, as someone addressed me from behind. 'What up, playa,' a young black man said to me. He was slightly shorter than I was, but with a stockier build and laughing brown eyes. Smiling, he introduced himself, 'The name is Maurice, but they call me Mo.' Gesturing casually to two other men over his shoulder, he continued, 'This is my boy, Dennis, and that's Sam over there. We're part of the local neighbourhood greeting team.' I held out my hand to shake his, but there was an awkward moment where he slapped me five instead. 'I'm Carey,' I responded. Cheerfully, he asked, 'Carey, where you from, nigga?' In complete shock, I blurted out, 'I'm not a nigger! Don't ever call me that again!' There was a tense silence after my outburst. Thankfully, Mo just looked at me strangely for a moment before laughing. 'Yo, this nigga's not from around here, y'all! He needs to be wearing a turban,' he called out, seemingly to no one. Looking at his cheerful face, I decided to change my demeanour; it was clear he had meant no offence and, in truth, I couldn't afford a fight with the neighbourhood greeters on my first day in the city.

'Don't worry, he cool,' Mo drawled to his friends, still smirking. 'Come on, man, let's walk these fine young ladies to the nearest Y.' I hadn't noticed, having been so absorbed in the logistics of my own anxious arrival to Chicago, that the three men had helped several young ladies find their bags and were now escorting them down the street. 'Where're you going?' I directed my question to Dennis, who was walking a little in front of me. He informed me that they were taking the girls to the local YMCA, as they probably had no other place to stay. While not luxurious, it was better than the other fleabag hotels downtown and they would at least be safe there. Confessing that I too had no place to stay yet, he laughed and invited me to join them. 'But, man, where you from, talkin' like that?' he queried. Blushing, I realized that my carefully cultivated Bollywood-style accent would not carry me far here. Chicago was not Indiana, and these guys did not find it exotic or impressive, just strange.

We started to make our way to the Y to drop off the girls' bags. There were five of them, all somewhere between fifteen and eighteen years of age, looking as new to city life as I was. Noreen, the youngest, had pale skin and red hair and hailed from Murfreesboro, Tennessee. Alice was also white and was from a small Bluegrass town in Kentucky. Rhanda, a black girl from Flint, Michigan, seemed older and rather more seasoned than the rest of the girls. Chanice, another black girl, was from Peoria and carried herself with an unmistakable yet ineffable sense of sadness, her shoulders slumped and eyes down. Finally, there was Nicole H., a gorgeous, confident blonde from California, completely unlike the others.

Striding down the streets, Nicole H. exuded a 'don't-fuck-with-me' vibe that made me immediately gravitate towards her. Trying to be smooth, I offered to help her with her bags, reverting to my go-to Bollywood accent to try and charm her. Looking at me, she laughed disparagingly, 'Listen, Yogi, back off. I don't need your help, I got all this way more figured out than you do.' Dazed, I followed her. *Wow*, I thought, *this is a girl I could love*. She was no-nonsense, no-romance, entirely and simply focused on getting from point A to point B. I knew then that we would become best friends or more. Recovering, I grabbed her bag despite her protests. 'I got you, blondie, and the name is pronounced "Carey", not "Yogi".' She smiled and was, I thought, more than a little impressed.

After several minutes of walking, we finally arrived at the YMCA. We dropped the girls and their belongings off, and Mo, Dennis, Sam and I kept going, heading to their home on 63rd Street in Woodlawn. Their 'crib' turned out to be a dilapidated brownstone, housing thirty to fifty men, more like a group home for tough guys than a proper house. I was told I could room with Mo and Dennis, which meant that I could put my bags next to their mattresses and sleep next to them. Dropping my bags off there, we went down to the kitchen. It was a small, cramped room with a cracked stove presided over by Larry, a huge guy over 6'5" and about 320 lb. Spotting us lurking in the doorway, he offered to fix us up some grits, eggs, bacon and toast. Starving, I did not refuse.

I sat down at the rickety bench which had been shoved into a corner and enjoyed every bite of the makeshift but tasty meal. I finished and thanked Larry. The room, which had slowly filled while I was eating with various men of all shades—from dark brown to caramel and tan, began to roar at the sound of my voice. Above the rising noise, I heard someone shout, 'What the hell is that fuckin' accent?'

Suddenly, a deep bass voice boomed, cutting through the roar like a gunshot, 'India.' I watched, amazed, as everyone in the room immediately stopped what they were doing, jumped to their feet, saluted and shouted in unison, 'Yes, leader Stan!'

Squinting, I tried to make out the mysterious individual in the doorway whose presence had sparked such synchronized sycophancy. 'Dismissed, carry on,' Stan drawled from the shadows. As everyone relaxed around me, I listened in rising awe. 'Our newest soldier is from India, a country in the Asian continent. He has obviously been sent by God to help us achieve our goal of domination over Chicago, the United States and, ultimately, the world. Welcome to the El Quawai, brother.'

8

The El Quawai

While not outwardly physically impressive, Stan Jones's undeniable presence commanded the room. He stood about 5'9", weighed about 180 lb. His skin was caramel brown. His hair fell to his shoulders in Rastafarian dreadlocks, and he sported a thick black beard already liberally strewn with grey. His almost hypnotic voice, with a vocabulary to match that of a president, along with his tone filled his troops with intention and calm assurance. I learned later that he founded and led the El Quawai gang, which had sprung to life in the early 1960s as the Black P Stone Rangers. They were part-good guys of the Black Panther type, feeding children and protecting their neighbourhoods, and part-gangsters, selling drugs and forcing young women into prostitution.

At our first meeting, surrounded by his followers, Stan questioned me. 'Do you know what "El Quawai" means?' Grateful for my knowledge of Arabic, I responded: 'It means "the strong".' Stan nodded approvingly and asked for my name. Before I could reply, Mo yelled, 'One of the girls called him "Yogi".' This triggered a huge wave of hilarity among the crowd, who began laughing and suggesting a host of less-than-flattering nicknames. 'Like Yogi Bear,' one called out. 'C'mere, Boo Boo.' There was a fresh upswell of laughter.

As the jokes flew around the kitchen, I watched Stan's face as he mused. Finally, he remarked in a quiet voice that nevertheless served effectively to calm the men around us, 'We won't call you Yogi, because that's too obvious. But I like the idea of bear. Your name will be Yatah, which is Arabic for "bear".' Clearing my throat, I tried to correct him politely, 'You mean Yatahamal?' He stared back at me coldly, his eyes flint-like and face unmoving. In a completely emotionless voice that nonetheless chilled me to my very core, he spoke again. 'No, I mean *Yatah.*' I learned then never to challenge him in public, even if I was right and he was wrong. There are some types of leaders who brook no challenges.

As I lay on my thin, uncomfortable mattress that first night in Chicago, I recapped the events of the day. I had left my hometown, made it to the city, met a beautiful woman and been welcomed into the warm arms of the El Quawai. Although they were Muslim and not Buddhist, and mostly black rather than Indian, I still felt that they were my brothers. We were actually the same colour. That would do for now. Before falling asleep, I felt a twinge of regret in my heart, wishing that I could call my father to tell him that I had taken his advice—that I had walked into the storm and that it had paid off—but it was impossible. Dad died an untimely death chasing a storm and had been gone for about a year now. It was his death and Mom's remarriage that precipitated my journey to Chicago. At least just knowing he was right was comforting.

7 October 1988, less than one month after I turned eighteen, Dad went out on a routine excursion about 500 miles north-west of Dakar.

'Baker Baker 123, We've got a depression which appears to be morphing into a tropical storm about 100 knots north-west of Dakar. Colonel Asanga, we need you to go there ASAP and map out the parameters of the eye. We think this has the

makings of a category 4 or 5 widow-maker. Get there quick before it actually becomes a storm and the winds become too dangerous.'

Colonel Asanga laughed, 'Too dangerous, we have flown into category 5 at their peak. A full bloom storm is nothing. Gentlemen, full operational mode...let's go.'

Dark vicious cumulonimbus clouds met them as they neared the storm. 'Colonel, this has the makings of a cat. 4–5 for sure. Those clouds are dense and about three-miles wide. We need to go down to about 700 feet to determine the Coriolis effect. If it is whirling east to west as I suspect, we should enter from the backside.'

'Roger that. Let's take this baby down and get ready for the rough ride.'

Col. Asanga had piloted his Lockheed WC-130 successfully for over forty-three missions since 1973. These Hurricane Hunters were tough planes designed to handle the vagaries of all types of tropical cyclones. In fact, none had ever crashed in the history of the programme. He was confident that his plane could fly under, over or through any tropical storm to complete its primary objective. The most important determination is whether the winds are whirring east to west or the reverse. The precision of the Weather Service prediction is based upon an analysis of the storm's Coriolis effect. The art is to fly under the storm and to fly up at the right moment in the same direction as the wind current. Hurricane Hunters developed a sixth sense and could accurately predict the direction just before entering the storm. As they flew under it, Col. Asanga looked above to predict the direction.

'It is clearly east to west. I can see the debris accumulation on the west side of the clouds. I can't see the eye yet; these clouds are larger than anything I've ever encountered. No problem. Let's get in and get out and convey the numbers.'

The eye was not visible because of the Fujiwhara effect. This wasn't just one cyclone, there were two. The second cyclone came from the south and was far more powerful. It was literally merging with the first just as they entered the clouds. It shifted the wind direction from west to east. The plane was tossed about like a rag doll when it entered the counter winds.

'Colonel, we are being torn apart from both sides, how is that possible?'

'It is a double hurricane, we have been thrown into the second cyclone which has a reverse Coriolis,' Asanga called out.

Upon entering the second cyclone, the left engine stalled and the WC-130 was thrown into an immediate tailspin. Unfortunately they were so low to the ocean that they had little or no time to recover from the spin.

'Let's keep calm; we've been through this before, initiate falling leaf procedures!'

The navigator initiated a counter-spin from the rudder in hopes of stopping the spin. If they were 1,000 feet above the ocean, they could have completed the manoeuvre. However, they were only 500 feet above the water and they could not. Their ship angled directly into the raging Atlantic which eagerly swallowed it whole.

Gandahara Lama Asanga accepted his fate just as he taught his son. He entered his watery grave with no fear, no regrets and a knowledge of a life well lived. He headed into the depths of the ocean full tilt, for he knew that the end of this particular physical existence was not the end of him. He accepted the transition with grace.

Stan was a quick thinker and valued equal intellect and discretion in those around him. I quickly became one of his top soldiers, his off-the-books accountant who tracked his finances mentally without leaving a paper trail. Unfortunately, most of the other members of the El Quawai were not appreciative that I, an Indian, was climbing so high up in their hierarchy. Thankfully, I stayed close with Mo and Dennis and together we explored the streets of South Side Chicago, whenever Stan would let me out. Dennis knew how to talk to the women, Mo was fearless and smart and I went along for the ride. They were part-friends and part-bodyguards, never letting me carry any drugs or become involved in anything that would get me arrested, as per Stan's instructions. He liked to keep me behind the scenes as much as possible.

In addition to accounting, I also became invaluable for my observational skills and operational suggestions, sort of like a gangland efficiency expert. I saw patterns everywhere. The cop cars came in twos, with the first car followed by another in approximately three minutes, approaching from behind so it would not be seen until they had closed off the perimeter. A dirty cop would hesitate just slightly before engaging, so as to allow our guys time to make an offer. Generally, most of the cops were somewhat corrupt; in their hearts, they knew they couldn't stop the flow of drugs, guns and prostitution in the city. Their goal was simply to maintain the façade of order. Therefore, so long as we didn't obviously disrupt the neighbourhood, they would let us do our thing. However, if a relative showed up at the police station claiming we had taken one of their girls, there would be hell to pay. We adapted to this by hanging around the bus and train stations, preying on the ever-plentiful supply of runaways. Very soon, we had no need to bother the local girls at all.

Despite my abstract knowledge of what went on in the El Quawai business, I was still very removed from its realities. I wasn't allowed to attend the indoctrination sessions for the girls who were trained as hookers and basic drug runners. Occasionally, if they were really attractive, some of the girls would be reserved exclusively for cops and politicians. Nicole H., the stunningly beautiful girl I had met on my first day in Chicago, was one such of these. With her long blonde hair, perfect face and witty banter, she was the perfect honey trap for corrupt cops and officials and quickly became our top spy. She only 'dated' cops who were captains or of higher rank and aldermen who had pull with the mayor. In recognition of her value to his organization, Stan kept her away from drugs and the more common prostitutes, both of which his boys were allowed to help themselves to on a Saturday night if they were bored.

9

The Nicoles

Six months passed by and I had more than proved my value to the El Quawai. As a reward, Stan put Nicole H. and me up in a brownstone apartment on the north-west side of the city. As I was half white and half Indian, no one suspected that I was involved in any gang activity. I looked like a smart yet naïve guy accompanied by his gold-digging blonde girlfriend along for the ride. Later on, I met Nicole B., a lovely black girl with ever-changing hair from Gary, Indiana, and she soon moved in with us. I loved them both as sisters—well, maybe not quite so fraternally, especially as we shared a bed every now and then. Those women taught me all kinds of things, from how to please a woman in bed to how to get a girl to really fall in love with you.

Meanwhile, the illicit business of the El Quawai was thriving. For the most part, I was kept insulated from its ugliness by my friends, Mo and Dennis. I didn't see the runaways being forced into lives of drug addiction and prostitution. I didn't witness the brutal murders of opposing gang members. My life revolved around my Muslim brothers and my new-found sisters. Doubtless, my perspective was made even cloudier by the copious amounts of sex, drugs and money. Although I never did heroin, not caring for the way it caused its proponents to nod off into oblivion for hours at a time, I did like the quick energetic pick-me-up effects of blow. I loved the way it made my heart quicken, intensified sensations and seemed to sharpen my mind.

The Nicoles and I settled into a rhythm. Sundays were the best. I would awaken from the previous night's debauchery sprawled in our large bed with a Nicole on either side. To my left would be Nicole B., whose smooth chestnut brown skin and ever-changing hair drove men wild. She moved with the sheer lithesome grace of a gazelle. Her smile could light up the entire room. She grew up in the nearby town of Gary, a few hours from my hometown of Kokomo. Despite her incredible intelligence, by the time she had reached high school, most of the nearby schools had closed. She had no high-school diploma, nor the possibility of college. None of her older brothers were employed and her dad had been killed in the crossfire of a gang-related drive-by shooting years earlier. The family eked out a meagre subsistence with the earnings from her mom's minimum-wage job. Seeing her neighbourhood for what it was—desperate, uneducated, economically impoverished, with no sign of change to come— Nicole B. began to self-medicate with weed and alcohol. Soon, she was walking the streets to make money to support her habit. Ashamed of how her family would react if they knew, she moved to Chicago and reinvented herself. Thus, Julissa Brown, the sweet smart girl, became Nicole B., the tough and streetwise beauty.

While I adored Nicole B. and our shared Indianan roots, Nicole H. was my great love. I was enthralled by her tight and toned body which always looked as if she spent half of her day at the beach or, this being Chicago, the gym. Beneath her toughened exterior, she had a genuinely kind soul and good heart. In reality, she should not have been out on the streets as she was, but unfortunate circumstances had dictated otherwise. After her parents' divorce when she was eight, her abusive stepfather moved in when she was thirteen and began making forced weekly visits to her room after midnight. Her mother either refused to believe her or did not have the strength to confront her new man. Finally, Nicole H. ran away at fifteen and had been on her own ever since.

Both of the Nicoles were my safety net and we formed an ersatz family. Our North Side brownstone was a haven from the outside world and seemed completely removed from the craziness of either the South Side or the West Side. Most of our neighbours were white yuppies, and were extremely liberal. No one looked twice at an eccentric household consisting of a brown Indian man, a gorgeous blonde white girl and a stunning black woman sporting, on alternate days, red, blonde or brunette hair.

10

Let's Make a Deal

It was 6.30 a.m. on Monday, 17 December 1990. Suddenly, the early morning stillness of the brownstone was punctured by the relentless shrill *Baaa, Baaa, Baaa* of the buzzer. Cursing my headache from the night before, I rolled out of bed, making half-hearted half-drunken attempts not to disturb Nicole B., who was passed out beside me. There was no sign of Nicole H., but I wasn't worried. She had her own life and knew how to take care of herself. Throwing on a silk robe over my naked body, I stumbled down the stairs. I hadn't been awake this early in years. Peering through the peephole, I saw the blurred outlines of two dark-skinned men. 'Who is it?' I barked through the door. The reply came back urgently, 'It's Mo an' Dennis, man, what you doin' not answering your phone? Stan needs you.' Blinking hard to clear my vision, I undid the various bolts and chains and came face to face with Mo, who looked singularly unimpressed with my dishevelled appearance. 'Now?' I asked, wistfully thinking of the warm bed and Nicole B.'s sleeping form awaiting me upstairs. 'Now,' came the implacable answer.

Resigning myself to the inevitable, I let them both in. Mo brushed past me, but Dennis paused to grab my right hand, hugging me with his left. 'What up, ya bear...' he began cheerfully. Mo interrupted him urgently, 'You ready?' I ran my hand through my hair and said I just needed to throw on a pair of jeans and a shirt and I'd be good to go. Glancing at me uncomfortably, Dennis shook his head. 'Nah, man, Stan said you need to wear a suit today. You can't show up lookin' like that.' Grumbling, I quickly headed back upstairs and returned in a few minutes in my best blue Brooks Brothers suit. Finally, there was a gleam of approval in Mo's eyes. 'That's how you do it, yeah, man!'

Once in the car, we headed south until we were just outside of downtown Chicago, near Halsted. Pulling around the back of an industrial grey meat-packing warehouse, I saw two Lincoln Continentals idling in the parking lot. Easing into the back of the first car, I found Stan sitting there, along with two white guys who looked to be in their early forties. Like me, they were wearing expensive blue suits with silk ties, though they also sported matching pocket handkerchiefs. Their hair was perfectly coiffed, their skin immaculate. I swallowed hard, aware of how rough my own appearance must look in comparison.

With complete equanimity, Stan smiled at me and introduced me with an elegant wave of his hand. 'Gentlemen, I'd like you to meet my accountant, Yatah. All proposals must be cleared by him. He has a rare mind and will remember all of the pertinent details.' Pausing, he glanced at me. 'There will be no need for anything to be written down.' I nodded in confirmation. Turning back to the other men, he finished with a flourish, 'So, please go ahead and make your pitch.' As the negotiations began, I thanked my lucky stars that I had snorted a shot of blow on the way over so that my mind would be sharp.

The two men shifted in their seats. 'Here's the deal,' the first one began, his voice rolling out smoothly and sounding somehow oily to the ear. He had platinum blonde hair and inscrutable eyes as grey as the cloudless winter sky outside the vehicle. 'We can bring in premium cocaine directly from Columbia. We want you and your gang to set up a distribution network, beginning in Chicago but extending eventually all the way south to St. Louis and Memphis, Minneapolis to the north and as far east as Cleveland.' Although his face didn't move an inch, I could feel hot excitement radiate from Stan as he sat beside me. Nodding in acknowledgement, he wordlessly waved his hand for them to proceed. 'We can provide as much as you can sell. But there's a caveat—no violence and no child hookers. We don't need that kind of attention.' Here, the blonde man leaned forward for emphasis. 'Especially the white girls, understood?' Grinning internally, I looked down at my hands and crossed my leg over my knee. *Especially the white girls.*

Meanwhile, there came two short sharp honks from the second Lincoln, which I would later learn held several Chicago politicians in the back seat, probably Aldermen. At this signal, Stan got out of our car, walked over to them and disappeared inside. There was an uncomfortable silence as the suits and I pretended to inspect the dreary view of the packing plant. Eventually, after five to ten minutes, I had to break it. 'Well, the Cubbies are sure doing well this year.' My attempt to initiate a conversation with a universal male icebreaker—sports—did not go down well. 'Don't give a damn about the Cubs, I'm South Side Chicago, born and raised. White Sox for life!' muttered one of the suits. I laughed, 'But doesn't it all fall under Chicago?' In disbelief, the other dark-haired man looked at me. 'No, the real Chicago is the South Side. It's where all the power is, both black and white.'

Thankfully, just as the silence was again reaching the stage of discomfort, Stan re-entered the car, this time accompanied by Nicole H., her mysterious absence from my bed this morning now explained. Immediately, the demeanour of the two suits changed. They were furious to see Nicole, a beautiful young white girl, sit beside Stan. 'Hey, this is exactly what we were talking about! Youse guys can't have girls like that on the street.' Stan and I laughed aloud at this but said nothing, knowing that Nicole was not one to hold her tongue. Haughtily, she leaned forward, her long sheet of blonde hair gleaming in the dark interior of the car. 'I am not a streetwalker and, what's more, I really don't care what you think about who I am with. My life is my own.' Both guys looked taken aback. Seductively, she placed the tip of one manicured finger on the dark-haired man's knee. 'Understood?' Before either of them could regain their equilibrium, Dennis pulled alongside the Lincoln in our own car. Stan looked at our hosts and exclaimed, 'Gentlemen, it has been a pleasure! My guys will get in touch with yours to work out all the details and firm up the logistics.' To Nicole and me, he barked 'Ghost!'

With that, we immediately left the warehouse and headed back to our own territory. Although he never usually showed much emotion, Stan seemed remarkably pleased. It made sense—under his leadership, the El Quawai was about to enter a phase of extreme profitability. We had just made a major distribution deal that, in one swoop, had essentially eliminated all local competition as well as assuring ourselves of major muscle behind us in light of our new links to both organized crime and City Hall. We basically now had a golden pass. Everyone looked happy, except for Nicole, who seemed concerned and distrustful. But then again, that was her default attitude, so I paid little mind to it.

That night, we celebrated the deal back at the brownstone. Nicole H., Nicole B., Dennis and Mo partied with me well into the early hours of Tuesday morning. Aided by Courvoisier and Coke, our refreshments of choice, we reminisced about the bad old days of four years ago and gloated about where we were now and how the El Quawai was taking over. As the party wound down, I sat there, alternatively sipping whiskey and sniffing blow, and contemplated my present circumstances. I had a strong brotherhood around me to protect me. I had two beautiful roommates who understood that romantic love was for suckers. We had each other's backs without any unnecessary sentimentality. *Not a bad life, not bad at all*, I thought to myself before heading upstairs.

11

Cloudy, with a Chance of Rain

Two weeks later, on a Wednesday night or Thursday morning, depending on your perspective, I was abruptly awoken by the beeping of my cell at 3.30 a.m. After my late arrival at our negotiations with the suits, Stan had given me an earful about keeping my phone on at all times of the day or night. Sitting upright in bed, I answered the call. 'Yogi, I need you to come here now, no bullshitting, right now! It's all gone wrong!' As Nicole H.'s fierce instructions filled my ears, I jumped up without a second thought and headed off to help my girl. Between harsh breaths, she told me that she was in a mansion just off Dearborn and Goethe, in the Gold Coast area. It was a palmy neighbourhood up north, just outside of downtown Chicago. As I made my way there in a taxi, racing past the affluent mansions and upscale restaurants and shops that lined the streets, I knew that her client tonight was either very wealthy, very well connected, or both.

I arrived to a scene straight out of an Al Capone movie. Nicole was sitting on the floor, smoking a cigarette. Her red lipstick was smeared down her chin and her eyes were dark and blank. Behind her, lying across a white King Louis XVI couch with gold trim lay the body of a balding, middle-aged white man. He was wearing a tuxedo, minus the pants. Oh, and there was the added feature of a giant gaping hole in his chest cavity. 'Nicole, what the...' was all I could say as I stared at them both in shock. Looking away from me, Nicole spoke savagely, 'He had it coming, Yogi, I swear! He told me to blow him and then, when I started, he put a gun to my head.' Taking a drag, she looked over her shoulder with pure loathing at the corpse behind her, 'He said that when he had finished, he was going to shoot me… and, if I stopped halfway, he was going to take me out back and bury me alive.'

At Nicole's harsh words, a tsunami of white-hot rage filled my soul. I urged her on, 'What happened next?' Though she still wouldn't look me in the eyes, she seemed reassured that I believed her. She continued, quickly tapping the ash from her cigarette onto the marble floor, 'I gave him probably the best blow job he ever had. He relaxed and, once he did, I grabbed the gun…' At this, her voice faltered. On the floor, I noticed the gleam of a 9 mm Glock lying diffidently beneath the couch. 'And I shot him first,' Nicole finished, her voice flattened and dead.

This was bad. My next question, and I really did not want the answer, was to find out who this guy was. 'Please, Nicole, for the love of God, tell me that he wasn't well connected.' Suddenly, a voice rang out from behind me. 'Unfortunately for you, he's extremely well connected. That's why I'm here and, coincidentally, why you two are going to die.' I spun around to see a man standing behind me looking the very essence of a classic Italian hitman. He was 6'3", weighed maybe 240 lb, had dark-coloured overly oiled hair, deep-set eyes and a nose that looked like it had been broken more than once. At his next movement, my attention quickly focused on the Remington 870 pump-action shotgun cradled in his hands, its black nozzle unambiguously pointed in our direction. With a cruel mock-bow towards Nicole, the hitman continued, 'Congratulations, signorina, you have murdered Salvatore Vincenzo, known to the world as Tore Vince, executive assistant to Alderman Bruzzi.'

At this, Nicole went into action. Quickly wiping her face free of lipstick, she sensually yet casually raised herself from the floor in a series of slow cat-like movements, delicately smoothing her mini-skirt over her thighs without breaking eye contact with the gunman. 'You haven't told us your name,' she purred. I could see her trying to slide the Glock out unobtrusively from under the couch. Indicating the shotgun in his hands, he replied, 'This is the only name you need. And if you take another step towards that gun, I'll blow your brains out.' I quickly jumped in, 'Whoa, man, everyone has a price, don't they? What's yours?' Glancing at me gratefully, Nicole echoed in a wispy seductive voice, 'Name your price, Mr Remington.' There was a harsh cascade of laughter from the gunman, which faded abruptly. After a pause of ten extremely long seconds, he said, 'You have one hour to bring me $100K or you both die.'

For the first time, I could see a shadow of fear cross Nicole's face and desperation creep into her eyes. She had been so strong, so resilient up until this point; but she knew that there was no way Stan would pony up such a large amount for one of his hookers, even if she was one of the best in the business. 'Sure,' I said, 'give us an hour.' I began to back away, but stopped hurriedly as the shotgun swung in my direction. 'Do you think I'm stupid?' Mutely, I shook my head. 'The girl goes, you stay. She won't be hard to find if she skips out on me.' The gunman quickly kicked the Glock away from us both and proceeded to tie my hands together behind my back with duct tape. As she waited, Nicole looked across the room at me. Her concerned eyes said what her lips could not—*we don't have that kind of money.*

But Nicole didn't know the whole story. In my capacity as accountant for El Quawai, I had become perfectly adept at tracking a huge amount of financial data in my head, including the difference between expected and actual profits. This year, we had far exceeded projections and that little discrepancy had been quietly siphoned off and currently lay in my private vault in the form of hundreds of thousands of bills of cold, hard cash. Shaking my head at her, I told her, 'Don't worry. I have the money. Go to our place; behind the picture of my Uncle Justa is a safe. The combination is left to six, right eight, and then...' Here, Nicole interjected, 'And then right eighty-eight.' Our eyes met. 'The day we met,' she whispered. I nodded, not wanting to say anything more in front of the eyes of the amused yet sardonic hitman.

Nicole left without a backwards glance and I stayed where I was. Surprisingly, time moves exceedingly slowly when your life is at stake. Death row inmates pass through innumerable snail-like days as they await their fate, right up until their very last day when their execution looms before them. *Will the governor call with a last-minute reprieve? How long is each bite of my last meal? Is the journey from my cell to the electric chair really a mile?* Simultaneously bored and yet aware that each moment could be my last, I waited with the gunman in complete silence. My hands began to itch, bound as tightly as they were behind my back. As the clock ticked towards the final few minutes of the allotted hour and I saw the hitman growing impatient, I mentally steeled myself for death. While I was aware of the fear that filled my soul, I chose not to surrender to it. I was, after all, Gandahara Asanga's son. This was just another storm.

Providentially, Nicole returned with seconds to spare, carrying with her one of our dirty pillow cases clearly stuffed with bank notes. My relief was palpable, although I hoped that she had more sense than to try to short-change the gunman. She strode towards us and, looking more beautiful and haughtier than ever, threw the bag at the feet of our nameless hitman. 'Here,' she spat. 'Now let us go and take care of this mess.' She waved callously in the direction of the late Tore Vince. 'Give him the acid bath he so richly deserves.' The gunman sneered. 'I need to see you count it. I've played this game before, sweetheart. A few thousand alongside some torn-up old newspaper won't work on me.' Nicole paused and glanced at me. 'Well,' she reasoned, 'at least untie him so that he can help me count. The quicker we do that, the sooner this whole nightmare is over.' Seeing the sense in her words, he acquiesced, ripping the duct tape unnecessarily roughly from around my wrists.

Nicole and I began to count the giant pile of notes as Mr Remington hovered menacingly behind us, his shotgun alternatingly pointing at the both of us. As we neared the end of our count, he relaxed. It had become obvious that the full amount was there, all $100K in neat stacks of hundreds, fifties and twenties. As I felt his attention focus on the money, I began to initiate the plan I had formed during my long wait as a hostage. Pretending to concentrate on the count, I began to slowly back up towards the gunman with tiny baby steps. As soon as we hit $99K, I suddenly spun around, grabbing the shotgun, forcing it upwards into the air. In his shock at the sudden attack, the hitman hesitated. It was a crucial mistake—as his grip loosened, I wrenched the Remington from him and hit him hard over the head with the butt of the gun. Before he could recover from the blow, I was the one holding him at gunpoint. 'Now then,' I ordered, 'this is how things are gonna go down.' Blood trickling down the side of his pale face, the gunman stared back at me in horror at his sudden reversal of fortune. 'Both of us are leaving. A deal is a deal. Your money is on the bed. Take care of Tore or whatever his name is.' I could see Nicole smirk from the corner of my eyes while the gunman nodded his head in confusion. 'We all walk away from this; you the richer, we the wiser.' Taking his silence for consent, I began to slowly back away, keeping Nicole behind me and the gun trained on the kneeling hitman. Finally, we ducked through the door and were out of the building. Our ordeal was over!

Ah, the elation of relief! We were weightless as we walked outside into the ever-expanding sky. It was a gorgeous early Chicago morning; trash trucks were lumbering around corners as the garbage men went about their business, birds were singing their morning chorus. As we slowed to a stop several blocks away from the mansion, the accumulated debris of dead leaves crunching under our feet, Nicole put her hand in mine and just looked at me. It was a look of true peace. In that moment, I felt an overwhelming flood of love and surrender take me over. We stared into each other's eyes, communicating to each other everything we had always wanted to say without uttering a single word. Finally, she smiled, breaking the spell. 'How on earth did you have all that money? You don't even have a car, proper clothes other than that one suit, and you never *ever* pay for dinner,' she gasped, shrieking with laughter. Chuckling, I shrugged, 'I'm a numbers guy. The big secret is not what you spend, but what you have.' Delighted, she leaned forward to kiss me and confided, 'Well, you have *me* for life.'

The first half of our long walk home went by in a joyous haze. We had escaped death and were ensconced in our love to the exclusion of all else. *Not bad for a guy who swore off love*, the fleeting thought ran through my head as I flashbacked to my first disastrous romance. However, sobriety returned as we moved closer to home. There was no way that we could trust Mr Remington to not betray us to the police, so we began thinking up an alibi. In this endeavour, Nicole turned out to be particularly smart and precise. Our defence was airtight by the time we arrived at the brownstone. Deep down, however, we knew that our days in Chicago were numbered. We would have to get out soon. Our luck was bound to run out and moving on before it did was our only option.

12

Quietare Coram Tempestate

Nicole and I had originally planned to leave Chicago before winter but, as they say, the best-laid plans often go awry. Instead, we engaged in six months of pure debauchery. The experience Nicole and I had shared changed us. We were no longer carefree kids. While our relationship mattered deeply, neither of us knew how to express our feelings or how to evolve from our previous personas. When she saw other guys, I hated it but pretended that it didn't matter. She feigned indifference as I self-medicated with whatever mind-numbing agent I could find. It was not pleasant. Denial never is. We were tiptoeing around the truth that, deep down, we knew we would eventually have to face. From my side, my feelings were terrifying. Dad had taught me not to fear death, but he'd never told me how to deal with a dizzying head-first plunge into true love.

One Sunday, I went about my normal routine. It started as usual with me walking blindly into my kitchen to make breakfast for my family. Cooking was, for me, a form of meditation. I put on some soothing jazz, Dave Brubeck's *Take 5* and some classic Miles, the perfect musical accompaniment for my culinary efforts. Coltrane was more suited to a wild rambunctious Saturday night. Grabbing six eggs and milk from the fridge, I cracked five of them against a silver bowl and whisked them gently—too much air and they wouldn't scramble well—before throwing in a pinch of salt, thyme and pepper. Next, I cracked the remaining egg and mixed it with milk, flour, some melted butter and baking soda for a pancake batter. Finally, once I had sausages sizzling in the pan, I brewed a big jug of strong black coffee to counteract the previous night's hedonistic blur of stimulants, hallucinogens and alcohol.

Pouring myself a cup, I sat down at the kitchen table while the pancakes and sausages gently sizzled on the stove behind me. *Knock, knock, knock.* It was a noise that seemed to signal the end of the all-too-brief morning peace and stillness. I tried to ignore it, but the knocking came again, harder and louder than before. I couldn't imagine who it might be. The police would have knocked twice and then busted down the door. One of Nicole's clients would have yelled and sworn at me to open the goddamn door. This disruption of a normal Sunday morning seemed portentous, but I had no real feel for exactly what it portended. But I knew enough to know that this was a knocking that would not go away by itself, so I tucked my gun into my front waistband, out of sight, and opened the door.

The sight that greeted me was startling, to say the least. I blinked in disbelief at the middle-aged Indian man framed in the doorway. Before I could say anything, he pushed his way into the brownstone, smacking me on my head as he walked past. 'Bhateeja, what took you so long? I'm tired. I've just spent the last three days travelling the entire world—all the way from Ladakh to Jammu to Mumbai to this dirty, crowded city, Chicago—just to see you.' It was Uncle Justa, the very last person I expected to see, the first of my family I had seen in three and a half years. He always knew how to make an entrance.

Uncle Justa stayed with me for ten days. It was fantastic. Even Stan approved, although he warned me that my vacation from the El Quawai needed to be quick because we had a lot of deals in the pipeline. For the duration of my brief interlude from gang life, Uncle Justa and I took long walks every day along the lakefront. We talked of everything, from my exploits with Nicole to the ways of the spirit. Then one day, as we were sheltering from the freezing rain under an awning, he turned to me with sad eyes. 'This is not the life you were meant to live, John. You are an Asanga. We have something that 99.9 per cent of the world does not—a direct connection with God.' As he lectured me, the shame began to creep into my soul. 'But, Uncle...' I tried to interrupt, but he held up his hand to stop me. 'Although you and your concubine have regaled me with stories of your bravery, how you have escaped death in dire situations, I am not impressed.' My heart was filled with lead. I knew that he was right, that my deeds during my time in Chicago had been far from brave. I was not the man I had set out to become.

'God has had his hand on you since you were born,' Uncle Justa continued, putting his arm around my shoulder as we stared out over the strong grey waves crashing onto Montrose Beach. 'Everyone thought that my brother, Harry, was the chosen one... but I knew, from the moment we met, that it was you.' At this, I must have looked disbelieving. 'And Harry knew it too,' Uncle Justa reassured me. 'He knew he was meant to mix with the Western world so that you could save it. You are the one that will show them the power of self-realization, show them in terms they can appreciate.' There was silence for some time, before I found my voice again. 'But, Uncle Justa, how is that possible when I don't even know what it means?' Uncle Justa laughed. 'Don't worry, you will,' he said, his tone one of absolute certainty. 'You will.'

13

Betrayal

After Uncle Justa left to return to India—his mission to set me back on my path completed—Nicole and I finally came to terms and agreed that our crab-like behaviour had to stop. Our tough insouciant exterior was merely artifice meant to hide our inner sensitivity from a harsh modern world not made for romantics like us. We settled into a workable rhythm. Outside the brownstone, I handled my business with Stan and the guys with focus and my normal detachment, while Nicole handled hers. But at home, we were completely different people—loving, compassionate and respectful. I felt like I was in heaven. I had made my way through the storm and found the object of my desire. Sometimes, though, the hairs on the back of my neck would stiffen and I'd feel a twinge of fear in the pit of my stomach. Everything was *too* perfect. I tried to ignore the feeling, disregarding it as the emotional remnant from years of bitterness and pessimism.

It was another Sunday morning when my world came crashing down around me. Once again, I had risen early to make breakfast, this time without a drug-induced hangover. I no longer felt the need to dull my senses with narcotics; I was beginning to understand who I was, and liking what I found. Lee Morgan's dulcet tones drifted into the kitchen as I began my breakfast ritual. Nicole had not made it home the previous night, but I wasn't worried. She could easily fend for herself in the Chicago wilderness. 'Nicole B.,' I called upstairs to my other best girl, 'five minutes till the waffles are ready!'

Then, there it was. *Knock, knock... BLAM*! I froze as the most feared sound in Chicago drilled its way into my skull as the front doorway burst open. Before I could begin to fully process what was happening and what I should do, a horde of policemen in combat vests and helmets were barging into my formerly peaceful home. 'On the floor, NOW, hands spread out where we can see them! Do it RIGHT NOW or we shoot!' Turning, I saw two cops of about 6'2" and 6'4" running straight at me. The first one shoved me and sent me sprawling face first onto the floor. He dug his knee agonizingly deep into the middle of my back, while the other whipped out his pistol and shoved the barrel into my temple. Leaning down, he hissed into my ear, 'Go on, make a move, rat boy. Just give me an excuse.' My cheek flattened against the floor, I focused on the remains of a piece of forgotten eggshell in front of me. Behind me, I could hear the other officers running down the corridor to the bedroom. My heart leapt into my throat as I thought of how scared Nicole B. must be.

Just then, two other men walked into the kitchen. In crisp tones, one of them snapped to the cop kneeling on me, 'Relax, don't get carried away. This one is worth far more alive than dead.' Grudgingly, the officer got up, hauling me upright as he did so. I finally got a clear look at the two newcomers. Unlike the police officers, they were in expensive suits. *Oh, crap, the Feds!* Looking through me, one of the men snapped open his phone and glanced at the screen. 'Who'da thunk this turban nigger would be the walking record for the El Quawai, eh?' Smirking, the second agent walked out of the room, heading upstairs with an air of complete assurance as if he knew exactly where he was going and what he would find once he arrived.

From down the corridor, I could hear his voice ordering the officers, 'Bag all this up. If one single dollar is missing, youse guys will be on traffic duty until retirement.' My mind was racing. *Bag this up? What was he talking about?* I had no drugs, at least not in any volume that would warrant a raid of this magnitude. The brownstone was supposed to be a safe house. At worst, I might get a misdemeanour for possession. No...they had come for my money, but how? No one knew how much money I had, except for Nicole, and I knew there was no way she would have told anyone. Dragging me from room to room, I watched as the officers tore up my place. For kicks, they ripped open every piece of furniture, destroyed books and photographs, all the while claiming that they were looking for drugs and counterfeit notes.

Handcuffed, I was escorted to the Dirksen Building, the FBI headquarters in downtown Chicago. They left me alone for hours in a dingy basement room, illuminated by a single neon white light, just like in the movies. Suddenly, noises begin to drift towards me from outside the room. *Clop... Click... Clop... Click...* I knew the precise sounds and rhythm of that walk intimately. I watched in stunned disbelief as Nicole, dressed like I'd never before seen her, in a dark grey pencil skirt and tailored jacket, walked into the interview room. She was accompanied by a man who I vaguely recognized, but couldn't quite place. Finally, it hit me—he was one of the guys who had been in the Lincoln with her at our warehouse meeting, months ago. 'Surprise,' he chuckled. Sitting down opposite me, he paused to light a cigarette. Exhaling, he leaned back and looked at me. 'I won't lie, I've been looking forward to this day for quite some time.' Not being able to help myself, my eyes found Nicole's and I looked at her in mute appeal. With guilt in her eyes, she cleared her throat and looked down at a cardboard file in her hands. In a clear cold voice I had never before heard, she stated, 'John Yogacara Asanga, I am FBI agent Charlemagne Scott and you are under arrest for drug trafficking and a host of other charges, which will be read to you in due course.'

My heart skipped a beat. I listened in astonishment as Nicole—or Charlemagne, as I suppose she really was—explained that she and her partner had been working undercover to expose the El Quawai for years, even back when they were known as the Black P. Stone Rangers. Slamming his hands on the table, the male agent leaned forward to look me in the eye. 'Look, here's the deal. You can either work with us or you can go to jail. The good news is that I can guarantee that your life sentence won't be too long, especially once we release what we know to the general population.' Staring at me, he jabbed a finger forcefully into my chest. 'Your arrest alone is enough to get you killed in about two weeks, John. Stan is a smart guy; he'll figure that you're already singing like a bird.' As much as I wished that what he was saying wasn't true, I knew deep down that it was. One of the many reasons that Stan had risen to the top and maintained his position of leadership over a large and violent gang was his ability to plan for and anticipate every eventuality, every potential betrayal. It was a skill I bitterly wished I had at this moment.

'So, think about it,' he finished. 'Talk to us, hold nothing back, and we'll see if we can arrange a plea deal.' He smirked, 'On the other hand, say nothing and everyone will still think you talked. It's really a "heads we win, tails you lose" scenario.' Even though I should have been thinking furiously, weighing my options—all of which looked increasingly slim—all I could see was Nicole's baby blue eyes watching me, looking on as my entire life crumbled around me. There she was my true love, Nicole, the agent of my downfall.

14

The Awakening

The Dirsken Building housed the Federal Courts, the FBI and, to my surprise and benefit, the federal jail as well. Even though the jail itself was small, I was kept apart from the general population. The Feds could not risk someone potentially harming the key witness in their struggle to bring down the El Quawai. As I sat in my cell that first night, I was overwhelmed. *Dad, you always told me to head into the storm, but this is too much. There is no truth to be found here. I need your help.*

I thought back to the last time I had seen my father, when I was seventeen. He was heading out to check on a burgeoning storm somewhere between the coast of Africa and the Bahamas. It would go on to become Hurricane Alba, the very first storm of the season. But his plane never made it back, crashing somewhere in the South Atlantic. In the aftermath of the news, I went numb. Mom was devastated. We moved from the Air Force Base to the big city of Indianapolis, into a modest house we managed to pay for using Dad's life insurance. About six months later, Mom met a professor from Purdue who was in town for some seminar. A thinking man just like Dad, Steve seemed to have a pleasant mien. I wasn't too happy with being the only Indian in the house, but there weren't many of us around and I couldn't fault her for gravitating to one of her own. They married and we moved to West Lafayette, a small university town, soon afterwards.

At first, Steve made an effort to act fatherly towards me,

but there was a distinctive air of distaste in his eyes every time he looked at me. One day, he mentioned that I needed to start planning for the future and preparing for college. Trying to get along, I asked if Purdue would be a good choice for me. Glancing at my mother, he cleared his throat and offered to take me on a tour around campus. As we rounded one of the college buildings that evening, he looked over at me. 'The way I see it, Johnny, you need to go as far away from here as you can.' Startled, I asked him why he thought so. 'Your mother only received a limited amount of money, and we're trying to build our relationship. She's re-establishing herself in the community. The last thing she needs is a reminder of her…shall we say *dubious*…past.' 'Excuse *me*,' I interjected. 'In what way is her past "dubious"? She was married to a brilliant Oxford scholar who went on to become a decorated officer of the United States Air Force!' 'Don't be a fool, Johnny,' Steve shot back. 'She was married to a turban head, no offense. It was tolerated, but not ideal.' His pale features shone in the darkness. 'Now, she has a chance to be part of normal society again…that is, once *you're* gone.' Needless to say, those words were the impetus for my move to Chicago six months later as I searched for my own truth.

Unfortunately, my so-called quest for truth had led me to the jail cell in which I was now sitting, brooding over the past. Looking back, I could see that all my actions had been spurred by a desire to belong and to feel loved, with lamentable results. Despite my intellect, I couldn't seem to get past being the *other*. Just like Dad, I was the Indian boy who had the temerity to think he had earned a place at the table, only to be thrown back into the kitchen. After a few days spent indulging in self-pity, I began to think clearly again. My problem wasn't the quest itself; it was the underlying foundation of my search. I did not need Lucy to know I was great, and I did not need the El Quawai either. I had thought I loved Lucy, but I had really just wanted a white girlfriend to confirm that I was just as good as my classmates. I had yearned for the love and respect of the El Quawai, even though I'd known that they were bad guys, forcing young girls into prostitution, selling drugs, murdering their competition. Sure, my friends were essentially doing their best to survive in horrible socioeconomic conditions, but no good can come from a business rooted in misery.

I needed to build my own foundation. Not long ago, Uncle Justa had reminded me of my special heritage as an Asanga. He had told me that I was meant to teach the West the benefits of self-realization. It was time to discern exactly what that meant. I needed to hone my connection with the universe in order to find my path forward. I was loved by the universal spirit within us all, a love not dependent upon good acts or how I was viewed by others. Such love is unqualified, it simply is. I had to learn to accept that love and find my own purpose. Real storms would come. I didn't have to look for false storms to find my truth.

Jail is the perfect place for spiritual conversion. Most people, faced with a lot of time on their hands, either go crazy or obtain a laser-like focus. Malcom X is a prime example, but there are many others throughout history. I was quite pleased to join them. After all, I was being held without bail and my trial was at least six months out. What else did I have to do? My first task was to study the works of my ancestors, Asanga and his half-brother Vasubandhu, the founders of the Yogacara school of Buddhist philosophy. They believed that only awareness was real and that the objects of that awareness were, in the end, of little consequence. Thus, Yogacara is often known as the 'mind only' school.

The term 'yoga' in Yogacara does not refer to the asanas that many Westerners commonly associate with the word; these are merely the postures one uses during hatha yoga. Hindus consider yoga to be the union of an individual with the Supreme Being. My new goal in life was no longer to be limited to the receipt of love from others, but to hone the connection between myself and the Supreme Being, of which I was essentially one infinitesimal piece. This spirit was within me and within every sentient being. Self-realization was the process of understanding one's true nature and yoga, the practice of making that connection with the universal spirit. I was a part of everything and everything was a part of me. The answers to all of my problems were available to me because they were within me. I had spent my life seeking something I already had.

My yoga practice focused mainly upon meditation. I needed to develop the right concentration to achieve *samadhi*, that state where the personal self becomes one with the universal self. This state of unity with the universal spirit that can only be achieved once the five *kleshas* have been eliminated. *Kleshas* are negative emotions based upon fear. There are five *kleshas*: avidya, asmita, dvesha, raga and abhinivesha. Avidya is the fear stemming from the individual ignorance of one's true self. It a scary proposition running around in the world not knowing who you truly are. Asmita is the emotional fear stemming from identifying with one's ego. Some of us have inflated egos and think we are the smartest beings on the planet. This is a state of which I am all too aware. My ego has served me well. Getting me out of jams over various lifetimes. I think I am smarter than the universe. However, if that were true, I would not be here in jail right now. While others, suffer from a diminished ego and feel they are beneath everyone else. Raga is an attachment to previous pleasure (guilty once again). We fear we may never have that exquisite experience again so we drink way too much alcohol or eat way too many cookies...we overindulge. Dvesha is an aversion to painful past experiences. We will go to all kinds of extremes to avoid those unpleasant feelings again. So we put things in good and bad categories without thinking about them. Such categorization is not the result of mindfulness. For example, a prejudice against a race of people. Simply because one person from a particular race has done something bad, we put all people from that race or tribe in that category. We can't hate based upon a supposition. Simply put, just because I had a bad pickle once should not mean that I should never taste a pickle again. We must think mindfully and live in the moment. Carrying aversions based upon hasty judgments from the past to things, people or activities is not the way to go. Abhinivesha is a fear of death because of attachment. We fear that the people that we love will be taken away from us. We fear that we will die and be taken away from the ones we love. We must learn to let go of our egos (asmita) and our quick judgments (dvesha) and our attachments to give the spirit room to operate. The spirit is the true owner of our bodies and once we learn to trust it and let it do its work we are on the path to yoga. I realized I was far from *samadhi* and that I had a lot to learn. I humbly began the process of applying myself in earnest to the task.

One afternoon, as I was meditating, I heard my inner voice for the first time. *Know yourself and you will be known.* I had thought I knew who I was, but did I really? If I was essentially spirit, I needed to understand the true nature of the universal spirit before I could truly know myself. I began reading all of the ontological books I could find. I started with the *Tattva Mimamsa*, which appeared in the early *Vedas*, one of the four sacred texts of Hinduism. I moved on to the three *gunas* of *sattva* (being), *rajas* (activity) and *tamas* (darkness). Next, I studied the Greek philosophers, working my way from Parmenides to Plato and on to Descartes. I delved into the minds of Thomas Aquinas and John Locke, before finishing with the works of Vivekananda, my favourite swami who had learned from the mystic Ramakrishna himself that all sentient beings were an embodiment of the divine self.

I was an embodiment of the divine self. Once I recognized my divine nature, the universe would in turn recognize me as divine. It sounded a little tautological, but it wasn't—if we don't recognize that aspect of divinity within ourselves, we cannot understand the universe when it speaks to us, much like an English-speaking person trying to understand someone speaking a foreign language. I needed to understand the divine self within me so that I could communicate with the divine aspects of everything around me. I called it the Namaste concept. The God in me needed to understand the God in everything and everyone else. By connecting on a divine level, people can fulfil their divine purpose and leave behind mundane aspects of life, such as gratification of the ego. However, despite this personal epiphany, I still had to learn how to apply my new-found wisdom in my interpersonal communications with others.

My second task was to learn the law and free myself from my present circumstances. My arrest had been based upon deceit and, hence, the very foundation for the charges against me was weak. By applying my intellect and staying strong, I could find a path to freedom. Nicole, the betrayer, would not be my master. After all, she had killed a man, Alderman Bruzzi's executive assistant. She had weaknesses I could exploit—and I would do just that, and whatever else it took, to obtain my freedom.

15

The Belly of the Beast

My jail cell was a rectangular concrete box of about 42 square feet, 6 feet wide and 8 feet long, with no windows and a toilet. Inside, my only furniture was a small metal bed, a small chair and desk. Three times a day, guards would slide me a tray of mush with an unidentifiable side of something crunchy through a small opening in the door. There were no jazz-fuelled culinary feasts here. *At least the crunchy stuff is protein,* I told myself. To be honest, my days in prison soon settled into a rhythm, and not a particularly unpleasant one at that. Fortunately for me, I had no cellmates, as I was kept isolated from the rest of my incarcerated brethren. After all, the Feds couldn't have their star witness in *United States v. Jones* shanked by an El Quawai before the trial.

So, I took advantage of my solitude. I filled my cell with books. In six short months, I had gotten a hold of every major treatise of the Abrahamic religions. I had books about the Old Testament, the New Testament, esoteric Catholic texts, and books on the Kabbalah, the Koran and Sufism. Additionally, I had the Bhagavad Gita, the Vedas, all the Mahayana sutras and the *Bodhisattva Path to Unsurpassed Enlightenment*, written by my namesake, Arya Asanga. I read all these books from cover to cover in my search for self-realization. As I read more, my inner voice began to speak louder and louder until I could hear it quite clearly when in a state of deep meditation.

I quickly realized that the FBI had spent years putting this task force together and that Nicole was one of their key players. She had really hit the mother lode when she befriended me; I was the glue that was holding their case together, having gained Stan's trust and climbed so high in the organization. I was the equivalent of Al Capone's accountant; with my testimony, they could map the criminal activities of the El Quawai by tracking the flow of money. They could tell which politician was paid off, and by whom, which cop was on the take, and what precinct he worked in. But what Nicole hadn't counted on was that I would become comfortable in prison. I was focused on my yoga and making use of the time alone to find my true self. On a more prosaic level, I was also in no hurry to put a target on my back by ratting out my brothers. Yes, the El Quawai was a murderous group of drug-dealing human traffickers. But they met my number one condition for loyalty—they had accepted me as one of their own, showing me nothing but love and respect. With them, I was not the dark 'other' I had been treated as throughout the majority of my childhood. I was just another brother in their war against man.

In hindsight, it's not surprising that Nicole and her superiors realized they would need to shake up their game. My prison experience was about to enter phase two. Whenever one becomes too comfortable, life initiates change. I had my routine. My life had a sense of order, of complacent contentment. So, of course, it would soon be completely transformed. That's the way of the universe, always pushing us forward, always forcing us to evolve and adapt to ever-shifting circumstances.

I had been imprisoned for about six months. Today was Monday. Like every Monday, it started at 10.00 a.m. with my bi-weekly interrogation. Normally, my interrogator would be either

Nicole, her partner or one of the FBI's topmost psychologists. I enjoyed my interactions with the latter; we had great existential conversations, though his job was primarily to break down my barriers so that I would see cooperation as the only way out of jail. However, that morning, I had a new persecutor. A serious-looking man, he was about 6'3" and maybe 210 lb, with a meticulous and yet melancholic appearance. Every hair was groomed perfectly into place and his moustache/beard combination endowed him with a brooding look. As he walked in, he looked at me with eyes that seemed to pierce my soul. They were deep and foreboding, yet as I looked into them, something restless inside of me finally stilled. For an instant, everything was eerily quiet, as if the world had stopped turning and we were alone, sitting by a fire at a caravanserai. He sat down slowly in the chair opposite me, not breaking his stare. Finally, he blinked and introduced himself as Jim.

We continued to sit there mutely for several long minutes. There were a few moments when he almost said something, but instead lapsed back into silence. Finally, he rubbed his hands over his face and spoke in a somewhat exasperated tone. 'I don't know what to do with you, John. You're an important part of our investigation. And I've read your case file; I can see you're an intelligent man.' Idly flicking through the papers in front of him, he sighed and pushed them away. 'But you've been toying with us for too long. I've been ordered to release you into the general population.' My pulse began to increase, my heartbeat hammering in my ears. This was not a move I had expected. 'Let's face it—you won't last three weeks in there. The bounty on your head is too high and your so-called brothers think that you've already given them up.' As much as I wished it weren't true, I knew that he was right. Yet still, I said nothing. I knew my only chance was to keep my cards close to my chest and see how this played out.

Leaning forward, Jim clasped his hands together. 'So, I'm here to advise you, John...no, *cajole* you to make the right choice. Do you want to martyr yourself for a cause not your own? Right now, you're facing twenty-five years to life.' He went on to describe his offer. If I would work with him and tell him everything I knew, he would make sure I was granted immunity for my crimes and swore that I wouldn't have to testify in open court. Getting up from his seat, he finished by saying, 'This deal expires in twenty-four hours. After that, I can't help you, they'll put you in general.' As I watched him leave the room, he paused and looked over his shoulder. 'The next time I see you will either be the beginning of your end...or the end of your beginning. The choice is yours. Either way, good luck and Godspeed.'

16

Resonance

My mind was racing as I was led back to my cell. *Calm down, think this through.* Suddenly, I heard my inner voice again. *Know yourself and you will be known.* At first, I was confused. *What are you talking about?* I asked myself. Over the next twenty-hour hours, I purified myself, chanted and prayed as the clock kicked down on my deadline. I continually asked my inner voice to guide me. I needed to know what kind of life would work for me. Others may call it destiny or fate; I needed to know what I was meant to do and how I could move forward with confidence.

You know what resonates with you when you hear it, because the truth strikes more than just your ears. It vibrates within and activates your core. In fact, when someone tells me the truth, I often can't help laughing out loud because their truth resonates within me and tickles my soul. It's an involuntary reaction and can be quite embarrassing. Sometimes, upon meeting certain people, it seems like my head is on fire; their presence lights up my chakras and I can actually feel a physical tingling in my crown. When I fall in love, a chamber within my heart is activated. It's an almost indescribable sensation, as if that that person is physically present inside me and gently humming, the vibrations emanating from the upper left chamber of my heart. As I contemplated my next step in life, I knew I needed to experience those same feelings. Jim had activated my crown chakra, so that was a good start, but I still needed more before fully committing to his offer.

The wrong decision would mean certain death.

The Hindus say that the events we see as coincidences are actually messages from God, or the universe, depending on your perspective. The Muslims have a similar parable in which God, seeking to contact a man, first strikes him with a feather. The man doesn't notice. He next sends a pebble, with no reaction. Finally, God sends a boulder. Similarly, a coincidence may be the first feather of destiny; if we fail to heed it, we will soon receive another message we cannot ignore. I was looking for a message, a sign from the universe.

I had received signs before that were quite powerful. When I first met Nicole H., she told me she had a dog, a Malamute-Husky mix, back home. A few days later, as I was walking back to the shared El Quawai house, a Malamute followed me home. I tried to coax it into the yard with food, but it simply licked me and ran away. At the time, I was convinced that this was a sign that Nicole would be my girl, but in retrospect, I think the universe was telling me that she would soon abandon me and run away at the last minute. I guess I wasn't in the best condition to interpret signs back then, too much bravado and too many drugs. But my mind was clear now.

That evening, I settled in for an all-night meditation session. Gradually, I began to feel myself levitating after about an hour. As my soul hovered over my body, the physical world around me disintegrated and I saw a scene begin to play out below me. I saw myself far below, walking along a road, travelling through a dense forest and up a mountainside, only to end up in a desert. In the centre of the desert, surrounded by sand, lay an oasis shaded by palm trees, filled with the sounds of cool gurgling water. There were people bathing in the water. It seemed to soothe their souls. Slowly, I moved over the glistening pool, towards a castle-like building in the distance. Inside, sat a guru, a man of Indian descent. Lifting his head, he seemed aware of my ethereal presence and beckoned me. 'Come, I have been waiting for you,' he said. 'We don't have much time and there are so many things you must learn before you journey further.' Into my hands, he placed a single feather from a red-tailed hawk. Then, he extended his arms, embracing me like a father.

As the guru hugged me, I was enveloped in a fog which immediately bore me away from him up into the clouds. I began to fly like a bird, only at an incomprehensible speed, soaring higher and higher into the mesosphere. In seconds, I was back in my cell, my soul innervated and invigorated. My experience had affected me on a cellular level. The very electromagnetic flow of the universe was surging through me. I jumped and had chills all over my body when I looked in my hand and saw the red-tailed hawk feather lying next to me. I was so excited, I feared I would spontaneously combust, but I quickly learned to accept the energy, calming myself with some deep-breathing exercises. I understood now why novices were cautioned not to attempt astral travel without an experienced guide. I had strayed into dangerous territory, but thankfully had survived to tell the tale. I kneeled, prayed and thanked my ancestors for guiding me, particularly Gandahara. *Thanks, Dad.*

The next morning, however, the quiet of the cell block was savagely disturbed at around 5.30 by the wailing of a tornado siren. Thankfully, having grown up in corn country, I was familiar with the sound. It reminded me of my father—he'd been able to tell the strength and direction of the storm based on the sound of the wind. 'Don't worry, that's a category 2, coming from the south at about 45–50 miles per hour,' he'd reassure us. 'It'll pass in about seven minutes.' But this storm was ridiculous. As the guards marched us out of our cells, we could hear the wind intensifying outside, rattling the windows in fury. The harsh electric lights in the ceiling above began to flicker. We were brought down to the storm shelter on the lowest floor of the prison. I laughed. The move was not for our safety—we would most likely be fine in our dungeon-like cells—but for their own; if the power went off, the cell doors would automatically open.

Rumour has it that a prisoner escaped once during a building-wide blackout. Concerned about the storm, the guards paid no attention to the count until he was long gone. Funnily enough, they caught him only a few days later. He was on the South Side, hanging with his homies. Your first reaction might be to label him an idiot; after all, why would he return to an area where he was known and could easily be found? But, after being in jail for five years, he had become a creature of habit. He ate at 6.00 a.m., 12.00 noon and 6.00 p.m. He walked in the yard every day at 11.00 a.m., rain or shine. Every night, the lights went out at 10.00 p.m. The routine gave him strength; it became his security blanket. So, once he escaped, he sought out the next best thing—his old neighbourhood, his old friends, his old habits. The police set up an eight-block perimeter around his house and, sure enough, caught him sleeping in the very park he used to sell drugs in. Most people confuse routine with comfort, and become stuck in the same rut for the rest of their lives. Very few understand that, with the proper escape velocity, you can go beyond those boundaries. Such rare souls, those brave astronauts, are the ones who evolve and push society forward, no matter the risk to themselves.

Boom, boom...a double clap of lightning. That definitely hit something, and whatever it was, it was very close. From the howling wind outside, it sounded like a category 3 tornado travelling in a north-westerly direction at astounding speeds of over 70 miles per hour. Foolishly, I believed that we were safe. Such a storm would never affect downtown Chicago, the densely packed area surrounding us would cause it to dissipate long before reaching us. I was wrong. The storm hit with a vengeance. It was as if God was finally inflicting on Chicago the penalty that it so richly deserved. This is for the murders, *crash*. This is for the inveterate racism, *scaruunch*, the groans of trees snapped and buildings collapsing. This is for the harm to all my children, *kaboom!*

A huge stroke of lightning split the sky again, this time scoring a direct hit. The entire building around us shook, the lights flaring as bright as an explosion...and then everything went dark. The wind screamed like a locomotive bearing down on us as the category-3 tornado tore through the building. I could hear the sound of brick—Chicago brick, the best brick in the world—crumbling all around us like sand. Metal beams groaned as they bowed down to God's will. There was a moment of complete stillness and then the ceiling above us collapsed. Everything came down on top of us at once—bricks, wood, metal, glass. A huge object came tumbling down and struck me on the back of my head. Lying on the floor, trapped beneath a wooden beam, I drifted in and out of consciousness. In the distance, I faintly heard the sounds of people yelling, moaning...dying. And then, thankfully, nothing...

Hours later, I awoke. Far above me, I could see shards of sunlight peeking through dark grey clouds. The storm had passed, leaving in its wake a sea of devastation and wreckage. Pulling myself from the rubble that surrounded my bruised and aching body, I looked around. In the ruins of the crumbled jail, I saw several bodies; some were alive, moving around slowly, but others simply lay there, unnaturally still. My first impulse was to run. So, I did; actually, I limped, still aching from the blows the storm had inflicted. I was free! But would my liberation be temporary or permanent? Soon, I knew, I would be pursued by two captors—the government and the El Quawai. It was a toss-up as to who would be worse. I headed west, towards Maxwell Street, Jew town, where I was sure I could find new clothes somewhere in the bazaars. I would take whatever I could scavenge in the ruins of the storm. *Wait.* I stopped. *The storm.* I had found truth in the storm and freedom, albeit a freedom that I knew could not last. *Thanks, Dad, for the sign.*

I needed a plan. As I walked, things slowly became clear. To know yourself is to know that God dwells within you and that this same intelligence dwells within everything else; its light, love and power permeating all that is. But, fundamentally, like recognizes like—if you know yourself to be divine, then divinity will in turn recognize you. It was a leap of faith, but I could feel all the way to my bones that the FBI District Chief, Jim, was more than who he had appeared to be. He was a sign sent by the universe. I would accept his offer and deal with the consequences; no matter what, I was sure I was being guided towards my destiny. But I'd be smart about it; I would call the FBI and tell Jim I would give them a statement, but only if they put me into their witness protection programme. This was my chance! No one knew I had survived the tornado. None of the El Quawai would ever guess I was still alive and cooperating with the FBI. I could have a whole new life.

Impatient now that I had made my decision, I sought the nearest payphone. It took forever, long gone were the days when there were phone booths on every street. Finally, I found one on the corner of 18th and Halsted and placed a collect call to the District Chief of the FBI Chicago Office. After an eternity of mind-numbingly annoying elevator music, the operator came back on the line. In a high-pitched nasal voice, she stated, 'Sir, he is unavailable, would you like to leave a message?' In a curt voice, I responded, 'Yes, I would. Tell Jim I know the whereabouts of their escaped inmate. But, I'll only talk to Jim himself.' As she hesitated, I added '...and you'd better hurry because I'll only hold for another minute.'

After a much quicker interlude of elevator music, a man came onto the phone. 'Hello?' It was Jim, I recognized his voice instantly. 'I know where the accountant has escaped to,' I replied quickly. 'Can we meet at a safe place?' Nonplussed, Jim tried to rally. 'Sure, where are you now?' 'Nice try, Jim,' I laughed. Taking a deep breath, I continued. 'Here's the deal: he's agreed to testify, provided you give him witness protection and send him far away from this Midwestern tornado zone.' There was a short laugh from the other side, while I held my breath. This was it. Finally, he acquiesced. 'Tell Mr Asanga we have a deal, provided his information is worth it.' At that moment, we were cut off and the line went dead. A flash of lightning lit up the entire sky above me, followed by a thunder clap so loud the pavement shook beneath my feet. At that moment, I saw everything in high definition. The blue sky, the grey intermittent clouds, the green green grass and the fecundate flowers and the trees...and I saw my life coming together. Resonance...

❧

17

Paul Bunyan

A few minutes later, I was hunched in a doorway. It was the moment to find out if Jim had kept his word. I flashbacked to our conversation earlier that day. 'I trust you, Jim. Tell me where to go and I'll come in.' 'Stay right where you are,' he'd responded. Had I been wrong to trust him? Exactly three minutes later, I looked up to see a 4,000-lb black Lincoln Continental creep around the corner, right on cue. It would either be my saviour or my demise. Unease roiled in my gut; it looked suspiciously like a hitman's car from a gangster movie, with dark-tinted windows, matte black trim and wheels, and the conspicuous absence of chrome. As the car pulled up beside me, the window purred down. It was Nicole. 'Get in, quickly!' She opened the back door for me and, steeling myself, I got in.

Sitting across from me, Nicole looked as beautiful as ever. With one taut yet slender thigh crossed over the other underneath a tight skirt, she looked like a dream, one I was sure designed solely to titillate me. It was working. Her leather jacket was short, exposing her tanned and muscular midriff. 'Wow!' she said, wrinkling her nose. 'You're more than a little ripe. Where did you get those clothes, a drunken pimp's convention?' *Great*, I thought to myself, *Nicole's got jokes*. Choosing to say nothing, I stared out of the window as we rolled smoothly onto the Dan Ryan freeway, heading north. We were on our way to Wisconsin.

This time of year, Wisconsin is emerald green in the midst

of its rainy spring season. It's worlds apart from Indiana, even though both are part of the Midwest. In Indiana, the humid summers sweat corn into sweetness. In Wisconsin, it's all about the cheese. The emerald lush fields of the dairy farms are a cow's paradise and they respond by producing enough cheese and butter to supply the entire nation. But, originally, Wisconsin was known as a mining state due to the abundance of minerals hidden beneath the fertile soil. Lumber mills soon followed. Once upon a time, this was a state for tough hard-working men who could mine the earth and tame the forests. In neighbouring Minnesota, the legend of Paul Bunyan was told. A mountain man who could perform great feats of strength, he helped build the nation by supplying wood for its building and, of course, all the other paper goods we take for granted.

This was what I needed, somewhere completely different from the grit of Chicago and the bucolic memories of Indiana. After driving all day, we left the highway as the sun was setting, following a road that wound around a malachite lake. As the light faded, the surface of the lake glimmered in the dusk, its colour slowly melding into a deep forest green. We slowly made our way around the perimeter of the lake, until the headlights of the car eventually picked out a side road leading up over a hill. Eventually, we came to a stop next to an old lumber yard. Stepping out of the car, I stretched my cramped limbs and looked around. The place was Pompeii, as if everything had died on the same day and nothing had been touched for a millennia. I could imagine this same yard a hundred years ago, filled with lumberjacks regaling each other with tales of superhuman feats. I could smell blueberry flapjacks being whipped up in the kitchen, mixed in with the scent of robust coffee with a touch of molasses.

Alas, my anachronistic musings were just that. The dust and

rot had hardened over the years into a moribund reminder of the halcyon past. This broken-down dust-filled ruin, of course, would be my new home. I had expected a little more from the FBI, seeing as I was their star witness, but weighing the option of this relic from the past as opposed to trying to live in jail or Chicago with a target on my back, this place would do.

I had spent most of the drive ignoring Nicole, or whatever her name was, purposefully avoiding eye contact. I could not chance giving her the opportunity to see how much she had devastated me. She was one of my betrayers and I was not quite ready to look at her from a different perspective. I loved her. I confided in her. I risked my life for her, only to have her take it all away—my love, my freedom and all my money! Fixing my gaze into the distance, I reminded myself that I had survived being in a deadly gang, life in prison and the Federal government; this one lady would not see me cry. Behind me, I heard her climbing out of the vehicle and striding around towards the trunk of the car. Furtively, I took the opportunity to look at her closely while her back was turned. God, she was so gorgeous. Her Californian beach body was in full effect as she pulled out a huge duffle bag from the trunk. I could see her toned stomach peeking out from under her jacket. Although I only glanced quickly so that she wouldn't notice me admiring her, I could tell she still knew. Her hips swung seductively from side to side as she sauntered towards me with the bag and threw it to the ground in front of me. 'Here, I figured you might need some new clothes.'

Just as I leaned down to retrieve the duffel, she suddenly darted in front of me. Grabbing my face with both hands, she said urgently, 'Look at me, *look* at me!' Reluctantly, I found myself staring into the bottomless pool of her dark blue eyes.

'This wasn't just a job for me. I'm not some kind of unfeeling monster.' Leaning forward, she gently touched her forehead to mine. 'You're special, but you need to find your purpose in life. I found mine and, sadly, it conflicted with whatever could have been between us. But when I was with you—that was real.' Tears were now welling up in both of our eyes. But we were the same, she and I—too tough to actually cry, too proud to reveal our sensitive interiors. 'Yogi, people do strange things in the name of love. I love you, and I saved your life.' Slowly, she released me and drew apart, until only our hands were touching. 'You can't see that now, but one day you will.' At this, she leaned forward one last time and kissed me gently on the lips. Then, she let go and walked away. Looking over her shoulder, she told me someone would be in contact soon. 'Read the materials I left you so you'll recognize them when they do. Oh, and your favourite sweaters are in the bag, take care of them so that the moths don't eat them.'

The black Lincoln pulled away, carrying with it my second love and betrayer. *Women*...and then she makes a dramatic exit before I have a chance to respond! I saved her life, saved her stupid career and all she could say was that she loves me. *Right.* Sighing, I made my way towards a log cabin set back from the main yard. Mulling over Nicole's parting words, I frowned. *What was she talking about, my favourite sweaters?* She knew that I hated sweaters, convinced they were a fashion faux pas with no earthly reason to exist. Curious, I crouched down to unzip the bag, half expecting to see a group of horrid moth-eaten sweaters as a final ignominious joke. Peering in, I could see that, yes, there were sweaters at the bottom of the bag. I grabbed them, but there was something bunched up in the sleeves. I angrily pulled out wads of paper, ready to throw them away. But it wasn't paper. It was money, *my* money. That crazy blonde had stuffed the sweaters with at least $300,000 in cash.

Leave it to Nicole to not even allow me to properly hate her. Do women always have to have the last word? *Apparently they do,* I thought to myself as I read the instructions she had left for me. Two FBI cars would be coming for me in two weeks, two black Lincolns with two or three passengers each. One would have Illinois plates and the other Wisconsin plates. *Anyone not in a suit or who looks too casual is not FBI,* I read. *Watch from afar when they arrive. If they're not wearing suits, run.* Tearing up the note, I shook my head at her audacity. I didn't need her to tell me what FBI agents look like. I could smell those guys coming a mile away. I knew their haircuts, their lack of style and their general air of conformity like the back of my hand. She got no extra points from me for her cautionary words of warning. I would be just fine.

18

Log Cabin Days

Iset up inside an empty log cabin that had probably once been the administrative office/master residence of the yard manager. There were fireplaces in several of the offices and, naturally, one in the master suite. Apart from some kerosene lamps, I couldn't see any other source of heat, so I prayed fervently they would work—the chilly night air already stung against my skin. Fortunately, they did. I lit a few lamps in the master suite, chopped wood from some ancient cords that had probably been left outside for years and carried it inside to start a fire. Nicole had also provided me with food in her care package: Colombian coffee, my favourite chocolates and a few other items reminiscent of my former brownstone existence.

As I sat there eating the first dinner for months prepared by my own hands, thoughts gurgled in and out of my mind like the nearby tributaries. *How did I end up here? Who lived here before me? Will the El Quawai find me and kill me for breaking their code of silence? Do I deserve to die?* Feeling overwhelmed, I finished my makeshift meal and headed back outside. I needed to walk to find myself, calm myself. As I made my way into the yard, I was greeted by a wondrous sight. The Wisconsin sky above, unspoiled by light pollution, was scattered with thousands of stars, thousands of bright gods controlling their own ecosystems. Were there planets around those suns? Was there life on those planets? Contemplating the vast ever-expanding universe finally calmed me, bringing me the sense of perspective I desperately needed. Hell, even the planets themselves were miniscule afterthoughts within the universal whole. But, unlike Nietzsche, this thought did not lead me to the notion that 'Gott ist tot' (God is Dead). I am innately optimistic. For me, the innumerable constellations were proof of God's existence, not necessarily in the same sense as a religious zealot, but rather evidence of a spiritual core or essence that underlies everything in this universe.

Intelligent design is the concept that the universe was designed by an intelligent being, which some people refer to as God. In reality, it is just another way of discussing the relationship between the macrocosm and the microcosm. 'As above, so below.' These types of sayings emphasize the fact that God is reflected in nature and in everything around us. Just as the stars align and form vortexes, we humans align ourselves with local groups, political parties, countries and international alliances such as the United Nations. We, in a sense, mirror those rhythms which we see in nature. The divine lives in everything around us; for example, in the way the seasons change with such purpose. In the fall, the moon is full for longer and has different phases than in other seasons. These extra lunar phases provide more light during the evening, allowing us to harvest the crops grown from seeds sown in spring. Such rhythm is not surprising. When everything is broken down to its bare essence, one finds God—the energy within every living thing.

Certain religions portray God as a supreme personality that judges us, rewarding us when we are good and punishing us when we are not. From a Machiavellian perspective, such thinking behoves these religious institutions because it enhances their ability to control their acolytes. Their followers are taught that they are separate from God, and that only by following certain dictates will they be deemed acceptable and be allowed into heaven after they die. The modern view is more scientific and greatly influenced by Eastern religions such as Buddhism and Taoism; these philosophies view God as an impersonal force that does not judge us, and is an energy that vivifies all life.

The intelligent design to which I—and I think most modern spiritualists—refer is that God is the ultimate energy within us all. Therefore, if we act in accordance with the principles of universal harmony, we can ride the waves that flow from this universal force we call God. However, we must learn its true nature and respect it; you don't stick your hand straight into the fire, or put electrical items into water. Fundamentally, religion serves a legitimate purpose in teaching us how to communicate with God. However, I believe that they need to update their methods and teachings to match the evolving sophistication of modern society.

Religion has the task of monitoring what information is released and when it should be disseminated to the public. For example, some schools of thought claim that a wondrous place called Atlantis once existed, at a time when man enjoyed unfettered creativity. However, there are inherent dangers associated with limitless imagination. It is believed that, during this time, centaurs were created if a man had sex with a horse, while the Minotaur arose as a result of union with a bull. But God, while impersonal, always seeks balance and order. He caused Atlantis to disappear, not as a punishment, but in order to preserve balance. After the Great Flood, a new order was created in which esoteric and potentially dangerous knowledge was zealously guarded and withheld until the zeitgeist manifested a certain degree of readiness.

I believe we are now on the cusp of unlocking these ancient

secrets. Books such as Alice Bailey's *A Treatise on Cosmic Fire*, written in 1925, have helped to push us to this precipice. The Theosophical Society and other groups have been leading this new age since the beginning of the twentieth century. We are now in the Age of Aquarius, one stage beyond the Piscean Age, the age of Jesus. The concept of intelligent design should be embraced as something that will lead us forward, not a reason to go backwards as it is sometimes used by Right-wing Christians. It is our responsibility to understand our place in the universe and to manifest our true divine nature for the betterment of all.

This was a lot of thought for a solitary walk on my first night as a lumberjack. Shaking my head, I wondered if Nicole had slipped any leftover psychotropic drugs into the coffee. 'Never trust the government,' I muttered to myself as I returned to the cabin. That night, I slept on an old bed, on top of the sheets. I was not quite ready to fully embrace my surroundings and still held the attitude of one who may have to wake up and leave at a moment's notice.

Despite the uncomfortable bed, I enjoyed my solitude over the next few weeks. My days developed a rhythm. I would rise with the sun and walk around the lake first thing in the morning. During these explorations, I honed my skills of observation, looking carefully at my surroundings and for signs of intruders. Was everything still in place? Did a pile of wood move? Was I being watched? Aside from a few recalcitrant raccoons, all was good. Nevertheless, I stayed vigilant and developed potential escape routes and plans to defend myself, if needed. Although I knew my defence would be fairly limited as I had no weapons, I began gathering rocks, figuring that I could claim the high ground and hide in the tower to throw them at unsuspecting intruders. Accuracy was key, as I would only have a few minutes before I was discovered; so, I began practising my aim.

As I was completely alone, I no longer concerned myself with my appearance. My hair grew to shoulder length and became matted and unruly. I stopped shaving my beard, which kept me warm on cold days. I looked increasingly Brahmin-like with each passing day; Uncle Justa would have been proud, I finally resembled a holy man. I only needed sandals and a robe to complete the look. Although I missed my books, I found a couple of dusty tomes in one of the cabins, which contained some great stories about lumberjacks and some Midwestern folk tales. In my mind, I was the star of my very own folk tale, the Mahayana Jack. He was a lumberjack that felled trees with his mind. After becoming one with the tree, the tree would kindly sacrifice some of its branches to provide me with warmth and shelter. As a result, I didn't need to kill the whole tree. The Mahayana Jack had a heart!

19

Vengeance Is Mine

I had fun living in my fantasy world for about two and a half weeks—seventeen days, three hours and fifteen minutes, to be precise. Suddenly, as I was finishing my morning reconnoitre one day, I saw them. Two black Lincolns winding their way up to the lumber yard, unmistakably the Feds. It was time to handle my business. I was somewhat prepared for this day. I had taken the precaution of burying the money under my favourite oak tree. After an intimate conversation, she had agreed to take care of my belongings so long as I took care of her forest. Just like a mother to worry about her entire family and not only herself! I had promised that I would come back and make sure there would be no deforestation, at least not while I was alive.

As the first of the cars pulled up, I grabbed my packed bag and met them by the front door. Five white guys in off-the-rack suits exited the vehicles. They had the look and smell of FBI agents, with wafts of Old Spice and cheap haircuts. I was unusually happy to see them; it had been a while since I had seen another human face or heard actual voices. A dark-haired guy in a plain black suit and ordinary but finely polished black Florsheims indicated that I should get in the back of the second car. I obliged, noting as I passed that both plates were from Illinois. *Huh*, I thought smugly, *looks like Nicole was wrong.*

Clambering into the car, I froze in shock as I saw who was sitting in the back seat. *Dennis? Oh god, this can't be good.*

'*As'salamu alaykum*, my brother,' he greeted me. '*Wa'alaykum salaam*,' I mumbled ruefully. There was a tense silence for a while as I waited for the bullet I was sure would be coming. But the seconds ticked by and I continued to draw breath. Finally, he smiled. 'Yatah, we have been waiting for an opportunity to correct a bad situation. As you know, God is good, and he has provided.' I nodded, wanting with all my heart to explain myself to my former friend. *Dennis, you don't understand that what you guys are doing, well-intentioned as it may be, it is wrong. You can't sell drugs to your own people and you shouldn't let young girls sell their bodies so you can live a life of luxury.* I wanted to say, *Dennis, you're better than the rest; you could actually lead your people and uplift them.* But the words were caught in my throat like a fish bone. I sat there, silently, frozen in fear and regret. I wouldn't be able to keep my promise to Oak. I wouldn't get to spend my life chasing nirvana. I was headed to an early, and assuredly painful, death. Dennis, in turn, simply stared through me. I had to give him props, his face gave no hint of what was to come. God is truly a trickster.

As I felt the engine of the car rumble to life beneath me, I was filled with silent derision for how I had treated Nicole. She knew what she had done and I had given her no chance for redemption, no chance to say, 'John, this is why I did it'. Now life was coming full circle, fast. It was I who desperately wanted to explain myself to Dennis. But, I figured, it would be for the best to just remain silent. No forgiveness sought, no absolution given.

We rode south for what seemed just shy of two hours. I recognized the waters of Lake Michigan as we passed, but this didn't seem to be either Wisconsin or Illinois. We circled off the main highway onto an idyllic country road, surrounded by rolling verdant hills. Red barns, cornfields and wind lilting through tall grasses. Just beautiful! That's when it hit me—the tulip poplars, the peonies, the geraniums—I had come home to die. We were in Indiana. Looking through the window, I figured we must be near Michigan City. Stan had always talked about his place in Michigan City, but I had never been invited. Well, this wasn't quite the party I had fantasied about, but it seemed I was to be the guest of honour. We neared the beach and began driving past some lakeside cabins. Finally, we came to a stop in front of a cabin at the very end of a deserted cul-de-sac. *Fantastic*, I thought to myself, *I bet the lake itself is in the backyard. They can just dump my body into the water.* Without a doubt, this was the time to call on all my guardian angels. Either they would deliver me from this dubious ending or they could welcome me into the next phase of existence. *Come now, angels,* I prayed. Come now.

The head car screeched to a stop, did a doughnut in the driveway and drove back off as soon as we arrived. As we idled, two ersatz FBI agents pulled me roughly out of our car. Dennis exited last, instructing them to take me downstairs and that he would handle the rest. As I was frog-marched from the car towards the cabin, everything slowed down. For the last time, I saw the beautiful sky arcing overhead, framed by trees, and smelled the sweet perfume of crushed flowers underfoot. But the closer we got to the door, the more things began to speed up. Inside the cabin, they took me downstairs into the basement. It smelled old and musty, circa 1972. I looked around. A burnt-orange bean bag lay off to the side, with an old black pleather couch and a matching La-Z-Boy recliner next to it. This must have been the furniture of the original owners. A wet bar with metal stools was adjacent to the far wall. On the other side of the room, glass doors led to the beach and lakefront. Nice digs!

But the question was: would I last even a few hours to enjoy this place?

As his two henchmen finished tying me to the recliner, Dennis deliberately pimp walked his way across the room. 'LEAVE US,' he bellowed. The two men rapidly followed instructions. Dennis turned his back on me and watched them out of the room. Just before they reached the top stair, he cocked his hand, did a 360-degree turn and backhanded me across the face. 'This is what we do to mother fuckin' traitors.' *Slam...* the door had closed behind them. Dennis spun again, but this time came just short of hitting me. My eyes still stinging from the previous blow, I blinked up at him. The hard, implacable façade had crumbled. 'Man, you were my brother, how could you give us all up just to save yourself?' Swallowing, I began to speak. 'No, don't talk,' Dennis interrupted. 'I don't want to hear your eastern B.S., which, by the way, you don't even follow!' His eyes were furious and he began pacing backwards and forwards across the room. 'The only reason you're living through the night is because I convinced Stan that they would have to let him go once you don't show up at his prelim hearing. Then, he can come here himself and look you in the eyes when he stabs you in the heart the way you did to him...'

'Okay, enough of the drama,' I yelled. Dennis sputtered in indignation, but I continued, looking at his face. 'Look, yes, I wanted to blow it all up. But I wanted that because it was wrong, and you know it! Just because it's black men instead of white men making money off of the south side doesn't make it right! You guys are choke holding your own people with drugs and violence. Dennis, take the next step past your pride and love of control towards actual progress.' Spitting at me, he laughed. 'Even now, you think you can look down on me. Save me your meaningless pontification. You're not holy, you're a betrayer.' As he left the room, his last words echoed in my head. 'You're dead to me. Soon, you'll be dead full stop. You're only living so that Stan can finish this himself. So yeah, let's not talk. Enjoy your last week or so, 'coz that's all you've got.' It was a reprieve, albeit temporary. *Thank you, angels. Come now.*

I spent the next week and a half awaiting Stan's preliminary hearing and my impending death. I spent hours at a time in a meditative state. *Come now, angels, come now.* I focused on unity, on my true self, one connected, continuous and infinite being. We are all one. Once we understand that hurting others is really hurting ourselves, all of the pain will stop. I prayed that that day would come soon, like in the next week or so. Every morning, Dennis would come downstairs to the basement to gloat and rub in the fact that my days were numbered. He took sadistic pleasure in each daily update. 'I talked to the lawyers, they say the prelim is in four days, so you've got about five left.' *Thanks, homey, I appreciate the update.* But I said nothing out loud, preferring to focus all my energy on my meditation. By two days out, it was just me and Dennis in the house. My meditations were getting stronger. I could feel unity with all there is. I wasn't quite there yet, but I was close to true equanimity regarding my pending fate. *Come now, angels, come.*

※

20

Angeli Venire

On the penultimate morning before the preliminary hearing, Dennis was late for his daily gloating session. It wasn't like him; he never missed an opportunity to start his day with a laugh at my expense. Above me, I heard footsteps on the wooden floorboards, moving with a sense of purpose. Finally, at around 10.30 a.m., I head the basement door open and his measured tread descending the stairs to my makeshift jail cell. Brusquely, he began to untie the ropes that bound my cramped arms to the chair. 'Say nothing. We have to go, and we have to go *now*.' Pushing me in front of him, he marched us both upstairs and out of the front door into a waiting dark-brown Camaro. 'Sit low,' he barked as he shoved me into the back. I did. He slammed the door behind me and quickly jumped behind the wheel. The tyres spun out slightly as he accelerated us out of the cul-de-sac. We raced past the hills, past the corn, heading south. I caught a glimpse of the speedometer edging past 110 as we pulled into the fast lane. 'Dennis,' I couldn't help exclaiming, 'You're going to get us caught!'

At this, Dennis laughed and whipped out a CB receiver from his front pocket. Pressing the buttons, he called out in a business-like tone, 'Alpha Mike Foxtrot. We will be at the designated spot in two hours. Over.' Our eyes met in the rear-view mirror as I gaped in astonishment. Dennis smiled. 'You dumbass. Now, look, I've saved your life for the last time. You were right, the FBI did come to get you—in this case, me.' As he caught a glimpse of my bewildered face, he laughed again but sobered up quickly. 'Now, first things first, we have to get you to Peoria and then to Chicago by tomorrow afternoon in time to testify. This thing is much bigger than you know. The guys at District know that Stan could not have masterminded this operation alone. Black folks only sell drugs, they don't have the wherewithal to bring them into the country. Also, they don't have the capability to transport women across state lines, especially in the south.' Breaking off, he concentrated on the road for a second. 'So, that leaves us to the only possible conclusion. There's a mole inside the Bureau. And that's where you come in—whoever tries to kill you is our mole.' I finally found my voice. 'Whoever tries to *kill* me?!' Dennis nodded casually. 'Oh yeah, bro, you always talked about living in the storm. Well, you've got one tonight. There are several FBI agents who want you dead.' Sighing, I shook my head. 'I hope my angels are with me tonight.' Chuckling, Dennis retorted, 'Well, you'll need them, my brother, because you are the chum and these fish are *hungry.*'

We drove through the north-eastern Indiana countryside in silence as I tried to process all of this new information and figure out where I stood. Finally, I blurted out, 'So, you're FBI too. Did you come with Nicole from Cali?' Shaking his head, Dennis replied 'Although both Nicole and I were assigned to the El Quawai, I'm from Boston. I went to Boston College for undergrad and Virginia for law school. Nicole is a talented field agent, but I'm on a higher track, management. I was bored behind my desk and requested this assignment. My ultimate goal, maybe twenty years from now, is to be either the director or someone close to the top.' I could feel the ambition radiating from him and wondered how I had ever been duped into thinking he was a simple thug. 'I can see the headlines now...the first African-American director of the FBI,' he finished, his voice purring in satisfaction.

'So, when did you make me?' I questioned. 'Honestly, I made you from the first moment we met. I knew you were the one who could finish the job, the Punjab kid they would never see coming. Some people have souls too good to be a gangster.' I felt a small flutter of relief in the pit of my stomach. 'I knew you weren't in it for the same reasons as the others. And Stan knew it too, but his ego was inflated to admit it to himself and, what's more, he thought he could control you with women and drugs.' I felt shame rise again into my throat. He was right; I had been controlled by my very basest desires. 'I'll admit, we were worried about you for a bit, but once you shared your stash with Nicole to save her life, we knew you hadn't completely changed. That being said, you were at a tipping point, so we had to throw you a curveball and force you to see who you really were. A good guy, magnanimous at heart.'

Feeling like I was talking to him honestly for the very first time, I told Dennis about how I came from a long line of spiritual leaders, the Asangas, and how my father was destined to be the return of a bodhisattva. 'But he never wanted that responsibility,' I finished, 'so he left home and made science his religion.' I felt a wave of unspoken understanding flow from Dennis. Emboldened, I admitted, 'After he died, my uncle told me that I was the one who was meant to unite the East with the West and to change the world. I laughed at him. I'm not that being. I can't be the Golden Child.' Dennis laughed, 'I guess one day we'll know the truth.'

As we drove, Dennis regaled me with stories of his upbringing. He was from a strong black family that had survived slavery, Jim Crow and everything else this world could throw at them. 'My mother told me,' he mused, 'that we are made of tempered steel, heated by hate and quenched by knowledge. Like you, I have always been an outsider. But I grew to realize that white folks weren't actually superior to me, either physically or mentally, but that society gave them advantages at every level. So I had to be exponentially better than they were just to stay even. In the long run, it tempered me. I don't hate them, I don't waste time disliking those who don't like me. I simply focus on my own evolutionary path.' It seemed as if we were kindred in ways I had never imagined, Dennis and I. We were on the same path, home to the infinite.

Nevertheless, I was not quite ready to join my ancestors in the afterlife, so it was imperative that we use all of our guile to survive the expected onslaught that would take place over the next few days. 'Do you have any idea who could be the mole?' I asked, bringing us back down to earth. 'Or should I be ready to shoot any white person I see? Say, speaking of shooting, do I get a gun? Despite my many skills, I'm not some magical Indian mystic who can materialize bullets with his mind.' Smirking, Dennis indicated the glove compartment. Opening it, I found a .45 pistol inside. 'Yes, I know exactly who the mole is. Keith O'Conner, a good Irishman from Bridgeport who coordinated the unit that picked you up. He doesn't know that I was working undercover, I report only to D.C.' I nodded as I checked the safety of the gun in my hand. 'But don't worry. We probably won't confront any rogue FBI agents just yet. For now, it'll be the Italian and Irish mafia, far more vicious than the FBI.' Ignoring my glare, Dennis continued talking obliviously. 'The rogue agents will probably try to stop us from reaching the courtroom, once we're actually at the courthouse. They will come at you, probably either when you're in the john or during the witness transfer.' Finally making eye contact, Dennis shrugged at my look. 'It's complicated, definitely an adventure. All we can do is trust each other and communicate at all times.'

The back roads of Northern Illinois weren't that much different from Indiana. The bogs and rivers were populated by sycamores, white oaks and mulberry trees. I even saw a few oddly named black tupelos whose leaves were bright orange. As we drove ever closer to the coming fray, it occurred to me that state lines and borders were such a civilized construct. Two hundred years ago, the Native Americans had roamed between Ohio, Indiana and Illinois without any such distinctions, following the buffalo and other indigenous animals, living in harmony with nature. They took only that which they needed and left what they did not for those that would come after them. They made as little imprint on the land as possible, out of respect for the gods.

It's funny; for all the supposed superiority of the whites in this area, Chicago was founded by an African man hailing from Haiti, Jean Baptiste Point du Sable. He established a prosperous trading settlement at the mouth of the Chicago River and lived there with Kitawaha, his Native American wife of the Potawatomi tribe, and their two children. It wasn't until recently, in the last twenty years or so, that du Sable's role in founding Chicago was officially recognized. Rewrite history and you can control the narrative. I grew up thinking that all Native Americans were savages and that black descendants from slaves were a close second, with no redeeming values other than as basic labourers. Who knew that they founded the prodigious city of Chicago? And why weren't their descendants wealthy landowners today? Why weren't they afforded the same reverence as the pilgrims or the Daughters of the American Revolution? These were the types of discussions Dennis and I had as we travelled towards Peoria. Just the nervous musings of two young intellectuals who knew that a reckoning was coming and that they would not be the same afterwards.

21

Deliverance

It took us about one and a half hours to arrive at our fleabag hotel in Peoria because we avoided the freeways. The drive itself had been great. It gave Dennis and me a chance to talk, to solve the problems of the world and to really get to know each other, without all the false bravado associated with being a member of the El Quawai. Naturally, we settled in the black part of town; we figured it would be easier to spot any Irish, Italian or FBI types coming for us. The proprietor of our building, Mable, a beautiful black woman with a rich dark complexion that rivalled the darkest of chocolates, set us up in a room on the second floor with a good view of the street below. She also agreed to deliver meals from nearby restaurants so that we would not be seen around town. Our first meal, delivered in a bucket, was some delicious fried chicken and dumplings with buttermilk biscuits and Alaga syrup on the side. If you haven't had Alaga syrup, you better ask somebody and find some. It's the best cane syrup money can buy, not light like maple syrup, but closer to molasses; it comes from Alabama and Georgia, hence its name. I dipped my fried chicken into the syrup as well. Even Dennis enjoyed it; although he tried to act polite at first, eating his chicken with a knife and fork, but once he tasted the syrup, we were both dippin' and drippin'. Good eating, not fancy, but good.

I stood sentinel for the first few hours until around 1.00. Dennis took over after that because he wanted me to be fresh for my testimony the next day. At around 4.00 a.m., he gently nudged me awake and calmly yet firmly said, 'Get up. It's time. Grab your stuff, you can get dressed in the car.' Yawning, I quickly met his gaze and saw the look of sheer power and determination in his eyes. Hastily, I got out of bed and switched to alacrity mode. My movements were smooth yet swift. Looking out of the window, Dennis cursed quietly. 'Three white guys, probably Italian. Across the street. Coming fast.' Moving as quickly as we could, we made our way to the fire escape. I could hear crashes and indignant sounds from downstairs, sleepy residents being disturbed, as whoever was after us made a methodical sweep of the hotel, room by room. Thankfully, Dennis had rented multiple rooms under fake names so the intruders would not know our exact whereabouts even if they checked the registry. But they had their own tricks up their sleeve, hitting us with a delayed double pincer. The three men Dennis had seen approaching the front of the building had stayed outside, no doubt waiting for us. Inside the building, unknown El Quawai members were making their presence known. We could hear them yelling, 'Come out, Nigger, Punjab Nigger. We know you're there!' Internally, I responded with a chant of my own. *Come now, angels, come now.*

We negotiated the fire escape as quietly as we could. Moving with slow, fluid, cat-like motions, we stepped onto the ledge in unison, before climbing down and opening the last ladder so we could jump to the ground. As the alleyway was a mixture of dirt and gravel, we had to tread carefully not to be heard. *Crunch, crunch,* my heart stopped with every sound. Dennis and I tried to place each foot on the ground simultaneously so that our pursuers would not hear multiple footsteps. Once we were at least 50 feet away from the hotel, we started sprinting down the street. Dennis had the foresight to park our car about a block away down another alley. As we ran towards it, I heard small pops coming from behind us. *Zing, ping.* Bullets came flying from the darkness behind us, hitting the brick walls of the alley and the gravel of the ground. *Don't turn around, just keep running,* I chanted to myself. *Stay low, zigzag without rhythm so they can't predict your movements.* I zigged three steps and zagged two, zagged for four steps and zigged one.

Behind us, we could hear them gaining, the bullet sounds getting closer and pinging off the walls with more force. I knew that once we reached the car, they would catch us, surround us and probably kill us. But there was no time for thought or reflection, I just had to be one with the moment and react to whatever happened next. As we approached the last intersection before the car, our already dire situation got worse, much worse. Ahead of us, I could see five white guys turning either corner from both sides of the street, running straight towards us. My only hope was that they would miss us in the crossfire and shoot each other.

Strangely, Dennis was, if anything, encouraged by their presence. 'Duck down, bend your back and walk close to the ground!' he yelled as he sprinted for cover. Much to my relief, the white guys began shooting over our heads, towards the group approaching us from behind. As we got closer, I saw with a surge of intense relief the familiar cheap suits and shoes—they were FBI agents. Dennis's boys had come through! My angels had arrived! Running past us, the agents began to engage the El Quawai and their Italian compadres. We jumped into the waiting car and followed a Ford Escort away from the shoot-out, screaming down Hamilton towards Madison. As we crossed Madison, another Ford came from behind us to form a caravan. We turned right on Fayette and left onto the I-74. Once on I-74, we sped up to 100 mph. Man, these guys could drive. We stayed on the I-74 for about twenty to thirty minutes and then merged with the I-55. As the first tendrils of dawn made their way over the horizon, we were heading straight towards downtown Chicago. We were driving towards the light, towards my angels who were heeding my call.

22

Breaking the Cycle

As the sun rose to greet us, I slowly calmed down and the adrenaline rush of the shoot-out began to subside. I began thinking of the testimony I would have to give. I needed to change my frame of reference, prepare myself for the moment I would have to look Stan in the eyes and betray him. It's not easy to betray someone, even when you think it's justified. I was helping to send this man away for life, issuing a death blow to the organization he had spent his life building. Stan had joined the El Quawai as a teenager, when they were called the Blackstone Rangers. Blackstone was a street on the south-east side of Chicago that ran from 95th all the way downtown. It had its good spots but, generally, it was not a safe street to walk at night if you didn't have the right gang props. Stan and his boys had negotiated with the cops for this territory.

On his first night, thirteen-year-old Stan was approached by a cop who told him he had a choice—he could either be arrested every night or take a beating. This was the customary deal the cops would offer to young guys. Most guys preferred not to take the back alley beating. But the flip side was, if you were arrested numerous times, eventually you would be sent to Juvie Hall, a finishing school for thugs. Once having been sent there, your life would change. The pretty boys were raped, the tough guys beaten up and forced to choose a gang, where they were trained in the arts of selling drugs, pimping, breaking and entering or hotwiring cars. Stan chose the beatings. Three weeks later, the cop, having finally tired of practising his body blow punches on Stan, told him that he was smart. He didn't have to play this game. Instead, he should work directly for the cop. The cop would provide marijuana for Stan to sell.

That's how it worked out that Stan, at thirteen, entered the drug trade. His distributors were cops and he was their main salesman. He eventually devised a system and employed a crew of guys to sell the drugs for him, all under the protection of the Chicago Police Department. Their only requirements were that they be paid their share of the profits on time, that no kids under eleven be caught selling on the streets and that Stan occasionally rat out rival gang members to keep arrest records high. From this foundation, Stan built a formidable gang. By the time he was twenty, Stan was a daunting figure in the community. The street cops he had made deals with had by this point graduated to senior positions, so his police protection was broadened and strengthened. His gang had viciously dominated most of the South Side and had begun to move onto the West Side. He was also known for his largess within the community, having used some of the illegal funds to establish breakfast and after-school programmes and even day-care centres.

However, as the Blackstone Rangers grew in stature, they had to change their approach. While Stan's cop friends protected him as much as they could, even they could not exempt him from all prosecution. It was then that Stan judiciously decided to change the Rangers from a street gang into a religious group. As a bona fide religion, it would be much more difficult for them to be prosecuted. The courts could prevent gang members from associating with other criminals, but they could not prevent them from practising their faith; thus, the El Quawai was created.

Looking back, I know that the El Quawai sold drugs to kids, forced young women into a life of prostitution and murdered rival gang members...but they were also a source of strength for the black community. No one else had ever invested anything into this community. Sitting in the car, I considered my motives for testifying. *Was I prepared to blow apart this organization? Was I doing this to help others, or just to save my own skin?*

At that moment, Dennis must have noticed my sombre reflection in the rear-view mirror because he started talking. 'Listen, brother, I know you feel a certain allegiance to Stan and, in many respects, he is a good man. But he's not really changing the dynamic for us black folks. He's merely substituted himself as the tyrant of his people by replicating the abuse normally inflicted by whites.' Choosing his words carefully, Dennis continued, 'Real change can only come if you overhaul the entire system. These people don't need the pyric victory that comes with the drugs and sex trade. They need true participation in America's economic system. They need better schools, better jobs.' Deep down, I knew that what he was saying was the truth. 'Yes, this will be painful, but you need to break the chain so that new leaders can emerge with real education, not just knowledge of the streets. Although you're betraying Stan, you're freeing whole generations of kids who can go on to make the right choices and avoid this never-ending cycle of poverty, drugs and death.'

Dennis's prescient words were very much appreciated. Although I believed in loyalty and acknowledged that Stan was one of the first people outside of my family to truly believe in me, I understood that his actions were wrong. As difficult as it would be, I needed to look Stan in the eye and send him away so that the next generation of young men from Chicago could forge a better path. Everything is not always what it seems.

My apparent betrayal of Stan would lead to redemption for his people. I had not come this far *just to contemplate the sand and the trees*. I needed to testify and change the course of history for all South Siders.

23

Trial by Fire

As we pulled up to a makeshift building on Dearborn, the time for musing had ended. It was showtime! I laughed as I sized up the temporary prefab building where the trial would take place; it had only been months since the tornado, and the old building was still being rebuilt. God's wrath is nothing to play with and I hoped that those in power would focus upon the genuine administration of justice this time, especially if they expected the new building to last. Around the rear of the building, there was a special parking lot where more FBI agents were waiting to meet us and escort us into the back of the building. Remembering Dennis's warning, I decided to use the restroom while I still had the escort.

I entered the grimy room with a fair amount of trepidation, despite knowing that my escort was waiting for me just outside. I looked under every stall and only relaxed once I was sure I was alone. As I approached one of the urinals, I heard a sliding sound in the ceiling over one of the stalls. I had a brief moment of panic; I had heard about assassins hiding in false ceilings to ambush their targets. Thankfully, this being Chicago, it was only a rat scurrying around. *Of course*, I thought ruefully, *rats recognize one of their own.* After finishing my business, I walked out of the restroom and was escorted into the courtroom.

As I moved past Stan and his attorneys sitting at the defendant's table, I felt the almost physical weight of Stan's fury as he attempted to stare me down. From an inner well of strength, I managed to greet his stare with resolve. I was there to do business, it was no time to be mawkish. As I entered the witness box, Judge Robert Higgenbotham, one of the first black judges to sit in Cook County, sauntered in. He was a big man, about 6'3", with dark skin and a thick jet-black moustache. 'Raise your right hand. Do you swear to tell the truth, the whole truth and nothing but the truth?' And so it began.

My testimony went on for a full day. The prosecution asked me about my role as the accountant for the El Quawai, about my personal conversations with Stan and how the organization itself was set up. The defence attorneys reminded the jury that I was a criminal and member of the El Quawai and that I had made a deal with the prosecution, trading my testimony for jail time. What's more, Stan's defence rested on the allegation that I was actually the kingpin behind the El Quawai, and I was just trying to pin all of this on him. Throughout the ordeal, I just tried to focus on the truth. I told the court how I had started, what my role was, how I was trusted because I could keep records in my head. I was able to explain how El Quawai functioned through an analysis of their bank records, property records and by telling the jury who was paid to perform specific functions. It was not an easy task, delivering Stan's head to the prosecutors...especially when I saw my former friends in the gallery, making throat-cutting gestures to indicate I was marked for death.

At the end of the day, I was again escorted out of the back of the building, but I was not done. I had to stick around for a few days just in case the prosecution needed me again. During that time, Dennis and I holed up at Marina City, the iconic tower buildings from Steve McQueen's movie, *The Hunter*. I hoped that we would not be sent flying into the Chicago River like the guys in the flick! To be fair, I think they chose those buildings because they were round and we could see anyone approaching. One thing never changes: always seek the high ground when defending yourself.

Eventually, after a couple of nerve-wracking days, the case went to the jury. I felt a sense of relief. I had done my job. I just wanted to be officially done with this mess and enter the witness protection programme. I was beyond ready to disappear into the next chapter of my life. 'So,' I asked Dennis, 'when do we leave? I've held up my end of the bargain.' Dennis said nothing, but his eyes told a story that I didn't want to hear. 'Come on, Dennis, what's up? Give me the skinny.' At first, he was reticent. Finally, he looked at me. Whatever came next, I knew it wasn't going to be good. 'Look, John, your sentence is based upon the verdict. If the jury convicts Stan of the most severe charges, then you'll get time served and full witness protection. But if they only convict him of minor charges, you may get two to three years, probably at Club Fed.' Sighing, he rubbed his eyes with one hand. 'And, if he's found innocent…you're looking at a minimum of five years in a State prison.' I couldn't believe it.

Dennis held his hands up and wouldn't hear my protestations. 'John, at the end of the day, this is a national case! *Somebody* has to pay for these crimes. If it's not Stan, it's you. And before you start blabbering about justice, let me tell you that no deal is final until the judge has approved it. So, until there's a verdict, we stay put.' I struggled to control myself as I felt the blood rushing to my head. I'm not a violent person by predilection, but at that moment I wanted to punch someone or something. After everything I had done, I might still go to jail? And, worst-case scenario, if I went to State prison, I would either spend my time in solitary or have to deal with El Quawai inmates vying to shiv me. In the past, I would have immediately needed a scotch or joint upon hearing this kind of news, or most likely both at once. But not now. I took a deep breath. I needed to focus. I needed the forces of the universe to guide me through this storm one more time. There was no time for anger, hate or self-pity. I had to make myself one with the universe to find the path out.

I went into full meditation mode; initially, I had hoped the verdict would be returned hours later, but it turned into days. On the first day, there was no verdict and no questions. On day 2, the jury had a request—they wanted a portion of my testimony read back to them. As I was not allowed to return to the courtroom, I had to depend on Dennis to summarize their request. 'They wanted to hear about the drug delivery system; how Stan received the shipments protected by the cops and how you paid them,' he said. *That's not good*, I thought, *it cuts both ways*. It proved Stan and the El Quawai were engaged in illegal activities, but it also outed me as the one paying the cops. I hoped beyond hope that there was enough evidence showing that Stan had been at this long before I arrived in Chicago. Finally, day 3, noon. Dennis entered my room. 'Let's go,' he said curtly. 'The judge will announce the verdict at 1.30. If the news is bad, you're going straight into custody.' Looking back at me, he sighed. 'I suggest you call on your angels one more time.'

❧

24

Sentencing

We arrived at the makeshift courthouse at about 1:00. I was made to sit in a back room, near the judge's chambers, a small cramped room with speakers so that I could hear the proceedings in the courtroom next door. I now appreciate the stress that trial lawyers feel, because those thirty minutes seemed to last hours. In the end, I didn't feel it was right to call on my angels. I would be calling on them to send Stan to jail for life or, even worse, to the gas chamber—they had the death penalty in Illinois. I decided to take my chances alone. While we waited, noises filtered through the speakers. On the other side of the wall, the courthouse was buzzing, with members of the press jockeying for the best position and the deputies getting in place. Finally, a hush fell over the room. I surmised it was due to the entrance of Judge Higgenbotham. His deep voice came through loud and clear over the sound system. 'Are all parties and counsel present?' The sounds of assent. 'Good, then let's go on the record. Counsel, with all parties present, and before the jury enters the courtroom, are there any issues to resolve before we hear the verdict?' I strained my ears to hear the less strident voices of the counsel. 'None, your honour,' murmured the prosecution and defence lawyers. 'Good. Bailiff, please bring in the jury. All rise!'

Wishing with all my heart that I could see what was happening inside the courtroom, I struggled to interpret the sounds that filtered back to me as the jury entered the courtroom and took their seats. 'I understand the jury has reached a verdict,' boomed the voice of Judge Higgenbotham. 'We have, your honour.' 'In that case, bailiff, please retrieve the verdict from the foreman.' A few minutes of silence ticked by as I imagined the judge reading the verdict sheet. 'Very well, Mr Foreman, please read the verdict aloud to the court.' My heart leapt into my throat as I heard the verdict read aloud.

'We, the jury, in the case of the People of Illinois vs. Stan Jones, have come to the following verdict: As to Count One, the sale and distribution of illegal schedule 1 drugs, we find the defendant, Stan Jones, guilty. As to Count Two, the sale and trafficking of women for prostitution, within and without the State of Illinois, we find the defendant, Stan Jones, not guilty. As to Count Three, conspiracy to traffic women for prostitution, within and without the State of Illinois, we find the defendant, Stan Jones, guilty. As to Count Four, conspiracy to engage in felony murder, we find the defendant, Stan Jones, guilty. And, as to Count Five, commission of felony murder, we find the defendant, Stan Jones, not guilty. This verdict is signed this 20th day of June, 1990.'

The language was stark, clear, with none of the flowery speech used by the attorneys. This direct speech made it real. I felt dizzy with relief as I listened to the counsel poll each member of the twelve-man jury and heard each one give their assent with the verdict. The judge's voice again came to me through the loudspeaker. 'Let the record reflect that the verdict is unanimous. Mr Jones, you are hereby remanded back to the custody of the State of Illinois until sentencing, which shall occur no less than one day from today and no more than forty-five days from today. Ladies and gentlemen of the jury, you have completed your civic duty. You are free to go. Court is adjourned!'

I slept very deeply that night. I didn't count the seconds and had no more fear. I had done my job, as demon, angel and Judas. I had helped to clean up the streets, stuck a knife in a place the El Quawai could not reach. I could now move forward with my life, find a new direction, fulfil my purpose.

The next morning, I appeared before Judge Higgenbotham at 8.30 sharp. The prosecutor was waxing on eloquently in my support. 'John's testimony was vital in breaking up a major drug and prostitution ring; accordingly, our suggested sentencing is minor, your honour.' I bowed my head hopefully and rose to face the judge. Looking into his dark eyes, I felt that Judge Higgenbotham could see to the very depths of my soul. 'Young man, while you have done society a great service, I cannot divorce myself from the knowledge that you were also a major participant of the gang you have helped to break up. I've read the plea bargain agreement proposed by the FBI, but I am not inclined to follow it. I sentence you to eight years in State prison.'

As my future disintegrated before my eyes, I drew upon my inner strength. I did not flinch, I showed no emotion. Instead, I created a namaste moment. I was certain the God within me would be recognized by the God in him. I knew any show of disdain, anger, weakness or pleading would feed into further negativity. Thankfully, as I stood there compliantly, the judge continued. 'However, I will suspend that sentence and give you five years of probation, based on time served. But be warned; if at any time during your five-year probationary period, it comes to light that you are involved in illegal or nefarious activities, you will serve the remainder of your sentence which, based upon my calculations, is seven years and six months.' The sense of relief was almost overwhelming. 'I hope that I don't see you until your hearing five years from now. As I understand you are to be placed in witness protection, I hereby relieve you of routine probationary requirements such as checking in with a local probation officer, but make no mistake, I will know if you violate your probation and you will be brought to justice. Do you understand?'

'Yes, your honour,' I acquiesced gratefully. My heart leapt in my chest as I left the room, a free man. I focused on my next course of action. First, I would go back to Wisconsin and pick up my money and complete my promise to the oak tree. Then, I was going home, maybe not for all of the next five years, but at least long enough to clear my head. And by home, I did not mean Indiana, but the place of my real Indian roots—Ladakh.

25

Flight or Fight

Although my flight from the US to India was long and bumpy—nothing like flying with Dad—at least, contrary to my nightmares, there were no goats or live chickens on our plane. As the pilot wrestled us incompetently through another bout of turbulence, I was sorely tempted to take the helm myself, but I had vowed that I would remain inconspicuous. In a duffel bag clenched tightly in my hands, there rested about $350K in unmarked bills and I didn't trust it out of my sight. I just wanted to make my way to Mumbai, deposit my stash in a bank that would ask no questions, catch a four-hour domestic flight to Ladakh and begin my new life.

As we touched down on the tarmac, I felt the Mumbai heat wrapping its arms around me like a suffocating girlfriend. *Welcome love, I'm so happy to see you*, she said as she squeezed the sweat from my neophyte American pores. The sun, not to be outdone by the humidity, proceeded to bake us all as we left the airport, turning our crust to a dry crumble. The locals were much darker than I, not so much as a result of the natural hue left to them by their ancestors, but due to their daily dose of UV rays.

Mumbai was the home of Maha Amba, or Mumba Devi, the Hindu names for Devi, the Great Mother Goddess. She fed the city with all that humankind could ever want or need. She paired love with hate, abundance with deprivation, and contentment with restiveness—all the dichotomies that cause one to seek the

Christ Consciousness, the bridge from Maya to the One. Like a good mother, she catered to all her children and gave each their own measure. Mumba Devi, mother of all. Everything could be found within her purview; you just needed to find the right people to experience contentment, pending the level of development of your soul. Were you seeking debauchery this time around, or to hone your knowledge of the Law of Economy? Well, Mumbai has plenty of that. Yes, there are places you can learn about the path of least resistance and how to travel as far away from the spirit as possible. Maybe you're a tad more spiritual, a bit of an older soul? There are plenty of temples and gurus to teach you about the Law of Attraction. Or are you a truly advanced soul seeking synthesis with, unlike Orpheus, the ability not to look back at your former life of passion? Yes, there are people who can help you, though not so readily available. These individuals have learnt to focus their energies on unanimity with God; their hearts and minds set on the North Star of the Spirit, not the Southern Pole of Matter.

My own goals weren't quite as lofty. I just sought temporary solace, a safe place that would allow me reasonable access to my money and nothing else. But God laughs when we make plans, and this was no exception. My initial goal of anonymity gave way to Western arrogance within minutes. Soon, I embodied the sophisticated traveller who had bested both South Side gangsters and the US Government. India would fall at my feet. No matter, I received a quick education. India has existed for at least fifteen centuries before Christ and is the birthplace of what many deem the world's oldest religion—Hinduism. While Westerners may think that they are naturally superior, India has seen and survived just about any circumstance one can imagine and devised a system to handle it.

I spent the next ten days dividing my money and depositing it into five different banks. Slowly, I was beginning to understand Mumbai. It was an assault on all five senses. The smells hit me like the blows of a boxer. A left jab of jasmine, a right cross of tamarind, a feint of curry and daal, only to be TKO'ed with an upper cut of human waste. I was overwhelmed by the sights, the magnificent temples, the grand hotels, and the cacophony of twelve million people constantly bustling around me, busily engaged in their daily lives. The city was a giant serpent, its jaws both welcoming and all consuming. Like a python, it eats its unknowing victim whole, numbing them so they don't feel it when they are being digested. Its fangs are the sensual, food, wine, sex, money and status, the quest for knowledge, for a glimpse of the Holy Grail, anything that separates us from each other or gives the illusion that we are separate from God. Above all, the serpent desires those who are lost and yearning. Curiously, it avoids those who have awakened their kundalini, that wondrous electrical current of the spirit that lies dormant in us all until activated. It is believed to be our connection to The One living inside us waiting to be activated. The serpent of matter stays away from those awakened souls, even when their awakening is nascent.

Finally, it was the eve of my last night in Mumbai; the next morning, I was headed to Ladakh. My last night in town had to be special. I could hear the hissing of the serpent through the tall grass. It called me. *Come, come, taste my fangs, they are the answer to what you seek. You have come so far, forget your pain. Experience mammon, it is all that you desire.*

As I wandered out into the humid night, I met an Indian, Nesh, who had only recently returned from New York, where he had lived since he was five. His parents had been quite successful and left him a large inheritance, which he promptly squandered. Upon hearing that I was a newcomer to the city, Nesh was delighted. 'Come with me, I'll show you the underbelly of Mumbai. It's unlike anything you've ever experienced.'

The evening was a blur as we went from clubs, to speakeasies, dance halls and strip clubs. As my senses became more and more overwhelmed, I dove further into the belly of the snake. We danced and drank exotic liquors such as Sazerac and Absinthe. We saw live sex shows where men and women coupled onstage before our very eyes. We tasted foods from all over the world— fresh monkey brains, elephant meat, lion stew and tiger eyes. At around 4.00 a.m., as the first signs of dawn began to emerge over the horizon, Nesh insisted that we go to one last bar that served Turkish coffees and amazing Nepalese desserts to finish our evening. There, I gorged on kheer and rasbari and Nepali milk balls. It was great to have a taste of home, almost like a harbinger of good tidings. Nesh, who had not paid for anything at any of the other clubs, insisted on settling the bill for these delicacies, to which I gladly acquiesced. After we finished, I decided to walk back to my hotel. Although I could still hear the hissing of the snake all around me, I had had enough and was no longer tempted. My curiosity quenched, I was ready to go home, study the word of God and find my purpose.

As Nesh and I headed back through one of the old Viceroy districts, the early morning air felt cool and refreshing against my skin. The alcohol was leaving my system gradually as I gazed around me in wonder at the ornate buildings with their black-and-white ivory sconces. About a block out from my hotel, I was about to bid Nesh farewell when suddenly the proprietor from the dessert emporium came running behind us. I half raised my hand to greet him but stopped, shocked, as the old man began yelling, 'Stop, thief, stop, you American thief!' I looked around in confusion, but he was pointing straight at me and Nesh. Before I could speak, Nesh took off and made a quick exit through an alley. Although at first I was inclined to laugh, believing Nesh had pulled some ridiculous prank, six Indian cops charged into the street in full force. Two of them tackled me to the ground. Paying no mind to my protests, the cops dragged me into a carriage and took me to the local police station.

The station house was an old building that could have doubled as a chicken coop. It was filthy and there was straw all over the floors. Despite the early hour, I was brought immediately before a magistrate. 'They say you are an American, but you look Indian to me,' he blustered, before I could say a word. 'I do come from America, Sir, I was just on my way back to my hotel when these officers brought me in,' I began. 'Typical American!' he interrupted, 'you all think you can come here and have your way! Well, I won't allow Americans to come here and steal from honest hard-working Indians!' I tried to explain to the magistrate that I thought my friend had paid for the desserts, and also that I had sufficient funds to cover the bill. Unimpressed with my explanation, he responded, 'Never mind that, what's done is done. Normally, the sentence for theft is five years of hard labour.' I stared at him in disbelief. 'But, in your case, I think thirty days at the Andhakshi Ashram will teach you not to steal,' he continued, already moving on to the next case. As the officer led me away from the magistrate's desk, I couldn't believe my bad luck. Less than one night away from going home and now I was being sent to an ashram as an indentured servant? *Really, Maha Amba*, I thought, *is this how you treat a prodigal son?*

26

Initiation

I was immediately carted off in the back of a dilapidated and foul-smelling van. As there were no seat belts, I held on for dear life to the roof handles at every sudden turn. The ashram was located near the centre of the city. Like the police station, it too was old, but had a certain charm to it. At my orientation, I was informed that it was an ashram for widows. Most widows in India have a horrible lot. Left destitute, shunned and presumed an unnecessary burden by society, they are deemed to have been the cause of their husband's death, regardless of how he had actually died. They have only two options. Either the widow is forced to marry her husband's brother—if there is one—or, if the brother does not want to marry them, the family's assets are forfeited to the state and she is placed in an ashram for life on society. Such women are often referred to as *randi*, slang for prostitute, and those who run ashrams often sell the bodies of attractive widows so as to keep the ashram solvent.

Maha's wise face was the first I saw upon entering the ashram. The kind proprietor of the ashram had gentle eyes and her speech was resolute but soft. Something about her touched me deeply, as if I had known her for many lifetimes. As she welcomed me to her ashram and explained my duties, I tried but failed to guess her age. At first glance, she looked to be in her late forties or early fifties, but at closer range, she may have been as old as seventy-five. Maha claimed she did not prostitute her women but encouraged each to paint their own portraits. Her job was to lead them to a realization of their own individual truths. 'We are not all on the same path,' she stated calmly as we walked down the corridor. 'Each of us has particular lessons to learn, specific to this lifetime. We run from the storm when we should run towards the truth it brings.' Looking at me, she smiled. 'But, you already know this,' she said. 'Rest now, for you will be tested soon.'

Resonance is a powerful force. I was immediately calmed by Maya's words. My purpose was unfolding before me. I was home and my spirit would rise to meet the challenge just like the spiritual warriors who were my forefathers. Initiations are best when one is just thrown into them, with no time to think or fear, only to react and reveal your true self.

The next morning, I greeted the sunrise ready to work. My first task was to clean out the chicken pens, scoop up goat dung and unclog the gutter. Accepting my less-than-romantic assignment, I began shovelling. I had finally gotten a good rhythm going when my heart stopped at the sight of an elegant goddess walking towards me. Her skin was the colour of a fall leaf, glowing like amber with a syrupy brown undertone. Her bright complexion was perfect, without a single blemish. She had liquid brown eyes, chestnut hair that flowed to the small of her back, an aquiline nose and full sensual lips. Her body was perfect, athletic yet lithe, and she moved with the nonchalant grace of a tigress. She was simply the epitome of beauty. I had never seen anyone like her before.

I came rushing back to reality as I realized she was approaching me. I looked down and swallowed hard. I was knee deep in sewage and, considering how hard I had been shovelling, it was probably all over my clothes and in my hair. *Don't run from the storm*, I reminded myself and, gathering my courage, I stood and smiled as she walked by. Catching my eyes, the beautiful stranger broke out laughing. 'Keep your eyes where they belong, dung boy.'

I blushed and she sauntered past, her every motion heavy with the knowledge that I was watching her. This was it; the woman I had been waiting for my entire life had presented herself. It was time to act.

In the past, I had always rolled with the punches. When I lost Lucy to James, I didn't hate, I became a *bon vivant*. When Nicole betrayed me, I endured and moved on. But not this time. This is where I decided I would make my stand. I would no longer take the path of least resistance when it came to love. I was not leaving here without Aanya. Yes, my love's name was Aanya.

27

Threes

I finished all of my jobs as fast as I could so that I would have time to prepare myself to talk with Maha. Surely she could be persuaded that my skills were better suited for nobler tasks. After listening to my persuasive arguments, she laughed. 'Well, you didn't fare well on the first test. Of course you don't want to be seen as the dung man in front of Aanya.' I nodded. 'But it doesn't matter,' she continued. 'You can't have her. She has a chance to remarry, but there is very little time. Each day, the temptation to become an upapatni, a woman of the night, or what you may call a courtesan, is great when it allows your family, all of us here at the ashram, to eat.' I balked at the thought of the lovely Aanya becoming a plaything for wealthy men. 'Help her to become more interesting,' Maha went on, 'Then she can make some nobleman a good wife. But sleep with her and you will ruin her life.' Although I understood, I was undeterred. I knew that Aanya would be mine when the time was right. I had money; all I had to do was to ensure that no one else married her in the next thirty days. But I had to keep my plans a secret and I couldn't tell Maha about my money. If she believed me, I was told by my fellow untouchables that she would take all of it because a master is entitled to all of their servants' assets during their servitude. If she didn't, she would think me a cavalier Lothario.

Seeing my worried face, Maha relented and offered me an olive branch. 'Come,' she said as she ushered me in. 'It's almost day's end, time to attend arati.' She always began the vespers with a quote or a topic for discussion. That night, she began, 'Shakespeare says the eyes are the window to the soul. What is he talking about?'

I jumped on this quickly. 'He is referring to the concept of "dependent arising". The eye is just another organ of the body; it is not capable of truly seeing or of independent thought. It is only through our consciousness—depending upon its connection to the eye—that we are able to look at an object and translate that object into something objective.'

Everyone seemed impressed, except for Aanya. 'You're quoting almost directly from Visuddhimagga's *The Path of Purification*. Do try to give us your own thoughts next time,' she said sarcastically.

As everyone laughed at me, I smiled inwardly. I knew that I had a formidable opponent in Aanya, but I was an Asanga, the very people who had started the Yogacara School. I would lovingly engage in this battle with my future queen; indeed, I found her intellect to be extremely attractive. Beauty alone gets boring after a while, but smart and sassy will keep you on your toes for life.

The next day, Maha started *arati* with another question, 'What is Aum?' 'It is the holy sound of God, the sound that started the universe,' Aanya responded first. 'It is an example of ear consciousness, the second of the Eight Consciousnesses proposed by the Yogacara School,' I added. Maha smiled at her two best students and allowed the discussion to proceed. Afterwards, Aanya deigned to speak to me directly. 'What do you know about the Yogacara School? You don't seem highly educated and you don't even have a proper Indian accent.' I laughed and told her that I had just been away from home for a while, but that my heart belonged to both India and to her. She laughed, 'Dung boy, you're full of surprises.'

The past is prologue—every step I had taken, every thought, every resonant action had led me to this moment. First my father and then experience had taught me that you need a plan of action to succeed. Yet, I was flummoxed by her beauty. She glistened like a mirage and carried with her the heavenly fragrance of honey and lilacs. I knew that I had to go deeper than mere desire if I wanted to be with her; I needed to turn to yoga for the answer. The next morning, I engaged in a few asanas to help me settle in, beginning with three sun salutations, or Surya Namaskar, starting with Tadasana or Mountain Pose, moving to Uttanasana or Standing Forward Bend, Phalakasana or Plank Pose, Bhujangasana or Cobra, Adho Mukha Shvanasana or Downward Dog and finishing with all three variations of Virabhadrasana of the Warrior Poses. Afterwards, I settled down into a state of deep meditation.

As I came out of nothingness, I relived my very first meeting with Aanya. At the time, I had felt ashamed that she saw me covered in mud and faeces. I felt shame and unworthiness and communicated those feeling to her. She responded appropriately. But I now saw our meeting in its true light; it was part of my first initiation. I was the lotus flower, rooted in the mud of desire, but blossoming far above the water on long stalks when the body and mind become pure. My first trial was to reach beyond my merely sensual fixation on Aanya's beauty and focus on my intentions for her. If she was to be my queen, I had to love her entirely—body, mind and soul. But first, I would have to purify my own body, mind and soul. *Know yourself and you will be known.* I had thirty days to purify myself completely to manifest my worthiness. I would spend ten days on each aspect.

The universe works in threes. Body, mind and soul. Brahma, Vishnu and Shiva. The Father, Son and Holy Spirit. The plane of matter (governed by the Law of Economy), the bridge (otherwise known as the Christ Consciousness plane governed by the Law of Attraction) and Yoga (governed by the Law of Synthesis).

Petit à Petit

The Law of Economy governs matter. It must be mastered before moving on to the Law of Attraction, also known as the Christ Consciousness, the bridge between man and God. The last stage is the Law of Synthesis. Everything returns to God or the universe eventually. Humans are born when their physical bodies are inhabited by a spirit. When the physical body dies, the spirit leaves and returns to the universe. Brahma is akin to the Universal God for Hindus. Vishnu is similar to Christ, the preserver and protector of all mankind who acts as a bridge between matter and spirit. Shiva both reveals and conceals the true essence of God; the being who, at the end of time, will be the destroyer who ends all physical existence and returns us back to God, the Alpha and Omega.

Water is the source of life on Earth. Most of the world's major cities are near oceans, lakes or great rivers. In the case of Chicago, the city was a bit of a late bloomer—it took about thirty years after the completion of the Erie Canal for it to boom. But once ships were able to travel between the Great Lakes, it grew exponentially. The strength of water is that it goes wherever it wants. In order to win Aanya's hand, I would have to bend nature to my will and remain firm to ensure that she did not marry another man. I had to make it clear to her, first, that I was physically the most viable choice and, second, that I was not going to honourably get out of the way for someone else.

People who get everything they want by not budging are often the ones called the most names by everyone; but they never compromise, and they always win, at least on the plane of matter. But there is more to life than just the physical plane. Others yield to these people because their goals are much broader. It may seem as if they are weak and the aggressive go-getters are strong. But the former are more developed and have moved beyond mere domination of the physical plane. Nevertheless, this advanced philosophy cuts both ways. Sometimes, we don't always get what we want on the physical plane but our souls are advancing spiritually. It can be frustrating at times living in societies that operate on pure Calvinism. *I am successful because I am blessed. My accumulation of things is proof of my blessings.* Corporations, for example, may ensure temporary material success while killing the planet through practices that don't respect the environment; this leads to involution, not evolution. A spiritually evolved being understands that the accumulation of *maya* is never a means in and of itself. It is merely evidence of the power to create. This ability to create is indeed an indication of our relationship with God, the ultimate creator. The accumulation of things is proof that one has mastered the plane of matter, but it takes a mastery of all three planes to evolve further as a person and as a species.

With the rule of three in mind, I focused the next eight days on mastering the plane of matter; but I had to do so in a way that respected karma. I wanted to succeed by manifesting to Aanya that I was physically superior to any other suitors, but I could not do so in a manner that would hurt anyone else. I, therefore, had to show my skills through actions that would juxtapose my strengths against theirs.

The ashram, while old and not well kept, was nevertheless a magnificent work of art. It had been built in the fifteenth century as an oblation to Mumba Devi by the salt workers and fishermen of the surrounding islands. The building had started life as an orphanage and a way station for bereft mothers who needed a place to stay. The architectural style was quasi-Greek classical with a strong helping of Asian artisanal flair. Columns lined the halls, sturdy and cylindrical, but each was inlaid with complex sculptures of Buddhist or Hindu gods. The level of craftsmanship and detail of each individual God or Goddess must have taken years to create. Each sculpture, and there were about fifty to seventy in the main building alone, represented a lifetime of work for that particular sculptor. The Giza Pyramids in Egypt are considered one of the world's wonders because of their size and mystical geometry. I can never understand why Hindu temples and other structures such as the ashram, which predate the Taj Mahal by about a hundred and fifty years, aren't also considered world wonders.

Inside the ashram, the rooms were designed efficiently. Like most of India, there was no indoor plumbing, but an ingenious ventilation system ensured that smells from the showering and waste rooms did not infiltrate the women's living quarters. Unfortunately, the rooms where the men slept were downwind of those facilities and did not benefit from those design features. Thus, the smell of dung soon permeated my clothes and my very pores.

On Wednesdays, young suitors would arrive at the ashram at around 10.00 a.m. for a cricket match. It was a friendly game among gentlemen of independent wealth, for only they had time to engage in a mid-morning game. The rest had to be at work. The women enjoyed gathering around the field, watching the males in action. They took the opportunity to whisper among themselves about eligible bachelors and play matchmaker. That

Wednesday, I took part; I had risen two hours before sunrise so that my chores would be complete in time. On that morning, I played with all my strength. I smacked the little cricket ball far beyond the next best player. As I celebrated my achievement, I looked around for Aanya. Nonplussed, she had seen my sporting triumph and could clearly hear the other women cooing. Still, she tried to act as if my achievement was as boring as a game of backgammon. I remained disciplined, I didn't expect an immediate reaction.

After the game, the men and women met in the parlour where, chastely chaperoned by Maha and her assistants, they were properly introduced to each other. I was responsible for preparing tea. I stoked the fire, boiled water in a large kettle and placed cups at each table. Sneakily, I made sure that I tempered the cup for Aanya's suitor in the fire right before I served him. I kept a straight face as I watched him struggle to pick up the burning hot cup. Looking over my shoulder, I was pleased to see a small smirk appear on Aanya's face as she figured out my mischief. I was not the guy who gave up.

That evening, after the suitors left, I accompanied the women as they walked around the lawn. They did this every evening after *arati* to preserve their figures. One by one, they each returned to their rooms until Aanya and I were left alone. A comfortable atmosphere descended. We acted as if we had grown up together. I would try to finish her sentences and she would cut me off with 'Wrong!' and we would both laugh. She told me her background; she had grown up in a wealthy Buddhist family in an area dominated by Hindus. At fourteen, her father had found her a wealthy forty-two-year-old Hindu husband. Unfortunately, after ten years of marriage and no children, he dropped dead from a heart attack. His brother refused to take on a barren Buddhist wife. Thus, she had landed at Andhakshi.

After this, our talk grew serious. She admitted that while I was 'cute', I was still not a suitable option as a husband and she could not waste time with me. However, my knowledge of yoga was impressive. 'In a different world and in a different time, maybe we could have been something,' she told me wistfully. But her responsibilities to the ashram and the other widows were too great and she needed a husband of means to take care of them all. I told her that I would take care of her and the entire ashram in due course. She laughed, 'I think that's what I like best about you, your unfettered optimism. But optimism alone won't feed hungry bellies; they need real food, which takes real money.' I wished with all my heart that I could tell her of my true net worth. Finally, as the silence lengthened, she stopped at the door to her quarters. 'Thanks for the walk. I enjoyed our talk. But now, back to reality. Goodnight.'

As I walked back to my own wing of the ashram, I was more smitten than ever. The secret chamber of my heart vibrated so strongly in her presence. What's more, 1 had looked into her eyes and saw that she felt it too. We came alive in each other's presence. She was beautiful, strong, intelligent and compassionate. She was the yin to my yang; prudent where I was headstrong, logical when passion blinded me. We completed each other and I had finally found my purpose—to love her forever.

❧

29

A Royal Competition

Regrettably, all of the headway I had made with Aanya was erased the following week. The first task given to me was to ensure that the receiving lounge was immaculate for that afternoon's tea. The entire ashram was in a state of frantic excitement; when I asked why, Maha informed me that a prince was going to be in attendance. Deep down, I knew that the prince wasn't coming for just any woman. He was there for *my* woman. My fears were proven true when I witnessed the buzz around Aanya. All the women brought her their best accoutrements so that she would be dazzling. 'The prince will definitely love this scarf!' My heart clenched. 'Aanya, wear my best shoes!' It was sickening. They went on and on. 'I heard he has three mansions! One in Mumbai, the second in Madras and the third in Delhi.' The high-pitched sounds of feminine giggles echoed piercingly in my head. 'Well, I heard that he's *very* handsome, an amazing athlete and a fearless hunter! Oh, Aanya, you're his perfect match!' It was all just too much. For the first time since I had left Chicago, I felt overwhelmed. Breathing deeply, I calmed myself. I was not afraid to ask for help. Now was the time to call for my angels. I had met my soulmate and I was not above using everything in my toolbox to make her mine. My angels had never failed me before.

Once again, the suitors arrived on the ashram grounds at 11.00 a.m. The buzz was amped up three times than normal as everyone awaited the entrance of Prince Amhad Bandezar. As he walked onto the field, he seemed every inch a prince. His measured gait was regal and he stood about 5'11". He was sinewy and his long jet-black hair was pulled back in a ponytail revealing his sharp features. He had a strong nose, high cheek bones and medium lips. His eyes were deep and mesmerizing. He spoke with measured confidence, looking you directly in the eye. His all-white outfit shone as resplendent as his easily confident smile. However, I detected a distinct lack of confidence upon closer inspection.

The cricket game began. Nothing is more difficult in sports than hitting a moving ball coming straight towards you at high velocity. It's both a measure of skill and bravery. Standing in the batter's box, you must judge the trajectory of the ball and hit it at exactly the right moment. It sounds easy, but when the small ball is flying towards you and comes within inches of your head, the bravery component becomes a key factor. In cricket, the ball comes in on a downwards trajectory and you can hit it after it bounces off the ground if you have good hand-to-eye coordination. With my baseball skills, I was counting on the fact that I could time my hit and turn on the ball, sending it farther than any of the other players.

The Prince was an excellent bowler; he hit the wicket with ease and left many batsmen frustrated. Finally, my chance came and I went up to bat. On the first ball, I easily timed the bounce and launched it well over the boundary for six runs. The crowd was hushed. No one had yet hit the Prince's bowls, never mind over the boundary! The Prince broke the silence by jogging up to me and shaking my hand, congratulating me on a job well done. It slightly bemused me—I hadn't counted on him being a good sport. My points for physical skill were counterbalanced by his sportsmanship. However, as the game continued, his affability waned. Cricket is a challenging game requiring both alacrity and athleticism. I had grown up with American kids playing baseball with a round bat every weekend. Hitting a ball with a flat bat on one bounce was not much of a problem. Time after time, I hit every one of the Prince's pitches past the boundary. With every hit, his calm demeanour diminished.

By the end of the game, the Prince no longer cared about impressing Aanya; he only wanted to destroy me, the apparent untouchable who had made him look silly. He refused to stay for *arati* or to walk around the gardens with Aanya. He announced that he needed to retire early so that he was ready for the next day's boar hunt on his private hunting grounds, to which we were all invited. Glancing across the grounds at me, he shot me a hard smile. 'Hunting—now that's a real man's game! There's nothing like hunting to separate the ordinary men from the kings.'

That night, I was a pariah. 'Did you see? John ruined Aanya's marriage chances by humiliating the Prince,' the contemptuous whispers echoed throughout the ashram. Aanya herself refused to speak to or look at me and her court treated me with equal disdain. I felt like a true untouchable for the first time. On the other hand, the men fell over themselves to congratulate me on my victory over the nobles. They regaled themselves with the retelling of each bowl, laughing uproariously as they drank their Kingfishers. Smiling, I couldn't help being apprehensive. Tomorrow, we common folk were to hunt wild boar armed with only bows and arrows while the nobles carried high-powered rifles. I hoped very much I wouldn't find myself on the wrong side of the scope. The Prince might not just have his sights set on boar.

30

The Hunt Is Afoot

The next morning, the Prince sent a fleet of cars to pick us up just after dawn, as was the custom. The women rode in four beautiful sedans, while the men made do in the back of old pickup trucks. By the time we arrived, the women were already set up in white tents enjoying a lavish breakfast of tea and cakes displayed on tablecloths of white eyelet lace embroidered with the prince's coat of arms. Every nobleman, woman and child were dressed to the nines in their finest clothing. Even the horses and dogs looked distinguished. In contrast, we looked even more drab and dirty than usual. It was clear to everyone that we had been invited as a form of amusement and entertainment for the nobles. Prince Bandezar wanted to clearly establish that, despite the previous day's trouncing, the untouchables were most definitely not on par with the nobles, especially me. Only then could he face Aanya again.

Oouu! Oouu! The sound of the hunting horn resounded through the clearing as the Prince led the way, bedecked in a white peacock-feathered hat, a long white jacket with a purple sash underneath, tan trousers and snakeskin riding boots. A machete was holstered over his right shoulder and a long gun lay besides him in his saddle. He looked sharp and ready for business. His compatriots were equally well adorned in long jackets, the colour of their sashes connoting their position in the hierarchy. We commoners were given rudimentary bows and arrows and red jackets so that we could be recognized by the nobles and not shot in the back. As there was no visible target on the back of mine, I donned it and began walking into the jungle.

Although I find traditions such as hunting to be outdated and crude, I must admit that the hunt itself was invigorating. Wild boars are no joke. They can grow to be about three feet high, five feet long and weigh as much as 300 lb. A full-grown boar is intimidating. Their manes run from their heads down their spines to their backs, making them look like porcupines on steroids. Even if you shoot them in the head or the heart, they don't roll over and die. No, they'll keep stampeding and trying to attack you until the very moment their hearts stop beating. Thus, the safest way to hunt them is on horseback so you can shoot them, ride away and then wait for them to die from a safe distance. During a hunt, the goal is to kill at least one or two boars. This would provide enough meat to feed the entire party. But strange events have occurred in the past at such gatherings. Careless men rumoured to have been stealing money from rich merchants have fallen victim to 'accidental' shootings. Mysterious deaths have equally claimed the young men of beautiful wives who have caught the fancy of a nobleman.

Despite the inherent danger, I was excited to be there. The poets say one is never as alive as when they are facing imminent death. There is some truth to that statement. My hair stood on end as we quietly waded through the jungle. This time, I couldn't call on my angels in good conscience. This was an exercise in human arrogance. We weren't killing to survive; this was 'sport'. This time, I had to rely on my own guile. I would have to master the physical domain to survive. Thinking logically, I knew that matter always follows the lines of least resistance. Both the boar and the noblemen would take the easiest paths to their goals.

The boar would react to the sound of hooves behind them and go where the horses could not—uphill through the trees. Meanwhile, the noblemen would avoid travelling to areas of the jungle that would require them to dismount. 'Head for the crest beyond the hills,' I quickly ordered the men around me. 'We can trap the boar in a pincer manoeuvre as they run from the nobles!'

My plan was brilliant until I realized that the boars heading uphill towards the crest would be running at full speed. An arrow through the heart would not stop them. We would therefore have to climb the trees adjacent to the crest and shoot down at them as they ran underneath us. Accuracy would be paramount. I instructed my men to concentrate their arrows at a single boar in the herd, and not on the biggest one. A medium-sized 150–200 lb pig would be more than enough. Finally, after about forty minutes of jogging, we came to our first resting point. The air was hot and humid, and we were already tired from lugging the rather unwieldy arms. After a quick breather, we continued upwards, following the path of the river in reverse. We avoided any open fields where we could be trampled by boar or easily spotted by the nobles. I estimated that we had just under forty minutes before the nobles would start to chase the boar uphill. Thankfully, our shortcut along the riverbed saved us at least thirty minutes.

As we came closer to the crest, I could hear the nobles engaging behind us. The sounds of shots fired, horses rearing, boars squealing and men shouting drifted up to us as we continued making our way up the hill. 'Over here,' I heard a man roar, 'to the left, no, to the right!' Then came the distinctive sound of the Prince's barked orders. 'Shut up, you idiots, you're just scaring them away. Follow me, I want the Prajapati so everyone will know I am God!' Even for noblemen, this arrogance was too much. Legend has it that Prajapati, the Hindu deity credited with raising the earth from primeval waters, first appeared as a wild boar. It was an extremely bad form and very risky for Prince Bandezar to make such a proclamation. Yet, none of his party had the gumption to tell him so.

The noblemen pushed on through the jungle. Struggling through the bush, we sweated in silence. It was getting close to mid-day and the temperature was rising. After another fifteen minutes, there was neither sight nor sound of any boar. The nobles were very close behind us and we could hear them murmuring among themselves. Someone ventured that the Prince had dishonoured the hunt and they were destined to come home empty-handed. Aware of the growing discontent in his party, the Prince tried to lift their spirits. 'Don't give up, men! Victory belongs to the hearty. We will not let the untouchables best us again!' 'But, Sire, it is not the untouchables we fear,' said one brave man finally. 'The Gods may be offended by your desire to kill Prajapati.' The Prince sounded angry as he spoke again. 'It was a joke, perhaps in poor taste, but nothing more. Don't let a creation myth ruin our day. Let's ride, gentlemen.'

But the damage was done. The boar had clearly felt their presence and escaped towards the hills. They would arrive at the crest just after we did. Quietly, we climbed the trees at the top of the crest and waited. As the herd stampeded below us, I drew my arrow and focused on the very last pig. A flurry of arrows flew down from the canopies; although we missed many, two began squealing in agony as the rest of the herd ran away. This was the worst part. The idea of hunting itself was primordial, a hearkening back to former times. But the reality stung. We had ended the life of a living being. We had to honour their sacrifice. After both pigs finally dropped to the ground, the men and I climbed back down the trees and mounted the carcasses on branches to carry them back to the tents. We vowed to use their remains respectfully; we would feed the party with the meat and use the bones, fat and other by-products at the ashram. We would not brag or claim victory; we would act like true hunters and give thanks to the universe for our bounty.

A hint of my second initiation was kicking in. The universe constantly guides us, although most people are lost in themselves and fail to observe the signs. My meditation was paying off; I realized if I focused my intentions on the well-being of everyone around me, I could win over Aanya while purifying myself at the same time. By helping others, she would see that we were on the same wavelength. After a brutal two-hour trek hauling the two pigs, we arrived back at the camp. The nobles had long since returned and I respectfully asked one of the nobles if he would bless our bounty and give it to the cooks to prepare for supper. But Prince Bandezar was in no mood to receive us. There was no hint of sportsmanship as he screamed in rage and railed against his compatriots. 'You soft, pathetic, cowardly weaklings, scared of an imaginary god! Gods don't rule us; strong men like me and my father rule!' His face was flecked with spittle as he turned towards our hunting party. 'Where is the Untouchable they call the batsman? Come forward, enough is enough. I will not suffer any more humiliation from someone who is so obviously beneath me.' A crazed gleam had entered his eyes. 'Let's race. The greatest man is the fastest man and I am the fastest man in all of southern India.' Nodding, I came forward out of the crowd. 'But let's up the stakes a little! If you win, you may have whatever you want in my domain. But, if I win, your head will adorn the spit alongside your boar.' The crowd gasped in dismay. I knew that I had no choice; he would have killed me anyway at this point.

As I readied myself, I watched the Prince pace out 200 feet. The finishing line, which he marked with his sash, was perilously near a large tree. As we got ready to sprint, a guttural braying sent chills down my spine. Just left of the tree was the largest boar I had ever seen, with a hide so black that it seemed blue. It stood there, staring at us, pawing its hooves on the ground in preparation for attack. Snot and foam dripped from its snout onto the ground. I took a deep breath. *Know yourself and you will be known*, the thought echoed in my head. *God is within you, God is within everything.* Without another second of hesitation, I ran forward towards the beast as if I had wings of fire. 'It is Prajapati!' a noble screamed behind me. 'She has come to kill us all!' The boar moved towards me and suddenly everything went black.

I awoke the next morning at the ashram, not in my bedroom but in one of maid's quarters. Besides me, I saw the kneeling forms of Aanya and Maha. Gazing up at Aanya, I asked, 'Am I in heaven? If so, I guess the boar got you too.' She giggled, 'Oh, you silly man! You want to know what really happened?' Between peals of laughter, Aanya recounted how Prince Bandezar had screamed for help and I had run to his rescue, before fainting. 'I don't know who's worse. And all because of a *mongoose!*' She gasped, clutching her sides in mirth. 'A mongoose?!' I exclaimed. 'No way, that was the biggest boar I've ever seen.' 'Well, so claimed all of the other men, but I know what we women saw. I don't know what you were drinking out there in the jungle, but it must have been powerful stuff! Anyway, I hope you're happy, the Prince has left town, probably never to return.' Aanya left the room in mock anger, but I heard her laughing as she rounded the corner. Turning my attention to Maha, I was pleased to see her looking at me with pride. 'Congratulations, John, you have passed another test. Rest now, for the others will be even harder.'

31

Solar Fire

Most people believe that Col. Kurtz's decline resulted from his love of the sensual: drugs, sex and the strongest aphrodisiac of all—power over men and nature. In actuality, Col. Kurtz's downfall was due to his decision to reject the light and seek darkness as his power base. Most humans straddle the middle ground, known as the Christ Consciousness, the bridge between the planes of matter and spirit, governed by the Law of Attraction. Christians are taught that they cannot know God unless they go through his son. As above, so below; the son of the father takes us to the father. He does so by revealing to all those who will listen that God is our father too and, thus, we are his children; secondly, he manifests to us how to be a good child of God.

So too is the sun a child of the universe. It teaches us the same lesson from a macrocosmic perspective. Every day, it puts on a passion play, filling us with brilliance in the morning, promoting fecundity, both physical and spiritual, throughout the day, before leaving us at dusk to forage in the darkness. How do we deal with its absence? Will we forget its presence and succumb to our base urges, or will we fortify ourselves and rest in preparation for its next visit? Night is the time when matter, the opposite of spirit, reigns supreme. But, in truth, spirit never leaves us. The stars above are a reminder that the universe is filled with millions of God's sons and daughters. As humans, we are part matter, part spirit. A physical expression of the divine, the one true God.

Great avatars, bodhisattvas and saints all have their commonalities: they love the universe and all sentient beings within it; they vow to uplift all sentient beings; and they forestall their own development, their own nirvana, to spend time on earth teaching us the primary focus of yoga—the union of the self with the Supreme Self, also known as God. If I was going to follow in the footsteps of Jesus Christ, Gautama Buddha and my forefather, C.E. Asanga, I would have to focus on more than just my own enlightenment. Once I was an avatar of God, Aanya would recognize her true self in me and she would see that we are meant to be together.

All in all, I had the next ten days to figure it out, starting from tomorrow. It would be difficult; after the dramatic finale of the hunt, I would be treated as a conquering hero by the men...and a fainting goat by the woman! *God is a cheeky fellow*, I reflected, *simultaneously boosting my ego while subjecting me to ridicule*. But this was all part of the plan. This was not about my greatness being recognized. I needed to show others that they were sons and daughters of God.

That night, I saw the antahkarana symbol during my evening meditation. This powerful sacrosanct symbol has been used by sages throughout the ages to represent the bridge between the self and the divine self for all living beings. It is the link between human consciousness, or *manas*, and the Buddhic principle. In Christian terms, it is the bridge known as Christ Consciousness, the effort to shift our attention from the mundane to the ethereal, from the needs of the physical self towards unity with the everlasting real self. So long as you seek goodness, the pathway between them persists. The thread is also strengthened through purification; only by ridding ourselves of the effluvia associated with the sensual life, can we build a strong enough bridge to withstand the cosmic fire of the highest consciousness.

I would teach those around me that all quotidian tasks were related to a higher purpose. We weren't just shovelling dung to rid ourselves of the smell—we were developing the bridge between matter and spirit so that we could cross over at the opportune time. Buddhists, Hindus and the adherents of most religions believe that a path to self-realization exists; it is the moment when you realize you are one with all that exists, an infinitesimal piece of the vast unending cosmos.

Most, however, focus on taking a gradual path to self-realization as this is a more reasonable goal. Such a journey entails illumination and purgation. We must rid ourselves of the unnecessary dross of matter before we can enter the pure tempering fire of spirit. Only once we have rid ourselves of ego and desire, and understood that all truth lies inside ourselves, are we able to withstand the purifying flames. For this reason, a quicker path to enlightenment is not encouraged because of the risk of spontaneous combustion. Although I was neither Jesus nor Buddha, I would have to engage in a similar task to theirs over the next ten days, by teaching both myself and those around me that the path to self-realization was an inwards one. We are born with everything we need: we just have to look within to realize the kingdom of God is all around us.

❧

32

Arati

Selflessness is an initiation. One does not knowingly enter its realm, but is driven to it by circumstance. Maha met with Aanya and I just before *arati* on the twelfth night of my sojourn. She said, 'Well done, both of you, I am impressed with your leadership efforts. Soon, I will be stepping back during *arati* and I want the two of you to lead after I have gone. Learn from my discussions and you will both lead the next generation.' From that moment on, I began to meditate not only for myself, but for everyone, so that they might all find clarity. My physical work as a cleaner and labourer now also had a broader purpose. I wanted us all to live in a clean environment, which would reflect itself in our clarity of thought.

I began to ruminate on the purpose underlying Maha's words during *arati*. Her talks with the widows were meant to instil them with the confidence that they were loved and one with the spirit. I wanted to turn *arati* into a yoga session focusing on the Eight Consciousnesses, of which laya-vijñ na—which Westerners call the Storehouse Consciousness—was the crown jewel. As time passed, Maha taught us how to lead, saying less and less each day. Yet, she would still drop cryptic lines to guide us. 'Love is like a never-ending electrical circuit,' she would murmur. 'If it is sent in a pure form, it will return to the sender strengthened in energy from all those who have received it.'

The time came for my very first *arati*. Although I wanted to impress those around me with my esoteric knowledge, I decided instead to focus on our recent hunting victory in an attempt to reach them with a more relatable example. 'A few days ago,' I began, 'we Untouchables were able to beat the nobles at their own games. We crushed them, first at cricket and then during the wild boar hunt.' I waited until the natural ebullience these memories sparked in the crowd had died away. 'How did we do that? Our strength came from our inner vitality, not our outer circumstances.' Getting into my stride, I went on to explain my message. 'If you strip life bare, the truth is revealed. Everything we do reflects, or should reflect, our goal to be with the One. But, we don't realize that the One is already within us. We spend our lives seeking that which we already have.' Looking around me at the sea of listening faces, I reached further. 'Jesus said, "If you think God is in the heavens, you should emulate the birds. If you think God is in the earth, the snakes are your guide." He said, "The Kingdom is within and without."' I paused, hoping beyond hope that my words were getting through to my audience. I could see people beginning to nod, as my message sunk in. Buoyed by this, I finished, 'Know yourself and you will be known. Rid yourselves of the desire for things outside of yourself. Abundance lies within. The nobles are not better than us, and we are not better than them. We are all children of the one true God, the Universal Spirit.' I had just completed by first discourse. I now had to walk the talk! My aspirations could not simply rest on Aanya's hand. I needed to aspire for an awakening for myself and all others.

Our lessons continued. Aanya recognized my goals and joined me in my quest to lead the ashram. She began with a discourse on breathing. It is no coincidence that deep meditation requires deep breathing. When we breathe, we connect with God. We are being imbued with the spirit. When we can no longer breathe, we no longer live. Our connection with God is broken. 'So, with that in mind,' Aanya finished, 'Enjoy every breath as, with it, you are receiving the Divine Spirit of God.' The next night, she discussed the concept of power. 'We are too in love with our own creations and we hoard them as evidence of our power. But true power lies in the process itself, the ability to create, which is the ability to act as a conduit of God's power.' Aanya went on to urge the followers not to fixate on the creations, as they would be weighed down by the desire to hold on to them. 'True power is the power itself, not its results. Focus upon the flow of energy, which is limitless, and not on the outcome, which is finite.'

With each *arati*, the women and men were listening, awakening. The ashram was no longer a brothel-in-waiting. People from outside of the ashram began to attend the talks. We developed a collective sense of purpose, with Aanya and me leading the others. Deep down, I could feel that Aanya was beginning to see me as I truly was. In her heart of hearts, she knew I was much more than an untouchable—and I, of course, knew that she was my queen. We had our namaste moment, silently. Yet, I waited. A warrior bides his time.

Later that week, I decided to begin the *arati* with an interesting perspective on failure as a jumping-off point for broader discussion. 'Everything always has a purpose,' I began. 'Every failure leads us in the direction God wanted us to go in the first place, usually as a consequence of us ignoring signals sent to us by the universe.' I explained that what we perceived to be failure was God's lesson to us in such a form that we would have no other choice but to listen, learn and move on. 'Think of it as a favour from God,' I paused and smiled as laughter echoed throughout the hall. 'Yes, I mean it, it is indeed a favour, because procrastination only delays the inevitable. My advice is to accept the lessons sent to us by the universe. All of the things that we deem to be bad or terrible are not punishments, but actually blessings in disguise. Instead of storing issues to be resolved in another lifetime, we are fortunate enough to be given the opportunity to confront them now, in this lifetime.' I concluded the lesson with my thoughts on evolution. 'The goal is always to evolve. Evolution is a painful process. It involves confronting weaknesses. But either you confront your weakness or you are destroyed by it. Either you adapt and survive, or you become extinct.'

The next night, Aanya focused her *arati* on rhythm. 'We all have our own internal rhythms. We need to listen to our true selves to discover that rhythm and try to live it to the extent we can. Find your rhythm, live your life the way you meant it to be lived.' That was a great evening; a couple of musicians attending the lecture had brought their instruments and began playing music. Soon enough, all of us broke out into dance. As the rhythm intensified, Aanya neared me. As we danced, I held her arm for just one extra second. Touching her was invigorating. I felt the electricity between us course all the way through me and, judging from the way she moved, so did she. It was a magical evening. We danced. We sang. We laughed. And we prayed together.

❧

33

Begin the Beguine

Unfortunately, as is often the case, our ultimate happiness was followed by travails. As human beings, we don't know how to handle bliss and so we subconsciously summon demons to torment us with the misery we think we deserve. Inherently, we don't understand or appreciate the wonderment that is within. We erroneously believe that we need to accomplish certain feats before we are worthy of love. But this is wrong—God, the Alpha and Omega, is immanent within us all. But, in this case, we had not yet come to that realization.

The morning after our reverie, we arose to find ourselves at the mercy of the heavy hand of the law, this time in the form of a police constable bearing legal papers. In dry, cold, matter-of-fact language, the documents stated that the ashram had been sold to King Bandezar, the father of Prince Bandezar. Our eviction would be effective in thirty days' time. Shaken but defiant to the last, Maha reminded the constable that only someone very high in the government could change the characterization of the property without notice. She would fight this decree with every fibre of her being. She, too, was not without connections.

At Maha's request, Aanya and I travelled with her to the City Government Centre to determine if anything could be done to prevent the sale. We were devastated when the authorities there informed us that the Viceroy had changed the status of the ashram a week previously. The ashram was in a prime

commercial location and King Bandezar had filed a request to
build a luxury hotel on the site; such a venture would bring
in significant tax revenue into Mumbai and, coincidentally, the
pocket of the Viceroy. Upon hearing this, Maha went into warrior
mode, refusing to waste her time and energy on anger. 'When in
war,' she stated, 'always take the highest ground available. The
Bandezars aren't the only royals in India. I have benefactors who
have allowed me to keep this ashram above the fray.' She looked
at me. 'However, they are men of power and only respect those
who can master their circumstances.'

At this, Aanya was perplexed. 'Why are you looking at him?'
she asked. 'He is nothing more than a charming janitor.' 'No,
my dear,' Maha replied. 'He is much more than that and it is
time that you see him for who he is. His name is John Yogacara
Asanga.' My heart fell into the pit of my stomach as I watched
Aanya absorb this revelation. Turning to me, she spat with
disgust, 'You are an Asanga. Yet, you pretended all this time to
be an Untouchable? Other people are not your toys, you liar, to
play with and tease and manipulate.' Before she could further
lose her temper, Maha jumped in. 'Now, Aanya, this is not the
time for recriminations. We must act now.' She shooed me out
of the room. 'John, go get cleaned up and put on a suit. Meet
us in thirty minutes and we'll start on our journey.'

Before my eyes, I saw all the trust I had established with Aanya
over the past fortnight dissipate like the morning fog. Steeling
myself, I left the room. As Maha said, there was no time to look
back. Move forward and eventually Aanya would see my true self.
That was all I could hope for. Exactly half an hour later, I met
them in front of the building. Both women were spectacularly
dressed. Aanya looked absolutely dazzling in a royal-blue sari
with a purple sash and scarf. The contrast between the deep

saturated marine colours of her clothes and her caramel-brown skin and deep-brown eyes was luminous. It seemed as if every part of her—body, mind and soul—shone through the colours. Her scarf revealed her warrior spirit, woven with precious metal strands of gold, silver and sapphire in the shape of her family crest. Maha was equally breathtaking, radiantly dressed in bright orange. Her very being seemed more ethereal than physical, as if she might flicker out of existence at any second. On her hair, she wore a headdress befitting a Goddess, adorned with gleaming rubies, lapis lazuli and diamonds over her third eye and crown chakras. Together, all three of us looked impressive, the women resplendent in their finery and I polished and suave in my modern business suit.

At Maha's directions, we made our way to the back of a building in what seemed to be the very worst, most sordid and dirty part of Mumbai. Looking around me in disgust, I muttered, 'This place is not worthy of our presence nor our magnificent presentation.' Shaking her head, Maha reminded me that the universe is a mystery and things are not always what they first appear to be. 'We are dressing for the substance of the situation, not its superficial appearance.'

We were led into a back room by one of the largest men I have ever seen. He didn't speak much and appeared to be of Tutsi warrior heritage. His beautiful black skin covered a body that was close to 7 feet and probably 275 lb. Despite his huge size, he walked with the rapid fluidity of a much smaller man. Swallowing, I felt shaken. Although I was willing to fight any man in order to protect myself, my family or my community, such an endeavour in this instance would likely spell my last fight in this realm. One might ask why you would even think about fighting this man. We men are not far from the Neanderthals;

we may not admit it, but our first thought upon meeting any man is 'Can we take them?'

We followed behind the man in a single file as he guided us through a maze of dark tunnels, each turn leading us deeper into the belly of this cavernous building. Finally, as we approached the end of a seemingly endless corridor, I saw light flicker under a foreboding door. The door was sealed shut and it took all of the strength of our warrior guide to open it. Finally, the door swung open to reveal an enormous cave lit only by candles and a giant roaring fire. The air was filled with smoke and the scent of burning pine and oak. The base of the pyre was solid gold, above which towered a giant silver structure emanating upwards. The structure had three platforms similar to an Olympic stand. On top of the middle and highest platform was a round golden and silver antahkarana. Inside of the round figure was a black mineral, probably obsidian. I didn't know what that figure was, but it stirred something deep within as if it revived memories from lifetimes ago. It drew me in like a Mark Rothko painting, one of his push and pull masterpieces. I wanted to drink it in. I was amazed at the pristine nature of the hearth in the midst of such a sordid cellar. Magnificent rugs and lavish pillows in red and brown hues redolent of Kashmir and Persia were scattered in a perfect circle on the floor surrounding the hearth.

After we had absorbed the scene before us, our Tutsi guide instructed us to sit down. Even at a whisper, his voice resonated throughout the cave. 'The Council will be in to see you shortly,' he told Maha before standing guard besides the door.

We sat down and I continued gazing around me, deeply impressed with our ornate and luxurious surroundings. Once again, Maha was right. Who would have predicted such an astonishing room would lie at the core of this rotten, dilapidated building? Suddenly, the wall behind us began to shift and, through a hidden door, into the cavern walked the Kings of Rajasthan.

Rajasthan is the largest state within India. Its name literally means 'the land of kings'. This is where my lack of growing up in India began to show; although I had heard of the King's Council, I had thought it just a myth. The Kings of Rajasthan were magnificent, both individually and collectively. Each of the great tribes of India was represented—the Yadavs, the Bishnois, the Meghwals, the Rajpurohits, the Bhils, the Meenas, the Jats, the Gurjars and the Rajputs. These nine families had birthed most, if not all, of the royal families of significance in India. As they filed in, all nine Kings took their place in a circle around the great hearth. As they took their seats, I realized that each of our pillows faced three of the Kings. Maha faced the Yadav, Bishnoi and Meghwal kings. Aanya faced the Rajpurohit, Bhil and Jat kings. I faced the Gurjar, Rajput and Meena kings.

Once each King had settled themselves comfortably on a cushion, the largest Tutsi guard stepped forward. 'Kings of Kings,' he announced. 'The Nine Tribe Council of the Ancients shall now commence.' With these words, he picked up a huge hammer and thrice struck a large golden gong at least three feet in circumference. *Bong. Bong. Bong.* Each boom of the gong resonated throughout the cave, sounding almost like *aums*, imparting a quasi-reverential tone to the proceedings. As the last echoes died away, the Tutsi warrior announced, 'Those who have business before the Council, announce yourselves.'

Maha stood up and told the Council our story. She told them how the ashram had stood on its grounds for over three hundred years. It was unique, one of the few ashrams for women that truly acted as a home and a religious sanctuary where widows and their children could honour God and live good, purposeful lives. It had not become a brothel, as so many others had. She went on to explain that she was responsible for saving many of the women, including Aanya, who had a destiny that had not yet been revealed to her, but nonetheless was very special. She told them of my arrival and my encounters with Prince Bandezar. She was careful to explain that my actions were not rooted in vanity or desire, but to fulfil my destiny of which I was also unaware. Finally, she told them of how King Bandezar now wanted to turn the ashram into a hotel. 'Please, most noble Kings, we request that you help us by investing in the ashram and superseding King Bandezar's offer.'

After she had finished, the Meghwali King spoke. 'There is a lot of uncertainty involved in making such a large investment.' Around me, in the flickering light of the fire, I saw other Kings nodding in agreement. 'We need to hear from these two heroes with as-yet nebulous destinies. If these two young people can acquit themselves well during our inquiry, we will consider your application. All three of you, return to us tomorrow. We will hear first from the beautiful lady warrior, then from the young man of dubious Indian credentials.'

∽◦∾

34

Explication

After we had exited from our audience with the Council of Kings, I pondered their comments. *Dubious Indian credentials, ouch!* In the US, my mixed Indian and American ancestry had been an asset. I could be whatever someone wanted to see. If they wanted the swarthy foreigner, I met the description. If they wanted just a touch of spice, *voila*. But, here in India, my lack of purity was obviously a shortcoming.

That evening, Maha, Aanya and I discussed our strategy over dinner. Maha was more serious than I had ever seen her before. 'John and Aanya, you have been honing your antahkarana over many lifetimes. Like a good seamstress, this thread has been made stronger with each life, with each attempt at purification. Draw upon that thread and walk now towards your highest level of consciousness.' Maha reminded us that we needed to focus on the energy we had developed. 'Rely upon as many lives as are relying upon you.'

The next morning, the sun rose at around 5.30. It was not a welcome sight; I felt like I needed more time to prepare for this ultimate test. Remembering my dad's instructions, I took a deep breath and reminded myself to face the storm head-on. I walked outside barefoot in the hopes of feeling my connection with the earth's core. As the first rays of light pierced their way over the horizon, I looked at the rising sun directly. *Give me energy and wisdom*, I prayed, *my celestial brother, son of the universe*. As I stared directly into the soul of the star, I felt it touch mine. In that moment, I felt simultaneously completely present while also being just a single part of eternity. I knew then that I was ready.

As he had done the previous day, the large Tutsi guard opened the Council session by striking the golden gong. 'The Kings shall now hear your requests.' However, it seemed there had been a change in schedule. I was to go first, followed by Aanya. King Matsya of Meena was my inquisitor. 'Young man,' he began, 'I ask of you: why should we listen to your entreaties, when you are not even a pure Indian? How are you worthy to stand before us now?' Bowing, I addressed the Council before me. 'Kings of the Ancients, King Matsya, thank you for allowing me to stand before you today. I understand your concern regarding my purity. Allow me to address this issue. My name is John Yogacara Asanga. My father, Gandahara Lama Asanga, was directly descended from Naha and Maitreya, one who has come and the other yet to return. My father was considered a Tulku. It may appear to some that he never fulfilled his destiny. However, he did not fail at his task; it is being completed through me.'

At this, some of the Kings protested. 'Why would a half-breed be capable of what he could not?' interjected King Hanna XI of Rajput. 'I am capable precisely *because* of my mixed birth.' I argued. 'His task was not just to bring enlightenment to India, but to the world. He was meant to bring the East and the West together. This began with his marriage to my mother, an American.' Looking at my inquisitor, I confessed. 'King Matsya, for most of my life, I was a fish out of water. I was too Indian to be accepted by the Americans and too white for most Indians. I spent my youth indulging my despair in a fundamental fact—I did not belong.' Pausing briefly, I continued my story. 'Then, when I came home, it hit me. My destiny manifested; I am an embodiment of the antahkarana on a physical level, destined to reveal to Westerners truths that emanate from the East.'

'All in all, the Christians are a good people and their religion has many of the right concepts; however, they need to understand that the highest self, God, is an impersonal force and not a superhuman. Indeed, scientists such as Albert Einstein have already come to this realization; so too did John Coltrane, who spoke of concepts of universal love and the mystery of the universe through his music. I was born to further that understanding. The world beyond India needs to understand yoga in its truest sense, which is a unity of the self with the highest self. As such, my Kings, I believe I have been guided here to complete that task. We will establish the ashram as a centre for self-realization. We will teach the world to realize their true selves, beyond religion. Our ashram will welcome people of all faiths, all countries and all ethnicities.'

'I wish to complete my father's life work,' I continued. 'I have faced every storm head-on, never hesitating to go right to the eye of the hurricane. Aanya, Maha and I will complete whatever task you assign us because we love each other, we love you, this world and the universe. I welcome the opportunity to be your emissary, for I have studied your history, great Kings. You too love the universe and you too walk in the footsteps of your fathers. Please allow me to do the same.'

I could not decipher how the stone-faced Kings had received my prayer. They whispered to each other in a language I had never heard. It wasn't Hindi, nor was it Sanskrit. Afterwards, Maha told me it was probably Tamil or Prakrit, both of which predated Christ by about two hundred years. Finally, King Sandhu, the Jat King, turned to Aanya and invited her to speak. 'Gentlemen,' she began, 'I am Aanya Devi Ghosa. I am an Indian Buddhist from the Buddhaghosa clan. My ancestor was the great Theravada scholar, Buddhaghosa, author of *The Path of Purification*.' With a wave of his hand, King Sandhu stopped Aanya from speaking further. 'Thank you, young lady. We already know who you are.' Blinded in disbelief, I thought, clearly, *they only wanted to hear from me, the outsider. No matter, I would make sure we succeeded in our quest...with or without their help.*

Before any of us could respond to the surprising announcement, the large Tutsi took five purposeful steps forwards and placed both hands on the large bronze hammer which hung on its stand next to the golden gong. The reflection of the fire made the hammer shimmer mesmerizingly in the heat haze, its golden movements reminiscent of a flame. He announced, 'The Kings of Kings, the Nine Tribe Council of the Ancients shall now retire to their chambers. Their decision will be issued forthwith.' At his words, the fire suddenly erupted, emitting a tremendous cloud of multicoloured smoke. He struck the gong nine times with such force that the sound boomed throughout the cave. As the echoes reverberated far beyond our present circumstances, each of the Kings seemed to disappear into the fog and smoke. Before we could speak, the Tutsi gave us a signal to remain quiet. Slowly, a reverent silence descended over us. I felt the presence of the Kings, as if they were still there, though invisible to us. After a few minutes, the guard beckoned us to follow him out of the cavern and directed us to an antechamber where we were instructed to wait until we were called.

Although we seemed to have retraced our exact footsteps from our initial entrance to the cavern, I could have sworn that we had passed no such room on our way in. Large comfortable pillows lay scattered over the floors, enough for each of us to lie down if we so chose. Delicious food and drinks were proffered on trays of silver by servers who seemed to glide to and fro without touching the ground as they walked. But I could not relax. Each second spent waiting was one less we could use to contest the sale of the ashram. As I paced back and forth, Maha clasped my forearm and stopped me. 'Rest now, John, while you can. If the Kings approve our prayers for help, the task they will assign to us will be undoubtedly harder than anything we have ever attempted before. It will take all our resources, our energy and, perhaps, our lives. This could be our last respite for quite some time.' She was right, as usual. I calmed down and settled myself cross-legged on one of the pillows across from Aanya. She was unusually quiet, not criticizing me as per her usual custom. Knees drawn up, she just sat there, staring off into space. Seeing her worried face, Maha hugged her and told her that all would be well soon. Aanya then looked at me and said, 'Well, if we do move on, I'm loathe to say it, but dung boy's entreaty may have played a major part in our deliverance.' She smiled at me for the first time in days. My heart lifted slightly. Even though I could see in her eyes that she was still unsure about me, even this small gesture was a major victory in getting her to forgive me. At least her voice was no longer dripping with derision when she spoke to me.

As we waited to hear the verdict of the Kings, we passed the time by telling stories of our greatest fears, failures and accomplishments. Maha regaled us with tales of growing up in the jungle. She instructed us on how to address an elephant before riding it. 'Elephants are keenly intelligent and communicate telepathically,' she informed us. 'You have to show respect for both them and their ancestors before they will let you ride them. But it's not just words! You must convey your appreciation for their species before sitting upon them. If you do so properly, they will bow down to you and allow you to ride. However, if your intent is not properly transmitted, they will wrap their trunks around you and throw you violently into a nearby tree or try to step on you.' Aanya laughed, 'But, Maha, when will we ever need to know this?' Maha just looked at her. 'Sooner than you think, my dear.'

35

The Assignment

We spent three days in the antechamber as guests of the nine Kings. Each meal was an amazing event, with a different representative of each of the nine tribes taking their turn to host us, feeding us regional delicacies and extolling the wonders of their respective kingdoms. Each night, we feasted on seven-course meals flavoured with exotic spices. I delighted in various novel culinary experiences, such as wild boar minced with quail eggs and aubergine masala. However, we were never served wine or any form of alcohol in order to keep our minds sharp. As we ate, we also received an education in Indian history and culture. We learned the individual manifestations of Brahma, Vishnu and Shiva that were particular to each region. For example, Mahadevi, the mother of all goddesses, was described alternatively as the source of all wealth, knowledge, forgiveness, peace and the absolute truth. Looking back, I believe the Kings were preparing us for our journey by giving us enough nutrition, both physical and spiritual, so that we could withstand the storms to come.

On the third night, dinner's end was signalled by the arrival of the Tutsi guard. He entered and strode to the front of the antechamber with a strong and purposeful gait. In a deep, foreboding voice, he announced, 'The Kings have made their decision. Please present yourselves to the Council at 9:00 tomorrow morning.' Realizing that this would perhaps be our last chance for a restful night, we meditated until we fell asleep. Just before I fell asleep, I reflected on how serene I felt; I had not felt such peace since my log cabin days in Wisconsin, which seemed several lifetimes ago.

The next morning, I awakened with an equanimity I hadn't known for some time. I was ready to accept the judgment of the King's Council. Much to my surprise, we found a table laden with copious fruits, juices and delicious pastries waiting for us when we arrived at the cavern. The setting was much more informal than I had expected. The Kings were relaxed, even festive, as they broke bread with us and entertained us with stories of past glories and future goals for their kingdoms and the world. It was easy to sense that, while they enjoyed the epicurean pleasures of life, their focus was on the future for themselves, their people, the world and, ultimately, the universe. These men of royal blood understood that sensual pleasure is an important part of life, so long as it is tempered with good works and a determination to return to Oneness with everything. Royals are sometimes considered to be God's emissaries on earth, rich physically because they are blessed spiritually. Some abuse that concept and live a life of avarice, corruption and greed. Others accept the responsibility that material wealth bestows and choose to be true leaders. They enjoy life full tilt while exemplifying the balance between *maya* and spirit.

Finally, Rajaram, the Meghwali King spoke, 'I hope you have enjoyed this banquet. Now, you must ready yourselves for a journey. You must now undertake a task of great import for you, your country, the world and the universe. It is something that must be done, but which has not been done during our time on earth. You must seal the door where evil dwells.' On cue, the distinguished Tutsi struck the golden gong and called us to the centre of the circle. As we stood before the nine Kings, the Council's decree was read out loud to us. 'Having heard the eloquent entreaties of all parties,' stated King Rajaram, 'The Kings of Kings, the Nine Tribe Council of the Ancients, has decided to support the mission and purchase the Andhakshi Ashram prior to the scheduled sale. In return, you must complete the following task. Failure to do so within thirty days and this accord will be null and void and the ashram will be sold to the highest bidder, regardless of his intentions.'

We waited with bated breath to hear our task. 'You must travel nearly 1,864 miles from here to the Kaziranga jungle located in the north-east corner of India and retrieve the original Antahkarana made of ivory, obsidian, gold and copper. It has been stolen by a king who has forsaken the path of enlightenment. Like many of those in whose heart evil dwells, he has been blinded by the ephemeral lure of matter over spirit and uses religion as a cloak to mask his physical greed. You need to retrieve the Antahkarana before it is melted down and buried, which will in turn effectively close off the bridge between humanity and the Universal Spirit. It could be the beginning of the end for all that is good.' The King's voice deepened as he continued. 'Be warned, travellers, that the Kaziranga jungle is one of the most treacherous terrains in the world. Your path will be blocked by rhinos, wild boars, Royal Bengal tigers and practitioners of black magic. Keep a wary eye out for Basamia, an evil sorceress who manifests as a white tiger with gleaming green eyes. You must find, capture and, if necessary, kill her. But do not be hasty in dealing with her, for at least one of her tiger eyes can open the safe where the stolen Antahkarana is being held. After retrieving the original Antahkarana, you must return it to the Council of Kings so that we can restore the bridge between earth and heaven.'

The sheer magnitude of our assignment was overwhelming. I was grateful to learn that we would have resources to help us achieve the task set for us. 'All of the necessary provisions for your journey will be given to you,' the King generously stated. 'But use them wisely as we have given you exactly what you need and nothing more. Three of our Tutsi warriors will also accompany you. Their ferocity is matched only by their loyalty; however, the same admonition applies, use them sparingly. They have been given to you for very specific tasks that will only be revealed at the right time. Today is 1 May. We will see you again on 31 May, hopefully with the Antahkarana in hand. Namaste.'

Outside, we were shocked to find a complete caravan already set up for us complete with six elephants, three for us to ride and three to carry our supplies. These were elephants fit for a king and they looked the part, adorned in red carpets and gold headdresses. Despite their regal status, they bent down immediately to allow us to board them. Nevertheless, I heeded Maha's timely advice, bowed my head in respect and requested the elephant's permission first before riding it. I, for one, did not want to be stomped on or thrown about.

ᘐᢞᕽ

36

Setting Out

It took us five days to reach our destination. Maha, Aanya and I rode on the elephants, whilst the Tutsis walked alongside us. The days were long, but the vistas were like nothing I had ever seen before. Above us, the sky yawned until it seemed like a mighty river. Every evening, we received the treat of sunsets so colourful that they seemed unreal, awash in unimaginable hues of red and orange and pink, like a magnificent painting. Once or twice, when we were near the river, I caught an elusive green flash of light as the sun descended into the orange waters, like a miniature glimpse of the Northern Lights, that awe-inspiring electromagnetic light show. It was a gentle reminder that God is everywhere, if you just keep looking for Him.

The tall elephant grass we waded through was also a thing to behold. Growing as high as four to six feet, the rich sea-foam green fronds tickled our feet. The elephants loved it. After drinking and bathing in the river, they would roll around in the grass, scratching their backs with the strong rough brush-like vegetation. I tried it once and quickly regretted it; my hide was nowhere near as tough as that of an elephant's and I had long, open scratches on my back for days. When she saw them, Aanya laughed and joked, 'Welcome to the jungle, city boy.' I had to admit it was funny. I hoped that at least my elephant had appreciated my attempt to join them in their end-of-day fun and games.

For most of our journey, we kept to the King's roads due south of the Indus Valley. Our path, though not paved, was surprisingly clear. The land around us was very rich and fertile. I remembered with some humour how I had once thought the poplars of Indiana to be pure heaven. Now, I was astonished at the multitude of exotic plants, trees and flowers of northern-eastern India. We travelled under the penumbra of the sacred Banyan, the heralded Bodhi, the healing Audumbar and the grace of the Neem. Under the shade of cotton trees, we feasted on gooseberries, tamarinds, guava, litchis, jamuns, bers and all kinds of mangoes. We conserved our supplies by dining on the fresh fruit we harvested from the land.

Although we travelled quickly, constantly aware of our impending deadline, I nevertheless enjoyed the journey. I felt as if, finally, my true home was revealing its soul to me. Aanya was also slowly getting over her funk with me, and we began to talk once again. As she was Indian born and raised, she had an amazing array of knowledge of the jungle. She knew all manner of local flora and fauna and their individual patterns and practices.

One afternoon, as I exclaimed in disbelief over some animal, she laughed at me. 'You're from Indiana, not India,' she stated. 'You may know your way around great American cities such as Chicago, but you know nothing of the jungle. In your one contact with wild beasts, you fainted!' She waved away my protests. 'Listen, I have only a few days to turn you into a jungle man. Lesson number one, elephants are your friends so long as you think of them in that way.' 'What?' I exclaimed. 'You act like they know what we're thinking!' 'But, they do, they're telepathic,' she said casually, almost as an afterthought. 'Did you not listen to Maha? Most animals are. The universal spirit flows through everything. Telepathy is just connecting with that spiritual element that runs through all sentient beings.'

I listened carefully as Aanya began to explain. 'Humans are semi-telepathic as well, but as we grow, we start to ignore that sense more and more. We learn to rely only on "provable" science, especially men. Women use their intuition far more, but men are so enthralled with their physical prowess that they ignore their feelings. Admit it, when your hair stands on end, you call it fear. But, in reality, it's a message from someone or something. So, lesson number two is that instincts and your intuition are communications from fellow travellers in the universe.' 'Is there anything else I need to know?' I asked. Aanya laughed. 'Yes, just relax and tune into the flow of the jungle. All will be revealed.'

As she said that, Aanya looked directly into my eyes. I was lost for what seemed like both a second and an eternity. It was weird the way she had that effect on me, the way she could make time itself become fluid and soft. It was unnerving because I liked to think linearly. I needed a beginning to analyse and an ending to predict so that I could fully process the situation. But I could not do that with her time-shifting; the lack of a known inception was entirely disconcerting. I had to throw out everything I thought I knew and just go with the flow.

My dad's exhortation made even more sense in this light: he had always said that I needed to run towards the centre of the storm to find the truth. It is not logical to run into a hurricane. Most people would be destroyed by the heavy weather. However, the man of spirit knows that matter ultimately has no power over him. It is all *sturm und drang*, all storm and stress. The true power lies in the eye, where pure spirit resides. According to Dante's friend, Guido Cavalcanti, secrets are not normally revealed to those who can return. We must swim out far enough so that returning to safety is not an option. At a certain point, we must evolve or die. The physical rules of matter are nothing, only the spirit that underlies all things is real. If we go with the flow, we will find the path home. There and then, I vowed to incorporate that type of non-thinking into my actions. I would take Aanya's advice and become one with the jungle.

As we neared Kaziranga, Maha outlined her plan of attack. We would split into two teams to search for Basamia. The evil witch was smart, she would not attack a large group. I was to act as a straggler, bait for Basamia. She would appear to me as a lost stranger who needed help in the woods. Once I let my guard down, she would shape-shift into a tiger and pounce. Aanya and the Tutsis were to remain hidden as my back-up while Maha would travel onwards alone. Fine, I had been bait in Illinois and survived. I could do it again. But I objected to Maha travelling alone. However, despite my fierce protestations, Maha simply laughed and fixed her gaze on me. Time stopped. I fell asleep and when I awakened, she was gone. Aanya shook her head. 'This fainting goat routine has got to stop.'

37

Kaziranga

Kaziranga is a small yet deep jungle that lies in the north-eastern Indian state of Assam. In the space of 25 miles, it rises from the relatively flat shores of the aptly named Brahmaputra river to 4,000-feet high at the base of the Himalayas. Long, long before our story, when India was just becoming herself, the people of the Northeast suffered a great famine. The good souls of that time prayed and prayed to the gods for relief. Brahma recognized that their prayers were sincere and he sent his son to help them. Brahma, of course, is one of the Supreme Gods and 'putra' means son. Thus, this river is the son of Brahma sent in answer to his people's earnest requests.

Kaziranga is home to the highest density of the Royal Bengal tigers in the world, along with elephants, the rare one-horned rhino, wild boar and a plethora of migratory birds. The river is strong, unpredictable and the God of the jungle. Its formidable floods, like God, can be both devastating and life-giving. Overall, the jungle is a hotspot of biological diversity, an important area of dynamic convergence. Everything meets here—the elements, animals, flora, man and spirit. Although the area around the jungle is densely populated, humans know better than to attempt to settle inside the jungle itself, where nature is still king.

A protected area since 1904 and designated a National Park in the late 1960s, there are many legends about how Kaziranga got its name; however, that is a story for another day. My focus now needed to be more observatory. I needed a quick education on the lay of the land and its indigenous animals and vegetation. Knowledge of the fauna would tell me who my allies were and which ones to avoid. The surrounding flora would help me track our prey, Basamia.

As we arrived at the jungle's edge, I looked at my surroundings with new eyes. At the behest of Aanya, I resolved to take a more free-flowing approach to facilitate our journey as we navigated the jungle and its denizens. For my initial reconnaissance, I tried to learn to recognize the interactions between the animals and their environment. After all, the birds are the bards of the jungle; their songs tell the stories we need to hear. They forewarn of flooding from the Brahmaputra, they tell stories of where the deer play, why the one-horns are angry, when the wild boar are rampaging and, most importantly, where Basamia was hiding.

The Royal Bengal tigers are magnificent animals, coloured a rich golden-brown with regal black stripes and a white underbelly. They are elusive creatures, seen only when they want to be seen. They hunt during dusk and dawn, the indistinct cracks between day and night. They make temporary lairs hidden away in the elephant grass near trees and lie there in wait, only to spring suddenly upon their unsuspecting prey. So too we needed to lay a trap for Basamia.

The three Tutsis were excellent guides. As promised, each was unique with their own particular set of skills. Babatunde was the leader and built like tungsten steel. He was at least 6'9" and probably weighed 270 lb, yet his appearance was lithe with high cheek bones and deep-set eyes. His skin was a deep powerful black and he spoke in slow measured tones that never gave a hint of excitement or fear. Each utterance was like a command; no one dreamed of refusing him. But his knowledge of our surroundings was unparalleled and extremely comforting. As the leader, he was the one to decide when we started and where we stopped each evening.

Our scout, Chacha, was much smaller at a mere 6'2" and around 220 lb. Unlike the chiselled features of Babatunde, his nose was a bit rounder and his lips were thicker. His skin was the same shade of chocolate brown as the soil itself, so he melded perfectly into the background. His eyes seemed to hint at powerful secrets. Every day, he ran ahead of our party until he was about two miles out and he would map out the lay of the land. He spotted tiger lairs, boar and rhino herds as well as sources of food and fresh water to supplement our supplies. I think he was also the medicine man for our crew; he seemed to have a strong relationship with nature and could call upon it to do our bidding, if necessary.

Aijeba was the last of the three guides. He was only 5'11" and about 180 lb, with powerful broad shoulders and a strong muscular body. He never spoke to us. He worked quietly but, to be honest, I did not know exactly how he added to our cadre. He seemed a bit disoriented most of the time and walked behind us. My guess was that he was trained to defend us. However, he radiated warmth and goodness, like a comfortable fire on a cold night. If you looked into his eyes, it was easy to lose yourself. He also seemed composed of a pure energy to which all animals responded in a remarkable way; he seemed able to calm them with only a brief caress.

As sunset approached on our first night in the jungle, Chacha suddenly appeared as if by magic and consulted with Babatunde. There was no sign of tigers thus far and the birds indicated this spot to be safe from rhinos and boars. At this news, Babatunde announced that we would camp here. The three Tutsi men set up a perimeter as we settled in for the night. After we had eaten a delicious well-spiced meal, we made ourselves comfortable around the camp fire. The Tutsis, Aijeba aside, were expert raconteurs. They had travelled the world to places we could barely imagine, a quieter and more discreet version of the Swiss Guards who protect the Pope. Our conversations reminded me of the caravanserai where my ancestors had regaled world travellers with stories of the spirit and nature over strong coffees and teas. This evening, we passed the time with each member taking turns telling stories of past and present, much like our own version of *The Canterbury Tales*.

Chacha told us of the jungle and how to recognize tracks. As he spoke, I saw corresponding images form in the smoke of the campfire. The Royal Bengal tiger is quite insidious, leaving few tracks; you can tell where a tiger has lain, but you rarely see where it has walked. Visible tracks are usually a trap for the unwary. In contrast, rhinos don't attempt to hide their heavy tracks. He also urged us to develop our sense of smell. The rhinos and boars are sweaty and pungent; although the former like the water, they don't clean themselves like elephants. Similarly, each flower, tree and shrub has a signature scent. Awareness was the key. Chacha warned us not to get lost in our own thoughts, and to be present and aware of what was coming our way.

We covered a decent amount of ground the next day. My elephant and I were beginning to develop a rhythm. As I rode, I occasionally stroked the back of her neck and sang to her so that she would know my voice. This way, she learned to assess my state of mind from the way I stroked her and the way I sang. When I was feeling well, she walked at a brisk pace. When I was curious about my surroundings, my singing would change, and she slowed down and allowed me to satisfy my thirst for knowledge.

Around noon, we stopped for lunch and to allow the elephants a forty-five-minute mid-day rest. They would eat, bathe and pour water on one another if we were near a river or lake, and socialize with each other, perhaps regaling each other with tales of pachydermic feats. As we ate, I watched them in quiet contentment. They are quite magnificent animals; so strong, yet extraordinarily sensitive to other beings. I wished that we humans could emulate their blend of power and awareness. We plow through forests to build new communities without a thought of how the ecosystem will be affected. If only we tempered ourselves with the sensitivity to listen to the earth and its other denizens, we could live in harmonious balance with the earth.

As I ate and mused upon these thoughts, Aanya came to sit next to me. She told me that she was impressed with the rapport I was developing with my elephant. 'You're starting to feel the rhythm of the jungle,' she noted approvingly. 'That's good, because you will need that to have any chance of dealing with Basamia.' Our conversation grew serious as we discussed how to go about our mission. 'She'll draw you in with her beauty and, once you relax, she'll pounce. So, in order to be prepared, you'll need to be able to feel her presence far before you actually engage with her.' Suddenly, she frowned. 'Now, if only we could cure your "fainting goat syndrome". Because if you faint while you're dealing with Basamia, she won't hesitate to tear you to pieces and eat you for lunch.'

At this, Chacha laughed. 'I have just the thing for fainting goats,' he interjected, reaching into one of his bags and bringing out six small sweet raspberry-like berries. 'These are special *shahtoot* berries that I have specially picked over time. They will cleanse your blood and calm you in times of stress, fainting goat.' At Chacha's words, I reddened but humbly accepted the remedy

he offered. Going behind a tree, I dropped the *shahtoot* berries
into the small leather bag that Maha had given me to store the
tools that I would need to complete our task. Inside, I had an
eye plucker that was the size of a small brass knuckle; this was
critical as, once I had captured Basamia, I would have to pluck
one of her tiger eyes to use as a key to open the safe where the
Antahkarana was stored. I also had a small bag of sweet ashes
that she and Aanya had taught me to use for protection. Prior to
my battle with the evil witch, I was to smear the ashes on my
wrist and third eye. Lastly, I had a small single-use vial of holy
water that Maha had blessed just for me. She promised that I
would know when to use it. The contents of the bag were all
that stood between me and certain death; as such, these items
needed to be on my person at all times. Aanya had taken it
upon herself to sew the small leather bag to the inside of my
underwear. The irony, of course, was not lost on her. *Don't even
say it*, I warned her with my eyes when she had handed the
sewn-in drawers to me. She didn't need to; her laughter by itself
was humiliating enough.

As we travelled, I took the opportunity to marvel at
Kaziranga's spectacular beauty. Around us, there were so many
birds and animals that I had never seen or even heard of before.
As we neared the river, I saw a mighty fish eagle circling overhead,
an enormous brown bird with a wing span of 6 feet, a prehistoric
reminder of a time when dinosaurs ruled the earth. With an
unnervingly piercing high-pitched call, it swooped down from
above us and, with ever-increasing speed, tucked its wings in
and dove like a missile into the water. After a brief moment
of stillness, the waters parted again, and it re-emerged with
a struggling catfish the size of my arm clenched tightly in its
powerful claws. Nearby, smooth-coated otters lay sunbathing on

the shore after a swim, guarded by Assam roofed turtles balancing on water-soaked logs. They looked like tiny soldiers with their green helmet-like bodies. *Nihil novi sub sole. There is nothing new under the sun.* Across a field to my left, I witnessed a couple of one-horned rhinos milling about in the tall elephant grass, huge creatures though not quite as large as elephants. Although I wanted to continue observing these majestic beings a while longer, Babatunde reminded me that we were on a mission. I was not yet ready to meet Basamia, confront my destiny and, hopefully, save the earth.

We continued through Kaziranga, sailing above the elephant grass, passing rivers, herds of rhinos, underneath the hot sun occasionally blotted by circling birds of prey. Around me moved a sumptuous Marsala of smells, tastes and vistas that resonated with my soul. It seemed to awaken Akashic memories I had forgotten lifetimes ago. As the light of the second day slowly faded from the sky, Chacha once again returned from his advance position. He whispered something to Aijeba, who in turn gave a look to Babatunde. 'We will set up here for the night,' Babatunde announced. 'Tonight, I will tell you my story.'

38

Babatunde's Exhortation

The cool blanket of night-time settled over the jungle, punctuated every so often by the calls of roosting birds, the croaking of frogs and the constant background ambience of buzzing insects. Far from home, it was in this exotic atmosphere that we waited in hushed silence to listen to Babatunde's tale.

'I am the son of a king,' Babatunde began in deep hypnotic tones, 'who was the son of a king who was the son of a king who was the son of a conqueror.' We listened, spellbound as he explained that the unparalleled physical prowess of his ancestors had been the key to their reign; men afraid of no one and nothing, the Original Vikings, conquerors of the African savannahs. 'My father was a great king. Though he ruled with an iron hand, he loved his people dearly and always kept their well-being and prosperity in mind.'

'However,' he warned, 'when your civilization is based solely on strength, it is destined to crumble. Invariably, there comes a time when a new generation of men and women arise, who see the world anew and adapt to their circumstances. They will grab the mantle of power; in doing so, they destroy the former rulers and everything for which they stood.' Gazing off into the distance, his eyes were sad and filled with world-weary wisdom. 'Such is the way of power, ephemeral, like all that is physical and tangible.'

I nodded in understanding. The universe is constantly

evolving and when it does, victory goes to those who foresee what is coming and are the first to act upon it. But all victory is based upon the laws of matter and is, therefore, pyrrhic. In time, all matter is destroyed; Shiva the destroyer comes so that Brahma can start a new cycle, which Vishnu will preserve until Shiva returns yet again. It is the way of the world.

'What my people failed to realize is that the only true reality lies within the spirit,' Babatunde continued. 'By whatever name you call it, the electromagnetic force that permeates the universe is the only true constant. Unless you are based in the spirit, you are doomed to come and go, to rise and fall like the many magnificent empires that come before us, after us, and which will surely themselves be defeated in time.'

The flames flickered before us, forming a single point of light in the darkness that surrounded us on all sides. Babatunde resumed his tale. 'Certain knowledge was withheld from mankind until we were deemed ready. My ancestors were taught that might makes right. While this is true in the world of matter, the world around us is not strictly all matter. As we evolve, we are given a peek behind the curtain, a brief vision of true reality. Great avatars have shown this to us—Buddha, Jesus, Krishna, and many, many more who came before and will come after. Yes, the physical is real, but not as real as the underlying spirit.'

'Africa, my civilization, my continent, my home, has fallen,' he confessed. 'We based our civilization on strength, on power which begat only the desire to obtain more power at all costs. This led to a mentality of tribalism, wars and, ultimately, the sale of our brothers into slavery. We failed to focus upon the underlying principle of spirit that is expressed through love. Love is a biological and cosmic feedback loop that gets stronger and stronger; if you send it out into the Universe, it will return to you threefold. Love is a radioactive force; once it starts to spread, it is uncontrollable.'

'I have devoted my life to spreading the knowledge of the spirit and its means of expression—love. This quest is as important to me as it is to you, because I understand that we must retrieve the Antahkarana, restore the bridge between man and God, and seal the door to evil. I was chosen to lead you because I am an initiate on the seventh plane and I have the physical strength necessary to guide you through this jungle. We have initiates of the eighth and ninth planes, far more advanced than I, who are here to help you complete the plan.' At this, Babatunde stood up. The time for tales was over; we needed to sleep to ensure that we were ready for the battle of our lives and there was still a lot of ground to cover.

39

Animal Spirit

The next day, we rose promptly just before dawn and breakfasted on a quick meal of dark, rich coffee, bread and a sweet jam made from local berries that Chacha had gathered and prepared overnight. We ate it spread on luchi, a light flatbread that is a cross between a beignet and a naan. The meal was delicious, but we wasted no time. As a result of his tale of the night before, Babatunde had imbued everyone with a sense of purpose. We were already a good mile on our way by sunrise.

The morning announced itself in operatic fashion. First, the night callers slowed their calls to a whisper and, for a second, everything was still and quiet. The water was placid, the wind non-existent, and there was a hint of dew on the ground and in the air. Then, from *pianissimo* to *forte*, the jungle awoke around us. The frogs took the bass section with their guttural croaking, while the tiny day fliers began flitting around and singing in light piping tones. The rest of the band followed soon after, each bringing its own unique tone to the tune building up to a slow crescendo. Even the elephants knew the rhythm and played their part.

I too played mine, observing every nuance of our surroundings. I watched the birds as they interacted with their kind and others. From the corner of my eye, I caught a wild boar crashing through the brush, either chasing lunch or being chased in turn. As I let the environment around me become my focus, I saw them all, the emerald dove, the swamp deer, the blue-faced langur and the peafowl, all magnificent creatures in their own right. I began to see the rhythm of the jungle and to feel its oneness. Its song played to me with every bird call, with the sound of the elephant moving through the grass.

Listen, listen to the stories of the trees,
Emanating in voices from their roots to their leaves.
The wind blows magnetic, it too prophetic,
For those with hearts and minds intertwined.

Listen, listen to the embracing call of nature,
Be wary that there is both wisdom and danger.
The jungle is free flowing, the morning fog all knowing,
Offering lessons from the past for all mankind.

The trail ahead is trampled by rhino and boar feet,
You must succumb to the jungle's tantric beat.
Lose your mind, your very sense of time,
There is a path revealed to those inclined.

Flow with the jungle whose past reveals the future,
Although I cannot guarantee you will arrive any sooner.
The road goes on ever onwards, you must continue forwards,
As the present changes and cannot be denied.

Follow this song and be guided by those who fly above,
The soaring eagle and the crooning dove.
The jungle teems with complexity, but moves with simplicity,
For those with eyes to see its hidden state of mind.

Know yourself and the path will be made clear,
You are a single part of this big blue-green sphere.
Heed these stories of the bold, warnings for the fold,
Listen to us that you may be aligned.

Listen, listen to the jungle song.

There is no dichotomy between good and evil in the jungle. In most situations, there is no time to question the morality of an action, just to react. The distinction between good and evil thus lies not in the intent behind the action, but in the focus. Evil focuses only on itself and on self-perpetuation, while good has a broader locus, realizing it is a part of the whole and the inherent responsibility this imparts. The goal is to focus on the union between all things, man and spirit, the personal and impersonal. Evil is ephemeral, good eternal; it is for this reason that the latter always prevails.

As the day continued, Aanya and I focused on honing our skills. As we journeyed through the jungle, she instructed me on the plants and animals we passed. I loved to hear her talk; her voice was low and soft, yet confident. Her Indian accent was enchanting, with just a touch of British inflection; however, unlike the English, her intonation did not stay at its lowest note. As she spoke, her tone became almost unconsciously song-like, with each lilting note revealing her moods, thoughts and even instructions.

As we passed a bush to our right, Aanya pointed out the small dark berries hidden beneath the green leaves. 'The *shahtoot* berries grow wild and are a good source of food year-round, though they're best in the early summer and a bit sour in the winter,' she informed me. 'But be careful, boar love resting in these leaves. Tigers, not so much, but they may still use them if they see boars looking too comfortable.' Her eyes sparkled mischievously as she glanced back at me. 'There's always a hierarchy in nature—just like there is between us. You know where you stand…too bad, it's far, *far* beneath me,' she laughed. I rolled my eyes in her direction but did not acknowledge her taunt. 'Speaking of which, have you picked your animal yet?' she asked. 'What?' I looked at her in confusion. 'Don't play stupid, you watch these creatures every day. By now, you must know which one you are. You'll need your animal spirit to fight Basamia. You should learn the unique skills of your animal so you can make use of them when you fight.'

'Oh, I see! Okay, this is getting interesting. What's yours?' I asked. 'I am a *cheela*,' she responded promptly. 'A crested serpent eagle, for those who don't speak our native tongue. It has a black-and-white crest, with yellow markings over its eyes and beak. Its black wings span over 7 feet and are framed by white bars. It eats snakes, lizards and sometimes small humans like you. The crested serpent eagle is just like me, beautiful, hungry and treacherous!' At that moment, I could see her as an eagle—soaring majestically in the sky above us all. I thought for a few moments about what animal form I would take.

Finally, it hit me. 'I am a *nol gahori*, for those that speak the native Assamese tongue.' Aanya looked at me strangely for a few moments, before bursting into uncontrollable laughter. 'A *pygmy hog*? Really, that's who you are? We're in a jungle filled with nature's marvels; authoritative one-horns, king-like Bengal tigers, huge Pallas's fish eagles who rule the air and seas, mighty water buffalo, wild boar and elephants who patrol it all… and you choose the tiny pigmy hog. Who are you planning on fighting, ants?'

'Pigs are magnificent animals,' I retorted hotly. 'There's a reason piggy banks are present in so many cultures; pigs are a symbol of abundance and strength. Also, they're extremely intelligent, probably the smartest animals on a farm. They have keen senses of smell on both the physical and spiritual planes. And the sense of smell is the third of the eight—' 'The eight consciousnesses of the Yogacara School, yes, I'm aware,' interjected Aanya. 'Well then,' I continued, 'You should also be aware that the pig symbolizes the ability to stand on its own, adapt to any circumstances and survive any storm. I've been preparing for this truth my whole life. Everything my father taught me relates to walking into the eye of a storm and not only surviving but thriving.'

Aanya absorbed my comments for a few seconds. 'Okay, fine, but why did you pick a *nol gahori* and not a wild boar? Oh, I forgot, you're afraid of wild boar. I guess you wouldn't want to faint if you ever caught sight of yourself in the mirror!' I waited till she had stopped laughing at her own joke. 'No, Aanya, I was never afraid. I never fainted. I just tried to communicate directly with the boar to stop it from harming us, to stop it from harming *you*.' She quietened at the sincerity in my voice. 'I also chose the pygmy hog because it has the type of intelligence I'll need when planning my attack on Basamia, a keen sense of smell to detect when she is near, and, because of its small size, I'll be imperceptible to her. She won't see me coming.' I had been thinking of Babatunde's speech from the night before. It's not always about power, but about spirit. 'What's more,' I added, 'It'll be a joint attack. I know a beautiful crested serpent eagle who will pluck out Basamia's eye at just the right moment, right when she's distracted by the pygmy hog that dares engage her.'

Aanya smiled and shook her head. 'Well, this is going to be interesting, at the very least.' She looked at me for a few moments. 'You're definitely a strange bird—you go left when everyone around you goes right. I think I need to keep watching you closely, strange Indian from Indiana.' I smiled but said nothing, glad that I had surprised her with my ingenuity. For the rest of the day, we kept to ourselves as we strode through the high elephant grass, each focused on our individual tasks. I spent time analysing the grass surrounding us, imagining how I would move through it with alacrity—pygmy hogs are known for their amazing speed through dense vegetation. This would be one advantage I could use against Basamia.

40

Aanya's Tale

As dusk approached, Babatunde instructed us to stop and set up camp for the night. After dinner, Aanya led the *arati*. Like Babatunde, she had decided to use this opportunity to tell us about herself and her journey and, more importantly, why there would be no going back should we not succeed in our mission.

'I was born Aanya Devi Ghosa,' she began. 'As we Buddhists are a minority in India, my family chose to shorten our name to Ghosa for fear of persecution. I was the oldest of five children, two boys and three girls. As the firstborn, I took the mantle of protector of my siblings.'

Aanya went on to explain that although her family was wealthy, the money did not last and so she knew she would marry a wealthy suitor to provide for her family. At first, she had objected when her father presented her at the age of fourteen years to a much older wealthy Hindu man; however, as a good daughter, she had eventually married him according to her father's wishes. 'I will always be grateful to him. He was a good man,' she stated. 'We were married for ten years. During that time, I did my best to be a good wife to him. I loved him. Although I never gave him a child, I took care of him and his household and, in return, he looked after me and ensured that my family never wanted for anything.'

At this point in her tale, Aanya's face clouded over.

'Unfortunately, he died suddenly of a heart attack one day while I was at the market. In an instant, everything certain and stable in my life was gone. All his wealth went by law to his family. My brother-in-law had the option of marrying me, but chose not to do so. Like many of our friends and neighbours, he feared that God had punished my husband and struck him dead because he had not married a good Hindu woman. He did not care to be saddled with a cursed, barren Buddhist wife. I was kicked out into the streets. After that, Andhakshi was the only place that would take me.' My heart ached as I imagined Aanya alone in the streets, with no money, food, home or place to turn to.

Aanya's voice strengthened. 'But this is not a sad story and I have not lived a pitiful life. I have always believed that every step I have taken has led me towards enlightenment. I have loved the journey thus far, and every day I strive to be present each moment.' Her beautiful brown eyes seemed alight with pure conviction. 'Babatunde was right: we have an important job to complete. We must restore the bridge between the realms of man and the *Deva-gati*. I know this is our purpose; I feel it is part of my past, present and future. It is as though I remember being there...so much so that I am obsessed with the possibility of return. So much so that I live this life without fear because I know I will return.'

'While I must admit it was disheartening to be a widow and social pariah at twenty-four,' Aanya admitted, 'I am grateful for my past because it allowed me to be here now, in this place, at this time, with the opportunity to do something that will matter for all mankind. This is the way I want to live my life, not the way that I am expected to—building a nest, bearing children, tending to a husband—although I would not object were my life to contain such elements. But, whatever happens, I want to truly live. I want to be in the moment. I want to connect with the universal spirit.'

She paused, taking a moment to examine each of our listening faces. She looked at me and I felt her gaze sear my soul. She saw through me, every inch; the man I was and the man I was becoming. 'I see that desire in all of you. None of us around this fire are living the lives expected of us. Babatunde, Chacha, Aijeba, you three are so far from home, selflessly devoted in the service of people of all ilk.' She turned to me. 'John, although I give you a hard time, I care for and admire you more than you know. No one would expect an American to be here risking his life for a cause not his own. You may have started by trying to impress me, but you changed when you decided to risk it all to save an ashram full of women. Now you are in the middle of a jungle, chasing a tiger-sorceress, with the destiny of the world hanging in the balance.'

My cheeks warmed; I had never before heard such kind words from her. The love inside me seemed like it could not possibly be contained within my body. 'But, let's be clear,' she continued, 'this mission is not about self-aggrandizement. Our goal here is to play our roles in the divine plan. We are subjugating our wills with that of the universe, crossing from the earthly to the transcendental. We must succeed in this journey. We must remain in the present, all the while remembering our past to access our true selves. This knowledge is essential if we are to succeed in sealing the door to the realm where evil dwells.'

After Aanya's inspirational talk, the group quietly separated and made their way to their sleeping areas. Her words were more important than ever before. Every second counted as we were nearing the heart of the jungle and our battle with Basamia would soon be at hand.

41

Past Meets Present

The next day, everyone had their own role to play as we began intense preparations for our battle with Basamia. Babatunde was busy organizing everything; he made sure every animal, every tool and every person was ready for what was soon to come. Chacha made shorter and shorter ventures ahead of us, reporting back every forty-five minutes or so as he tightened the net in his search for Basamia and the site where the Antahkarana was being held. We knew that Basamia and her ilk were planning on burying it deep within the mantle of the earth so that mankind's access to it would be lost forever. The mantle is just over 1,800 miles deep, so he was looking for a chasm of epic proportions. Chacha and Babatunde walked, testing the surrounding soil for any sink holes in case tricky Basamia had covered up the fissure.

The whole time Aijeba quietly accompanied us, never speaking; he would just hum quietly to himself, every so often performing some strange action with a set of bizarre tools. He would pull out tiny pickaxes occasionally to test rocks or sprinkle perfumed ashes over us occasionally while muttering some incantation. He also covered his face with another kind of mud or ash in the evenings. Something about him tickled me; although I could not fathom his purpose, a part of me seemed sure that he would nevertheless be of great assistance when I needed him.

Finally, it was time to say goodbye to the elephants, our

trusty transportation. They had carried us comfortably through most of the jungle, but the most important part of our journey now had to be undertaken on foot. We would have to move in stealth mode and the elephants could be heard from miles away. That night, we set up one last camp, at which Chacha would remain behind to tend to our animals and supplies until we returned.

The atmosphere that evening was fraught with anticipation and the silence around us was palpable as we ate our dinner by the fire. It wasn't fear or nerves, but pure concentration, rather like race horses lining up at Pimlico, each focused on what was to come. We could have used a good story to distract us, but we were all deep in pre-game mode and uncommunicative. Suddenly, a surprise visitor walked into the clearing, breaking both the silence and the tension.

'Maha!' Aanya and I shouted in unison. 'It's so good to see you,' Aanya exclaimed as she ran up to our mentor. Maha was suffused with an ethereal radiance; she looked as if she had just awoken from the best sleep of her life, completely recharged and rejuvenated. Her entire demeanour was different, she looked almost twenty years younger. Her face was bright, her eyes sparkling. Smiling, she looked around at us. 'I came to tell you a story on your last night of comfort before the battle,' she said. Without hesitation, we all sat down around her as she jumped right in.

'Three thousand years ago, just after the great battle in heaven, when many demigods and angels who were on the losing side were regularly seen on this earth, this jungle was very different,' Maha announced. 'The world was young and new. Women, men and demigods lived together. These demigods, fresh from heaven, performed amazing feats; of these, therianthropy—

the ability to shape-shift into an animal—was quite common. In some ways, this worked for the good; men treated animals as equals, because they never knew if they might be dealing with a powerful magical creature.

'Now, there are many stories about how Kaziranga got its name, but based upon my remembrance, this is the best of them. Two young lovers, Kazi and Rongai, lived in Assam during that time. They lived in the forest and took care of its animals. As a result of their love for the creatures and the forest, they were rewarded with abundance; they grew the largest, most delicious vegetables and fruits for miles around. People would travel from all over India to taste their blessings and all kinds of animals were attracted to their crops.

'Many a day, Kazi or her husband Rongai would find themselves feeding a stray animal, only to witness it transform halfway through the meal. Often, in such cases, the demigod rewarded them for their kindness. But the young couple always refused. "We do it for the love of all things, not for reward," they would explain. "We are all one. It is our duty as citizens of the universe to extend love to all beings."

'The lives of Kazi and Rongai were almost perfect. They loved each other with all their heart and soul; she the yin to his yang. Yet, one thing was missing—a child. They had been blessed with abundance in every way, except for an offspring, and this saddened them both. They could not understand how they had displeased God that He would not allow them to conceive.

'Now, the demigods were not perfect. They had fallen from heaven for a reason, so that they might learn lessons or work on themselves before they would be allowed to return. Of the demigods, one in particular—a young female named Basamia— was infatuated with Rongai. Despite her entreaties to leave Kazi,

Rongai refused and claimed that he could never leave his one true love. Basamia could not understand how he could choose a simple human like Kazi over her, and her jealousy and rage grew and grew. Eventually, she hatched a plan to take her revenge.

'Basamia told Rongai that the cause of his and Kazi's infertility was punishment from the gods because they had not obeyed their instructions. Rongai was puzzled. "But we live an abstemious life. We grow fruits and vegetables to feed the world, taking only what we need to survive. Our home is humble, and we dedicate our lives to the service of all. What can it be that have we failed to do?" Basamia shook her head sorrowfully. "You have not listened," she told him. "For some time, the gods have been speaking to you, trying to tell you that you must go on an important journey. But you have ignored this message because of your selfish infatuation with Kazi."

'Rongai was horrified and pleaded with Basamia to tell him his mission. "The path to the earth's centre lies somewhere in this jungle," she informed him. "Find and follow that path deep within the bowels of the earth. You will find a cave there and, within it, a door. Behind the door, you will find a box. Bring me that box and I will bless you with a house full of children."

'Poor naïve Rongai, he truly thought that everyone was good. But evil Basamia had decided that since she could never have Rongai as her lover, the rest of the world would suffer and be as miserable as she was. She had given Rongai instructions on how to find the centre of all evil, a place designed to promote division and differences. One of the rules by which all demigods had to abide was that they could not release such confusion into the young world themselves. The majority of mankind does not have the sophistication to understand distinctions; only advanced souls can see through the effluvia of surface differentiation and see themselves as truly homogenous, made of the one true spiritual essence from which all stem and to which all return eventually.

'Basamia knew that the release of this evil would set mankind off course for over a thousand years. Her selfish hope was that Rongai would come to her for help after releasing this awful force upon the world; in return, she would demand his eternal love. After he returned to their humble abode, Rongai told Kazi of the mission sent to him by the gods. "If this truly is God's plan, then we must by all means fulfil it," Kazi answered. "But we must first be sure that this is God's will before we act." Rongai agreed and so they meditated for three days straight, consuming only water and mangoes.

'On the first day, they began the morning with an oblation of choice yellow mangoes to the gods. They watched the sunrise and went about their daily chores. A few animals visited them and they fed them as usual. On the second day, once again they left mangoes as an oblation, watched the sunrise and meditated. They asked for direction from the universe in their meditation. On the third day, a luminous white tigress with brilliant violet eyes approached their home, just after sunrise. It was one they had never seen before. The tigress looked quite famished. Despite their own hunger and thirst, they offered her the rest of their water and food. After eating, the tigress transformed into a beautiful woman and spoke to them. "I am Mahadevi, the saint who presides over this jungle. I have watched your union from afar with great pleasure because your love for each other is true. But others are sometimes jealous of what you have because such a match is rare; they will come to you with lies. Don't listen: God gives you everything you need. You will have a child, but this blessing will come when the time is right. Don't be distracted from your task or take on foolish tasks for personal gain." With that, the tigress bounded away into the jungle, imbued with a bright unearthly light, moving so quickly that she blurred into nothingness.

'The next day, Basamia approached Rongai to ask if he was ready to complete her task so that he and Kazi could conceive a child. At this, Kazi turned to them both. "Mahadevi has shown us the truth," she stated. "And we will not play your game, whatever it is. The box in the cave will remain unopened." Angered by Kazi's insolence, Basamia transformed into a tigress, pouncing on the mortal woman. With her mighty paws, she clubbed Kazi around the head, rendering her unconscious. As Rongai shouted and began to run towards his beloved wife, Basamia tucked Kazi beneath her, holding her in place with her extended tail. "You will never see this pathetic human woman again," she yelled to Rongai as she ran away towards a nearby lochan.

'Although he ran after them as fast as he could, Rongai was no match for Basamia's speed. By the time he reached the water, Basamia had drowned the unconscious Kazi. "Now," Basamia said gleefully, "she is gone. You are free to love me." Wading into the murky muddy waters, Rongai responded, "My only desire, now and forever more, is to be with my beautiful wife." With that, he grabbed Kazi's outstretched hand and pulled her body towards him, wrapping his arms around her body as they sank to the bottom, as united in death as they had been in life.

'Rongai knew that he and Kazi would live forever in the eternal home of the true spirit. He did not worry about the end of this particular human experience; he knew that if he acted with true love—the governing principle of the universe—all would be well. Indeed, after they entered the lochan, it began to expand. At first it gurgled, then bubbled, in the centre a small water spout sprung up pouring water everywhere before erupting into a great lake. Years later, when the great King Singha, ruler of north-east India, was served fish from this lake, he proclaimed it to be the best he had ever tasted. After hearing of the origins of the lake and the reasons for its bounty, he named the entire region Kaziranga in honour of Kazi and Rongai.'

At this, Maha turned her gaze to Aanya and me and smiled at us. 'I told you I would see you again, Kazi and Rongai. Basamia wanted you to unleash what many call Pandora's box upon the earth. She and her minions wanted to keep the bridge between mankind and the infinite as a tool only for themselves. Their long-term goal is to build a cadre of selfish souls who think they can wage a battle for the heavens once again. Sleep well, for tomorrow we will set out to right the wrong that occurred many lifetimes ago, not just for you but for all.'

My eyes turned on their own accord to look deep into the beautiful brown eyes of Aanya, the doorway to her heart. They reflected what I too felt—surprise mixed with unquenchable warmth filled my entire being. Although on the surface I was surprised to learn of how deeply and intrinsically Aanya and I had been linked in our past lives, deep down the knowledge seemed to fit into my understanding of myself like a missing puzzle piece. Since meeting Aanya the first time, I had always known we were two halves of the same whole; for my whole life, I had been seeking the other part of me, and there she was, the beautiful woman staring back at me that very second. We said nothing; there was nothing in that moment that could be said out loud. It was truly an ineffable moment.

Maha cleared her throat and at that mundane sound, Aanya and I blinked and came back down to reality. 'We will recapture the Antahkarana and restore the bridge so that all souls who aspire to return home, all those who desire to experience pure love, and all those who long to experience complete union with the One—the source of all there is—will have access to it.' Clasping each of us by the hands one by one, Maha smiled before turning her back on us and running swiftly away from the camp. As she ran, her luminous figure shivered and began to blur as her distinctive human silhouette began to metamorphose surrounded by an ever-increasing angelic electromagnetic force. With each step, she was less human and more animal. First her face, then her arms, hips and legs in quick succession and finally her skin...until she was all tiger.

42

The Tiger's Den

Early the next morning, we were awakened by the sounds of Chacha returning from his scouting. He had finally narrowed down the area in which the great chasm should be located. On a map that he scrawled in the dirt, he drew a great circle; our plan was to split up into two groups, each of which would make its way around the opposite outside edge of the circle until we met in the middle. We would then slowly make our ways inwards in smaller concentric forays until we homed in on Basamia and the chasm. With the plan agreed upon, Babatunde and Aanya went left while Aijeba and I went right. As had been decided beforehand, Chacha stayed at our base camp to mind the animals and preserve our supplies while waiting for us to return—if we were successful in our endeavour.

'Remember to practise transforming, so you can do so at will,' Aanya said to me as we separated. Gently touching her hand as she passed, I whispered '*Squee-oink, squeee!*' I saw her slim brown shoulders shaking with laughter as she disappeared into the bush and a quiet high-pitched *kaeeeah, kaeeeah* in return. Then there was silence as Aijeba and I were left alone in the dense jungle. We were on our way.

Ah yes, therianthropy. I had transformed myself before but not at will, ergo the fainting goat moniker. I needed to be able to do this at will. I thought back to my first transformation after the boar hunt. I did not consciously command a transformation;

I was overcome with a desire to save everyone—well, Aanya to be honest—from Prajapati. My desire was so pure that it just happened. I evoked a response from the Monad, the Supreme Being, which was answered. It is easier, for some, under exigent circumstances to think clearer. Life and death as one's only options have a clarifying affect. I needed a trick to return to that state of clear desperation. I had to realize that every sincere call receives an answer. As Jesus says, if you have faith as small as a mustard seed, you can tell a mountain to move and it will comply.

I needed that type of faith, which I should have; after all, the universe brought me to this point. It saved my life innumerable times. It freed me from jail via a tornado in downtown Chicago and prior to that there had never been a tornado to hit downtown Chicago. It brought me back to India and when I thought I was making a quick stop in Mumbai before heading home to Ladakh, it brought me to the ashram and back to Maha and Aanya. By this time, I should know without any hesitation that God has my back. Okay, so with all the sincerity I could muster, I brought my attention to its highest point within my consciousness and applied the necessary tension to hold it there. Once there, I aligned myself with the Universal will, the Will of the Monad. Once I knew myself as a living example of God's will, I would be recognized by The One. The One never fails to answer the requests of those who completely align themselves with it in an unadulterated fashion.

I realized I am one with the universe and the universe rewarded my recognition by answering my call. 'I attest that my being shall now be expressed as a pygmy hog for the purposes of this adventure I am undertaking to save the world.' I believed it to be true from the moment I uttered those words. I felt disconcerted. I began to sweat, my heartbeat increased rapidly. I began to black out. *No, no, stay present, but at the same time, let go.* I relaxed. I knew my call would be answered. I saw only bright colours for a few seconds—bright reds, orange and yellow. I saw the proverbial stars one sees just as one is fainting or about to pass out, but I kept my tension, so I stayed conscious. Suddenly, my perspective swirled, it was dizzying. I lost all feeling in my body, first my legs, then arms, then trunk... I knew I was alive because I could hear my heart beating loudly and ever more rapidly. I was floating in space. Just as suddenly, it calmed. I could see but my eyes weren't normal human eyes. I couldn't see as many colours; my depth perception was skewed, but my field of vision was amazing. I could see at least 300 degrees and my eyes saw separately. Each eye had its own field of vision. I was inches from the ground and I felt much lighter. I had transformed! I looked down and I had little brown legs and brown hair. I was a 6 lb, two-feet-long pygmy hog! I tried to exclaim to Aijeba, I did it! It came out as *squeal oink, squeal oink.* Aijeba laughed at me and told me to stop playing and to communicate telepathically. *Wow, Aijeba actually talks* was my first thought. Next, I was impressed with my ability to take off and cut left and right with ease. With these skills, I could make millions as a footballer or rugby player. It was way cool.

As we walked, I would go back and forth between my human self and my new form as a pygmy hog. But, apart from transforming, I also had to practise my technique as bait as well. Basamia would not know me as a pygmy hog; she needed to see me as a human to recognize me as John...or Rongai... I wasn't so sure what to call myself anymore. We noiselessly continued our way around our side of the circle. Aijeba and I kept watch intently for the evil sorceress, hoping to catch signs of the white tiger. I applied the techniques Aijeba had taught me. One doesn't have to transform into an animal to make contact with nature; I asked the leaves and the grass about her and if they knew of any huge holes in the ground nearby. Nature does not hold back its secrets to those who bother to ask and listen for the answers.

My new friends were quite happy to share information with me. They indicated that something strange was happening about a mile westwards. Scores of chital, wild boar and barasingha carcasses littered the area, far more than normal. The birds had also fled the nearby area, heedless of normal migration patterns. All the signs pointed to the fact that a large carnivore had recently settled there—one with a big appetite. Given our knowledge, it seemed evident to Aijeba and I that Basamia was nearby. After some quick discussion, we decided on a game plan to flush her out. Once we had accurately identified her lair, we would scope out the nearby terrain in disguise, all the while looking for the chasm. Despite the risk of being a snack, I would investigate as a pygmy hog. If we found it without being discovered by the witch, we would retreat and regroup with Babatunde and Aanya. They would alert Maha and we would attack in full force. If we could not find the chasm, I would revert to my human form and hope to attract Basamia. I hoped very much that we would not be forced into battle with her just yet; I was not quite ready for that confrontation.

Aijeba and I continued down our path as quietly as possible. As advertised, about a mile in, we came across remnants of her kills. Chital bones, gaur and boar tusks gleamed in the dusky shade of the trees; in areas, there were still tufts of fur clinging to the wet bone. This was no ordinary jungle predator; tigers are usually solitary hunters and one gaur bull alone would be enough to satisfy several hungry felines. This creature had ravaged three rather large animals in a few days at most. The killings were so recent that the vultures had yet to clean up the mess; or, perhaps, they too shunned such evil.

Aijeba and I began our search for the chasm. Despite a systematic search, we saw no evidence of it; however, I did find two further dens under trees with more piles of carcasses. Thankfully, there was no sight or sound of Basamia herself. After approximately forty-five minutes, I decided it would be safer to switch back to human form as to not be mistaken for food; I couldn't help but notice that the surrounding vegetation was bereft of any other living creature. As a little pygmy hog, I stood a great chance of being mistaken for a light snack. After transforming, we rested for a while to try and clear our heads and think of a plan B. Suddenly, I became aware of the far-off sounds of running water. *That must be a mini waterfall*, I thought to myself. *After all this fear and running on high alert, it would be nice to cool off and refresh myself before I continue the search.*

Tracking the sounds, Aijeba and I turned the corner and discovered my surmise had been right; deep in a densely set grove of fruit trees was indeed a small waterfall, probably about six feet tall. The water dropped down in a long white cascade from the top of a hill and bled down into a small muddy lochan next to the trees. I reached out and plucked a low-hanging pummelo from a nearby tree. I thanked it for its offering, peeled it and took a large bite. Partially from hunger and the relief of not having been eaten up myself, it was the best fruit I had ever tasted. Juicy with the right mix of sweet and tart. As I finished, I waded into the cool waters. *I deserve one minute of relaxation, what with all this work to save mankind*, I thought. *Just one minute and I'll get back to work.*

The waters soothed me. I looked to my right and caught sight of movement about fifteen yards away on the other side of the pond. *Probably one of the deer common to Kaziranga*, I thought. *Perhaps a chital, sambar or even a barasingha.* 'Hey little creature, whatever you are, be careful: there's a mean tiger nearby with a voracious appetite,' I called out. 'Well, I hope it doesn't eat women,' a lilting voice responded sweetly. Thrown off by the presence of another human being here that was not one of our party, I looked in confusion towards her. Part of me knew I should run and yet being naked in the water, I felt rooted to the spot. That voice...so sweet, and with such a captivating cadence. It was a voice filled with love, with love for me. A voice that I had forgotten eons ago, yet one I knew as if I had heard it only yesterday. It was the voice of Basamia.

43

Temptation

We are always told that there are clear distinctions in life. Black and white, sweet and sour, good and evil. The truth is that the real choices in life are never easy, because they are influenced by nuance. I had forgotten how much Basamia loved me. Sure, her love was selfish, and she did not care to help anyone outside of her cadre, but nevertheless it was a real form of love and one that was insatiable from years of longing. What's more, she was a demigod; her power to attract was far more alluring and difficult to resist than that of a regular woman.

Without making a ripple, Basamia began walking towards me through the lake that divided us. She moved with all the confidence and assurance of divinity. I could not tear my eyes from her, though I felt Aijeba pulling at me to move me away. Somewhere in the distance, he seemed to be shouting something. My thoughts grew confused and it became hard to think properly. *I know she's evil, but doesn't the love she feels for me deserve some kindness on my part? After all these years, she is still so beautiful... so charming...that scent on the wind...like the most fragrant of roses.* Seeing that I had fallen under her spell, Aijeba threw a handful of ashes from his pouch into my eyes. Suddenly, the haze lifted and I was brought back to reality for a second. I dashed to put on my clothes as I remembered how she had tricked me centuries ago; how she had killed Kazi, my soulmate, right in front of me. Anger bloomed in my stomach as I fought hard to regain my senses.

Stepping barefoot onto the muddy shore, Basamia ignored Aijeba's presence completely and continued directly to me. As she came closer, my perceptions of everything else faded until she was all I could see. Laughing, she spoke playfully to me. 'Good day, handsome stranger. Who might you be?' Her eyes were completely beguiling, changing like lightning with her mood on a spectrum between lavender and grey. *She is everything I could possibly want, all that I need… Oh, heavenly goddess…* In a distant and supremely unimportant universe, I vaguely felt Aijeba blow more light ash on me; this time, I brushed it off impatiently. Nothing should impede my view of Basamia. *Anything, oh beloved one, whatever you want, I am yours forever more.*

Maha's clear voice broke through the white noise in my head. 'Don't focus on her eyes, John,' came her wise words. 'Look past the lovely shell, feel the dark spirit within.' Slowly, the world around me swam back in focus. Although it took more effort than I realized I could make, I managed to break eye contact. Almost immediately, I felt better and staggered backwards a few paces. Realizing what was going on, Basamia released a growl of rage and quickly turned from me to aim a dagger of energy towards Aijeba. He avoided it and transformed himself into a fly so she could not see him as readily.

Just as quickly, she turned back to me with an innocent smile. 'What is a handsome young man like you doing here in the jungle? This is not a safari for the inexperienced and you look like a city dweller,' she laughed airily. 'I came in search of my future past,' I replied guardedly, still trying not to catch her eyes. 'Is that from a song?' she asked in amusement. 'The past is the past and cannot be changed…at least not without the help of the gods.' Smiling archly, she asked, 'Do you know any?' As she spoke, I noticed that she was wearing a necklace with an amulet on it in the shape of an antahkarana. If I could only grab it now and be done with it! My fingers twitched in anticipation.

Seeing my interest in the amulet, Basamia threw her head back and laughed. 'Let's stop these silly games, Rongai. I know you know who I am.' Slyly, she reached down to stroke the amulet. 'And this is just a replica, the real Antahkarana is down below. Once the sun sets in a few hours, I will seal it. And that box...the one you refused to retrieve for me last time...will be released. All mankind will be destroyed.' She floated closer towards me. Leaning in, she whispered into my ear. Behind the fake scent of honeysuckle and rose her magic had produced, I could smell the stench of rotting meat on her breath. 'But, Rongai, you will be the one exception...if you marry me. Our offspring will be glorious—half human and half god. We can repopulate the earth the way it was meant to be; a home for the gods, not these ignorant feeble savages.' She gently laid one hand on my cheek. 'I will save you because you are my love. Despite your betrayal of me last time, I still love you.'

I thought furiously. The last time this had happened, I made a choice that caused Kazi to sacrifice her life to save mine. I would not allow that to happen again. 'Okay,' I finally responded. 'You're right, Basamia. I've always loved you. I will marry you... on one condition. Aanya is a good woman and she deserves to live. If you can guarantee that Aanya and her ashram lives, I will marry you.' Behind me, I knew that Aijeba was listening to the entire conversation and relaying it telepathically back to Maha and Aanya. I could imagine Aanya's face as she heard the news of my supposed betrayal. Her heart would break; she would be disgusted with my perceived weakness and refusal to fight.

Once again, I heard Maha's calm voice in my head. 'Whatever you do, John, don't believe Basamia's lies. She needs a human to open the door to unleash evil and to seal the Antahkarana from all mankind. She needs you. For centuries, she has been waiting for your return to complete this task.' There was a pause before Maha continued. 'At the end of the day, the fate of the universe depends on who you truly love. If it is Basamia, then the two of you can seal the bridge to the seat of the soul. But if it is Aanya, only the two of you can open the door to the Antahkarana. Get Basamia to show you the way; we will meet you there.'

I could feel Maha's uncertainty in the mental connection between us. More than anything, I wanted desperately to tell her the truth. I wanted to reassure them all that I had regained my senses after the brief moment I had been caught in Basamia's fragrant spell. I wanted to tell them all, especially Aanya, that I had a plan. It was a plan that had been evolving over many lifetimes, awaiting this moment for fruition. Instead, I could not tip them off. Instead, I looked at Basamia as I spoke aloud to both her and Maha, 'Yes, that is the plan. It has been the plan all along. After tonight, I will spend eternity with my one true love.' As Basamia smiled in delight, I prayed in my heart that Maha had heard my words and understood.

❧⤬☙

44

Into the Darkness

U pon hearing my fateful promise, Basamia smiled at me and took my hand, tugging me away from the muddy shores of the lochan. She walked joyfully, almost skipping in sheer childlike abandon. I followed obediently as she guided me through the tall grass. Suddenly, there, behind some low-hanging leaves, appeared the hidden chasm. The passage was not what I had expected; it wasn't huge or dramatic, nothing like a chasm destined to take us to the fiery core of the earth. It was just a nondescript tunnel sloping gently downwards, big enough for maybe two to three people walking side by side. However, once we set foot into it, the walls and floor morphed around us, transforming into a surreal glowing wormhole that spiralled dizzyingly around us, the abyss yawning below us. As we travelled deeper into the earth, we seemed to be moving in every direction; sometimes I was sure we were upside down. I was reminded of Dante's pilgrimage through Hell. Glancing behind me, I heard Aijeba buzzing and was relieved to know he was trailing behind us. It would be his job to defy gravity and lead Maha, Aanya and Babatunde to me, so we could all fight Basamia together.

The walls of the tunnel were truly unique. I gently brushed them with my fingertips as we travelled. They were spongy in consistency, yet metallic. Their colours shimmered unceasingly with our direction, ranging from bauxite to sapphire to outright obsidian when we were horizontal. Without a word, I let Basamia lead us ever deeper into the earth. It was at least an hour before we stopped; a huge cave had opened out in front of us. The walls here were the exception to the previous pattern. Although the cave was indeed horizontal, it was not obsidian; the colour was closer to burnt amber, tinged with gold from the reflection of flames. A fire flickered from an ornate twelve-foot hearth in the centre of the room. All around the semi-circular room, there were smaller caves. Although I couldn't see anyone, I shivered. My skin crawled from the pressure of unknown eyes.

I heard a tiny noise behind me and realized that Aijeba had left and began his flight back to get the others. I needed to stall Basamia until they arrived. Clearing my throat, I tried to think of potential ways to postpone the sealing of the Antahkarana. 'We have to wait until sundown before we can begin,' I said casually. 'That won't be for at least another two hours, so why don't we enjoy each other's company until then?' At this, Basamia laughed scornfully. 'Your simplistic notion of time means nothing here, my naïve little mortal.' Seeing my disappointed face, she relented. 'But, it's true, I'm impatient to spend time with you. I've waited such a long time to enjoy you, my love, and this time, Kazi is not here to interrupt us.' I thought quickly. *Well, that would be just the perfect picture for Aanya to walk in on—me making love to Basamia! But, on the other, I do have to stall her, so sacrifice I must...* No, there I went again, falling for her powerful spell. I needed to find a way to delay Basamia while still honouring the one I truly loved. I needed to find a way to 'yoga' the situation and the answer would come to me. Silently, I prayed.

The answer came to me almost instantaneously, as if the universe had just been waiting for me to ask. A husband is entitled to ask a few questions of his prospective wife. After all, if she is to be your match for eternity, your decision should be well informed. Turning to Basamia, I questioned her. 'Since we are to be wed, shouldn't I know your full story? I have so many questions, oh wondrous one. What is heaven like? Is any part of you human? What about the other demigods? Will they be destroyed by your box as well?' She laughed, dropping her defensive posture for a moment. 'You're right, my love. I will tell you a little about myself, so you know who it is you are marrying.'

'I am part of what some may call the second tier of gods; however, I prefer to think of us as advanced souls who have successfully evolved over many eons. We could not stay in our home dimension because we were too advanced. Here, we upset the balance of things with our mere presence.' As she spoke, I watched Basamia's face. There was no modesty in the way she spoke of herself or her kind—she believed in her inherent superiority to all living things.

'But why do you wish to get rid of mankind? Surely we could live in harmony?' I pleaded. In response, Basamia shook her head. 'Humans are limited in so many ways,' she mused disdainfully. 'They are generally oblivious of their power or its source. Fear and self-loathing accompany those who don't understand their true nature. They fear the unknown and look down on themselves and others, frustrated by their lack of power over their circumstances. As lower beings are wont to do, they project their own fear and inadequacies unto others.'

Sashaying closer, Basamia ran one claw-like finger over my cheek. 'Why should I live in harmony with such pathetic creatures? Humans are forced to invent instruments to harness the most rudimentary powers of the universe.' There was a rapid flash and, with a wicked grin on her face, Basamia was suddenly at the very other side of the cave; she had teleported at least fifteen feet away in a millisecond, with no visible effort. 'Look at me!' she exclaimed exultantly, raising her arms in triumph. 'I don't need a car, boat or an airplane to travel. I go where I want when I want, simply by deciding and willing it to be so.'

Before I could regain my composure, she reappeared in front of me, smiling with egotistical enjoyment at my shocked expression from her parlour trick. 'You think that you are rooted in the expression of you. You give this expression too much power. You build it up and, after a while, it becomes tied down, frustrated by its lack of real power, bound by the effluvia of your fear and negative thoughts. While I appreciate my form of expression, I know that it is only that—a means of expressing my spirit. My spirit is attached to the source of all there is and so I have the power of the entire universe at my disposal.'

'But we could learn!' I blurted out. 'You could teach us! We could be like you!' Basamia spat in disgust on the floor of the cave. '*Pah*! Great beings have spent *decades* on earth, trying to teach these concepts to you, manifesting all that an authentic self is capable of if they just understood they could do so. Instead of learning, you humans stupidly deify your teachers, believing these skills are gifts from God that can never be replicated. Jesus Christ walked on water, healed the sick and revived the dead; this, along with countless other miracles performed by the avatars who have visited the earth, should have pushed you into understanding your true selves. Such ignorant, lesser creatures do not deserve to exist.'

There was silence for an instance before Basamia continued. 'I, along with my ambitious cousins who were sent here after the great battle between Satan and the Archangels in heaven, have grown tired of mankind's ignorance. We will clear the earth of your kind so we can attract more advanced souls dispersed throughout the universe. They will join our battle to take back what is ours. This time, *we* will win. We will beat those arrogant beings who sent us here because we did not have enough so-called *love* for those who rise so slowly on the evolutionary ladder. Love is wasted on pitiful souls unworthy of it.'

Basamia's lilac eyes gleamed fanatically in the light of the fire. 'That's why we need the Antahkarana, my darling. It will act as a bridge to bring our kindred souls to this planet. After the battle, we will take control of the universe and bend it to our will. Power, not love, is the only force of any worth. And you, my sweet one, will be the father of a bolder, stronger and more complete race. You will be a king on Earth. For all your lives, you have been held back by the inferior dregs around you. But no more.'

I didn't know quite how it had happened, but Basamia had me gripped tightly. While she had been talking, long algae-like tendrils of her hair had slowly and insidiously curled around my forearms, climbing down my arms, into my pants and encircling my neck like they had minds of their own. I was enmeshed, bound to her, drowning in her hair and sickly-sweet perfume, falling for her seduction. 'Now do you understand, my darling?' She breathed into my face, drawing me closer and staring deep into my eyes as I struggled to clear my head. 'I need you to open the door to release the forces that will bring all this into play. I cannot do it alone. Two are necessary to open that door. One human and one advanced soul. You...and me.' I struggled desperately against her grip as she drew me inexorably closer, the last dregs of my strength beginning to ebb away. As I pulled away, I saw that she was not interested in seducing me; she was merely distracting me while she removed my bag of tools stitched to my underwear. You won't need these stupid tools where we are going, my darling; you are about to become a god on Earth. You can soon accomplish anything at will, no need for instruments. Wow, no eye plucker, no ashes or any of Aijeba's wondrous tools to save me.

45

Battle Royale

'That's enough, Basamia. Why don't you tell John the truth?' came Maha's calm, firm voice from behind me. The spell was broken; I managed to turn my head to look at Maha, tearing through the hair strands. 'Tell him you need someone with a pure heart to seal the Antahkarana. Your black heart is only good for releasing evil. Tell him that you have no intention of saving Kazi. As long as she is alive, she and John have the power to defeat you. Love is the most powerful force there is... You lost once because of it and you will lose again this time.'

With a banshee-like scream, Basamia released me and whirled around to face Maha. There was no trace of beauty left in her features: she looked the very epitome of ancient evil. 'I won't lose to you!' she shrieked and leapt with lightning speed across the cave towards Maha. The two women raced towards each other, each step a marvel in transformation. In nanoseconds they changed, first their legs became muscular tiger hind legs, then their arms each with fiercely clawed paws, next their trunks grew broad and strong and finally their faces, until they clashed as two enormous white Royal Bengal tigers in the middle of the cavern. The acoustics of the cave enhanced their growls until the air itself was filled with snarls. Their claws were out, and their teeth gleamed menacingly in the darkness as they began to tussle.

Boxing aficionados describe the sport as a sweet science, while others call it barbaric. I had always been of the latter camp, but I now found myself appreciating the beauty of up-close warfare. And these were no mere 200-lb men throwing jabs and blocks; these were two magnificent eight-foot, 340-lb Royal Bengal tigers going at it at close range with every iota of incredible strength and deadly intent. It was invigorating. Unlike a boxing match, there was no preliminary announcement, no 'In this corner, weighing in at 200 pounds...' Instead, the two big cats circled each other with low guttural growls. *Pppahbaa grrrr, pppahbaa grrr*. With lightning speed, one would suddenly pounce on the other, striking with all 340 pounds of sinewy strength.

It was difficult to distinguish them once they began fighting. They were both magnificent beings, moving rapidly with flow and power. Although Maha was a pure white and Basamia had traces of red around the eyes that glowed emerald green, their markings were quite similar and they soon melded together as one mass of fur and muscle, teeth and claws. Dashing towards Aanya, I asked desperately, 'How can we tell which is which? We must help Maha before Basamia kills her. And we need at least one of Basamia's eyes!' With an inner calmness that I sought to emulate, Aanya told me to look at them more carefully. 'Focus on their auras, John,' she told me quietly. 'Although they wear similar skins, they could not be more different on the inside. Focus on their hearts.' Taking a deep breath, I tried to take Aanya's advice. Staring hard at the two tigers, I tried to focus on their auras. Then I *saw* them. Maha had a translucent aura and a bright pink heart. Basamia's aura was much murkier, and her heart was dark; not black in the literal sense, but like it had become clogged due to inactivity.

The fight grew more vicious. The speed of battle became less intense, but more savage, every slash and bite inflicting great pain. It was clear they both were adept fighters, feinting and striking like seasoned warriors. As we watched, Maha retreated to the back of the cave, gathering her speed and power for the next attack. Suddenly, she raced directly towards Basamia and attacked her straight on. But Basamia eluded her lunge, fading away to her right, causing Maha to miss. Staying on the attack, Maha quickly spun around and gashed her opponent's side with her front claw. The scent of blood filled the cave. Seemingly stunned that she had been struck, Basamia feigned weakness and appeared to hesitate; but it was a ploy to trick Maha into exposing herself. Maha complied by attacking straight on again, this time aiming for the throat. As Maha closed in, Basamia suddenly jerked to her left, striking Maha with a ferocious blow using her rear right claw. Each bleeding, they retreated to opposite sides of the cave to lick their wounds and gather themselves for the next attack.

Aanya was not one to wait for the outcome. Transforming into a crested serpent eagle, she flew over the fray. Timing was key; she had to attack at the right moment to injure Basamia, and not Maha. Focusing on Basamia's dark heart, Aanya melded with the rhythm of the fight, darting back and forth with each blow, left then right, up then down. Just then, Maha rammed Basamia's left side, causing her to fall onto her right side for just a moment. Aanya dove down, attacking Basamia's vulnerable left eye, slicing through the extraocular muscles with her razor-sharp claws and plucking the eye clean out of Basamia's head with her beak.

As Aanya flew off with the eye, Basamia released a terrible scream of agony. A huge colony of black bats, larger and more vicious than any I had ever witnessed before, swarmed out of holes in the cave walls and began to attack Aanya in mid-air. I immediately changed into my pygmy hog self and scurried out into the open. Seeing me, Aanya released the eyeball. There was a moment of breathless silence as everyone, human and animal alike, focused on the little green orb falling through the air. Seconds seemed like minutes and hours as the eye wafted down towards me. Thankfully, the bloody gooey eye landed right into my waiting hooves.

Taking advantage of the distraction, Aanya rapidly flapped her huge wings, creating a tremendous gust of air that threw the bats off her temporarily. She quickly joined us on the ground and transformed back into her human form. At once, Aijeba clapped his hands commandingly and a force field shimmered into being around us, repelling the bats. Stunned, they flew back to their caves to regroup, though I felt sure they would return to attack us again soon.

Meanwhile, Maha attacked Basamia from the left. Taking advantage of her opponent's weakness, she bit deep into Basamia's throat and tore it out of her body. Bright-red blood sprayed out of her and onto the surrounding walls. With another shriek, Basamia turned back into a woman and squirmed pitifully in agony, flailing as her life blood ran out of her. Using her claws, Maha ripped through her chest and wrenched her heart out of her. Shaking her large tiger's head, she flung the dark organ onto the cave floor next to us. Immediately, Aijeba sprang into action, reaching into his bag and pouring an acid-like substance on it. In front of our eyes, the heart hissed and bubbled, before dissolving away into nothing more than a little pile of ashes.

In the centre of the cavern, Basamia was dying a slow and painful death. As her heart dissolved, she was losing her ability to transform. For a while, she pulsated back and forth between feline and female, Royal Bengal tiger and Basamia; each time, the image of the tiger grew weaker and weaker, until at last she gave up. Meeting my gaze with her one remaining eye, she gave me a look of pleading and stretched her hand out to me in desperation. Her soulful gaze called to me and moved me to pity. It was as if her dying request was that I hold her hand as she returned to eternity. Having played my part in killing her, my guilt and compassion could not deny her last request. As I reached out to take her hand, Aijeba smacked my arm away. 'No, John! She's trying to jump into your body and steal your essence before she dies!' Shaken, I hastily snatched back my hand before she could grab it. I had to give her credit; she was a deceiver until the very end.

Once we had witnessed Basamia's final breath, Maha turned to us. 'Your task is not complete, my dears. You must still seal the door where evil dwells and restore the bridge between mankind and heaven.' She told us that only Aanya and I could open the door where the Antahkarana was being held. Basamia had told me the amulet she was wearing was only a replica, but I hadn't believed her then. We weren't that lucky, we had to find the real Antahkarana. Her evil plan had been to have me open Pandora's box, causing massive damage to the wormhole and sealing the path to the Antahkarana until they had killed all humans. Thankfully, the Antahkarana amulet would act as a beacon and lead us to the real one. However, Maha gave us a dire warning before she left. 'Be very careful; if you open the wrong door, you may still release the poisonous forces of Basamia's dreams, completing her mission and dooming all mankind.' Gulping in apprehension, Aanya and I exchanged worried looks. 'How will we know which is the correct door?' I ventured. 'Trust yourselves,' Maha laughed, before vanishing as if she had never been.

My favourite phrase is 'Know yourself and you will be known.' I didn't mind having it thrown back in my face. It would be a chance to prove what my father had taught me, although

I had to admit that saving the world from potential destruction was just a little bit more pressure than I had bargained for. Well, no matter. I could have no better partner than Aanya. If I was going to die, it might as well be next to her.

46

Orpheus and Eurydice

Aanya and I were not completely alone after Maha left. Aijeba stayed with us. I now knew that his accoutrement, far from being an unimpressive tool bag, was actually a full-fledged hospital and armamentarium. He had powerful potions, powders, tools and just about anything one could ever need to get out of any situation. He had prevented Basamia from transforming back to her demigod self by disintegrating her heart with acid and he had saved me from her love spell with ashes. Considering he could also transform himself into a fly, I was quite impressed with Aijeba. I had learned my lesson not to judge people or things too quickly.

After he had healed our scratches and bites with a salve, Aijeba informed us that we would not be able to rely on his shielding powers. We would have to figure out how to open the correct door and avoid the bats on our own. He said that Basamia's demonic minions would probably attack either just before or just after we opened the door; their goal was to prevent us from leaving with the Antahkarana. Aanya and I took a moment to settle ourselves. Only two options lay ahead of us—dying together once again or saving the world.

'So, husband,' she remarked sardonically as we rested for a few moments on the cavern floor. 'How is it that you keep falling for this Basamia chick, if I am supposedly your soulmate? Were you actually going to comfort her while she was dying?

You men are so weak. Why you are considered the stronger sex is beyond me.' Turning my head, I responded, 'Oh no, wife, we are most certainly *not* the stronger sex. Don't you get it? Men subjugate women because you have too much power, power that we can't control. You produce our progeny from your womb, so it is you who decide if our genetic material and our name are to live forever. Men are insecure and so we control women to protect our lineage...'

'I see,' she interrupted, 'If I choose you that means that I've apparently already decided to create a lineage with you. Yes, you *are* insecure. A woman decides on her mate based upon a myriad of subtle factors. Yes, looks and security are a part of it, but so are bravery, intelligence, spirituality, resilience, ingenuity, as well as compassion for others and a respect for the earth.' Chastened, I looked away. 'Yes, it is our job to produce beings that will bring the world forward,' she continued. 'I may enjoy parlour tricks such as feats of strength or amassing a fortune, but my mate must have much more than merely physical skills. My mate, above all, must have love, discernment and a respect for the spirit. I chose you, in the past, for your ability to show love and compassion for all and for your connection to the spirit.'

'Yes, Aanya, we are all connected,' I said earnestly. 'Every man, every animal, every plant, every mineral. We all come from the same source, all one with that source. Let's hug as hard as we can; we will become one heart, one mind, one spirit, one endless, unchanging, infinite being. Then we will know which door to open.' Blushing prettily, Aanya laughed. 'Okay, I'll hug you, but the only thing that should get hard, mister, better be our hug. This is a time to focus, not a time to get your jollies!' I laughed, 'Oh, I have plans for you when this is over, my dear, but right now, we need to concentrate on the situation and the answers will be revealed. We will know which door to open and how to get past those ridiculous vampires who seem to have a taste for hog.'

With that said, we hugged each other. Instantaneously, we lost all sense of separateness. We became one. First with each other, then with our surroundings. We were the sandy floor of the cave, the worms, beetles and gnats beneath that. We were the mice and the rats in the darkness, the puddles of mud, the pools of green water, every pebble. We were one with the rocky walls of the cave, one with the doors, one with the minerals that comprised the rocks, even one with those pesky bats. I felt them and understood that they were just following instructions to save *their* world. They, in turn, felt our love and changed their attitudes.

We *saw* the path forward. All of them, from the microbes to the amoebae, from the prokaryotes to the eukaryotes, from the copper and iron ore to the nickel deposits, everything spoke to us.

The door on the left contains erroneous thoughts, fears and misguided acts of the past. Open it and unleash confusion, fear and selfishness, the forces that will destroy the world. On the right is the door where the Antahkarana is being stored. Open it and you will restore the bridge between earthly beings and the universal source for all sentient beings, the indescribable, ineffable One from whom we all come and to whom we all shall return.

Slowly, Aanya and I returned to ourselves and released each other. We knew without speaking that each had gone through the same experience. Arm in arm, we walked to the right door and opened it. Her left hand under and my right over, we turned the handle. Behind it, on a scoria-coloured igneous rock altar covered with a cloth spun of gold, was the Antahkarana. It was a sight to behold. Encased in pure silver, it was elliptical with an obsidian base, encrusted with magnificent gems of all descriptions—emeralds, amethysts, sapphires, rubies and diamonds. It gleamed in the dust, an alchemist's delight. More so than its physical appearance, I felt breathless in its presence. I could sense that it contained all the love, intrepidness, resoluteness, discernment, compassion and strength needed to evolve and expand throughout the universe. It radiated pure spirit. It was the very embodiment of Yoga.

47

The Returning Path

Having retrieved the Antahkarana, our next task was to return to the surface so we could complete our mission in a timely fashion. The Kings had given us a strict thirty-day deadline to save the ashram. We had planned for twelve days in and twelve days back to give us plenty of time to accomplish the mission. According to our calculations, it was day ten; therefore, we had a good two days to return to the surface. This seemed more than reasonable; after all, it had taken us mere hours to descend to the cave in the first place. But what we had not counted on was that the ascent would be far trickier. On the way down, we had been aided by magic. This time, we were solely reliant on our own efforts. The euphoria from the Antahkaranic victory soon faded.

We laboured upwards, our backs scraping the dirt off the roof of yet another tunnel, our palms stinging from grazes inflicted by jagged rocks that seemed to bar our path ahead. Panting, I asked Aanya how she was doing. 'How much further?' she gasped. I shook my head. I didn't know. We were lost in the bowels of the earth. 'Now, I know the plight of the Jews as they left Egypt,' I mentioned bitterly. My only hope was that we too would not be there for forty years. Trying to take her mind off our plight, Aanya analysed my comment. 'The Jewish people were lost in the wilderness for a reason. God wanted them to rethink their mentality; they had believed they were separate from God.' Her words seemed amplified by the acoustics of the tunnel, bouncing from wall to wall and echoing in the cramped darkness. 'They could only enter the promised land when they believed that they were one with God, when they had inherent trust in the Spirit.'

'We are lost,' she continued, 'because we don't fully believe in yoga. We're holding on to the belief that our relationship with God is transactional: that if we do good things, we will be rewarded with love.' A drop of sweat stung my eyes as I contemplated her words. 'While karmic cleansing is part of the evolutionary process, it is not a prerequisite to receiving God's love. We are one with God—that is the way of true yoga. We will always be evolving and honing that relationship so as to reach further levels of understanding, but we must above all understand that we have been and will always be connected.' She paused for a second. 'I think that we need to consciously focus on our connection with all things. Once we stop doubting and start trusting with all our hearts and souls, we will *see* the path forward.'

She was right. *What a beautiful soul!* I wanted to stay with her forever. Reaching behind me, I crouched in the dark and held Aanya's hand. Closing our eyes, we focused on the bond between the small personal selves and the Divine Self that is the essence of all. Slowly, the universe around us provided guidance. Slowly, we followed instructions and moved from one channel to the next. We went through tunnels and holes, jumped over rivers of magma and crawled over craggy rocks. Finally, after fifteen days of arduous climbing, we reached the surface. Babatunde, Chacha, Aijeba and Maha were there to greet us. Chacha had brought the supplies and elephants to expedite our return trip.

After the enthusiastic welcome, neither Aanya nor I could look them in the eyes. We knew that our almost two-week delay meant that it was all but impossible to meet the Kings within the designated timeframe. The ashram was all but lost already. Seeing our downtrodden countenances, Maha was puzzled. 'Why the long faces after such a successful journey?' 'We have failed you and all of the women of the ashram,' I acknowledged. 'It will be impossible for us to meet the Kings and fulfil their mandate.' Maha and the Tutsi guides continued to look confused. 'What are you talking about? We still have fifteen days to return.' Aanya and I glanced at each other in puzzlement. 'But we kept track of the days,' Aanya pointed out. 'We were underground for over two weeks!' Shaking his head and smiling, Babatunde held up three fingers. *Three days? Or fifteen?* Time is a relative concept that becomes skewed as you travel closer to the earth's surface. 'Don't worry, we're still on schedule,' Maha informed us. 'You have both done well. Now, hide the Antahkarana in this case. We don't want the wrong forces to know it's above ground just yet.'

We spent the next ten days riding back through Kaziranga to meet the Kings. The journey was joyous. As we had done on the way there, we told tales in Canterbury fashion each night. This time, Aijeba proved himself to be an amazing raconteur, regaling us with tales of past adventures before taking up the post of camp sentinel every night while we slept. However, relations between Aanya and I became somewhat strained. She vacillated constantly in attitude towards me, sometimes flirting and all but admitting her attraction for me and other times, ignoring me completely and keeping her distance. Even then, though, I would notice her darting furtive glances at me when she thought I wasn't looking. I was a little hurt that, despite our adventure and all we had been through together, she still did not know what to make of me. Nevertheless, being the somewhat overconfident boor that I am, I tried to look on the bright side. *It's a good thing,*

I consoled myself. *We're still new to each other and the fact that I keep her off balance will keep our love fresh over the years.*

Balance is the key to life. As Buddha says, you must walk the middle way so that you do not fall thrall to sensual indulgence. But the middle path is a foreign concept for me; I had survived thus far by being all in, putting all of my heart and soul into a decision. After all, had I walked the middle way, this adventure would never have happened. I would have done my thirty days at the ashram and headed back home to the wonderful shores of America or continued on my way to Ladakh. Instead, I had fallen in love, my Akashic memories had kicked in and I had followed my destiny on a perilous yet invigorating adventure. Although I understood the wisdom of Buddha's words, and promised myself I would strive for his middle path, I made a decision. As of today, I was still all in.

I guided my elephant gently next to Aanya's as the morning dawned. The sun had just risen and the world around us was hushed in a moment of anticipatory stillness. The beauty of the early morning sky over Kaziranga was unparalleled. The soft orange hues graduated gently until they kissed the bushy tops of the elephant grass on the horizon. Such breath-taking stillness is an opportunity to inhale the unity of the universal spirit. The sun has returned to light our way, to create the new day, one filled with potential for joy and pain, love and hate, success and failure. That morning, I looked upon the new day with excitement. In all my years, every time I had prostrated myself to the universal will, it had produced tremendous results. It had saved my life, released me from jail, and brought me home to my country and my future wife.

Turning to Aanya, I greeted her softly. After she had acknowledged me, I decided to embrace the moment and tell her how I felt. 'Aanya, this time, this moment, I want it to last forever. I want to create a legacy that will help the rest of mankind find the same union with divinity that you and I have discovered. It starts with community. It starts with family. I want you in my life forever. I never want to lose you again.' Looking into her wide brown eyes, I proposed. 'Will you marry me?' Although I wanted that last question to come out strong and confidently, my nerves betrayed me, and my voice cracked.

Aanya, resisting her normal urge to tease, smiled sadly. I waited desperately for her answer as she looked off into the distance. 'No,' she responded softly. 'I cannot marry you, John Asanga. You're a wonderful person, but too impetuous and naïve. You think the world is a great fairy tale and that all will be well with the right attitude. I see the world as a cruel, difficult place where, if we're lucky, we may find momentary glimpses of happiness. For me, life is about struggle, hard work and living to help others.' My face pounded with the beat of my pulse. 'But I thank you for the honour of asking me. It's nice to receive a proposal again.'

Breathing deeply, I resolved to remain undeterred. The day was young. 'I understand, Aanya,' I replied. 'Life with me *is* risky. But wise ventures make life worth living. Evolution is for the bold who strive forward, not for those happy with the status quo. Yes, the world can be a place of struggle and frustration, but only for those weighed down by limitations. We understand that God is inside all of us. Our job is to teach these concepts to the rest of the world. Once the world becomes self-realized, its potential is limitless.' At my words, she smiled, but still shook her head. Undaunted, I continued. 'I figured you would say no. I respect your choices, so I will only ask you three times. If you turn me down three times, I will leave you alone, my love.

But, know this: some people are in your life for a reason or a season; others, forever. You and I are in each other's lives forever. Someday, I know we will get married again, either in this lifetime or the next.'

With that said, I moved on to speak with Aijeba. We had a discussion on the nature of trees and how we were all part of one huge organism. I was fascinated. He was extremely knowledgeable about a variety of subjects and every day taught me more about the connection between science and spirit. He believed that science does not disprove religion; in fact, that some scientists can prove the existence of God. 'The question is,' he mentioned in his calm, quiet voice, 'what is your definition of God? If you seek some kind of superhuman, you're wasting your time. But, if you look at God as a unifying, vivifying force underlying all that exists, well then...' We continued discussing this and other concepts as we journeyed back to the Kings. The Tutsis were the best. The best intellects, knowledgeable of ancient African religious teachings that went back to 2500 BC, well before Hinduism and Zoroastrianism began. The best magicians, as their ancestors had been practising magic even longer than religion. The best athletes, due to a training regimen superior to even that of the Swiss Guard. They were generally just some of the best guys to hang around with—no ego, no fuss, just focusing on living life at its most basic yet fantastic level.

Aijeba shared some of his vast wisdom with me during our conversations on the way home to Mumbai. He told me, 'When one truly lives in the moment, that person touches eternity. It is the paradox of life that if we focus on the past or future, we miss out on the present. But if we are fully present in the moment—and I mean totally focused on that which is happening now—the past and future open to us. When we achieve perfect awareness of the present, we enter the realm of the spirit which is eternal. The here and now comprises all that has been and all that will be.'

These are the kinds of contemplative discussions that the Tutsi guides, Maha, Aanya and I engaged in on our journey. However, sometimes our talks were far more mundane. For instance, I was well aware that bets were being made behind my back between the Tutsis and Maha regarding whether or not Aanya would accept my marriage proposal. Unfortunately, no one deigned to share the odds with me.

48

Elephantine Wisdom

Pachyderms are amazing animals and, as I was reminded, telepathic. Asian elephants live an average of forty-eight years. I rode a middle-aged bull that was about twenty-four years old. He mocked me, after hearing my conversation with Aanya. Male elephants are notoriously polyamorous. *I don't know why you humans value monogamy,* he seemed to say. He snorted, *I live free, making love to whomever I want, when I want.* I told him to keep quiet; my libertine days were behind me. He stomped the ground arrogantly. *Have it your way. Your life, your headache.*

However, as we approached a dense area of the forest, he spoke up again, this time not about Aanya. He sensed danger. He simply stopped and refused to go any further. My first impulse attributed his stop to arrogance; however, I realized his seriousness. I immediately alighted and ran to Babatunde to convey the message. He told us all to stay put while he, Chacha and Aijeba investigated. After several tense minutes, they returned. My elephant was right: a band of demigods, in league with Basamia, were nearby. They were scouting us to determine if any of us had the Antahkarana. Babatunde and Maha set up a plan. She would distract them by transforming into the likeness of Basamia; then, after they had dropped their guard and came out to meet their companion, Chacha and Aijeba would attack.

Demigods are powerful but have restrictions, especially when in other forms. They are not fully human and don't have the physical strength we have. These took the form of little elf-like men, suitable for hiding in a jungle. Demigods are also overconfident when it comes to fighting humans—they don't quite understand that some of mankind is self-realized. While such men are not yet gods, they do believe that the power of the universe flows through them. Our Tutsis were such men and soon made quick work of our opponents.

Six demigods came out of hiding to greet Basamia. They gathered around her like Snow White and her dwarfs. Maha removed her Basamia veneer and the fight began. They swarmed Maha with fury. Babtunde, Chacha and Aijeba attacked them from behind as they failed to use the proper military technique with their attack. The demigods quickly recovered and turned their attacks towards the Tutsis.

Chacha and Aijeba conducted a pincer-like manoeuvre, attacking the demigods from both flanks while Babatunde struck from the middle. Although it was six against three, the Tutsis were bigger, stronger and faster. The demigods had no time to transform into something stronger; they tried desperately to use powerful magic to ameliorate their disadvantage, conjuring close-quarter bombs that, while lethal, had a very limited range. Cunningly, our guides bound them in a web of their own making, by creating virtual mirrors so the spells reversed and boomeranged back on their casters.

As the little elf-men exploded into nothingness, we left hurriedly before we attracted any more unwanted attention from wandering malevolent creatures. As we rode, I sneakily gave my elephant an extra bunch of bananas. 'Keep talking, buddy,' I whispered, 'I'm all ears.' He snaked his trunk up towards me and blew hot elephant breath into my face. I laughed, 'We don't know each other that well yet, dude.' He responded with a stomp and a sly look from the corner of his right eye. *Oh, but we do. Same mother, same father, same universe.*

Once again, we continued on our way. This time, I found myself accompanied by Babatunde. 'You made quick work of those demigods,' I commented admiringly. 'Those guys never stood a chance against you!' Babatunde was silent for a moment before responding. 'It's all about controlling the energy,' he explained eventually. 'We were able to beat them using our joint powers. We have learned to partner with the universe when we need to. In this case, we used the power of the forest to create the shield.' 'How do you mean?' I asked curiously. 'We are all one, John. Every part of the forest had an interest in our success, from the minerals deep within the rocks and the soil to the deep roots of the trees... The collective spirit of the forest made its energy available to us.'

'At any given moment,' he continued, 'if we surrender ourselves utterly to the present, everything is available to us. You have done this unconsciously throughout your life. Do you remember pulling your dad's plane back up into the air just before crashing as a child? You did that by summoning all of the surrounding energy, the energy of the sky, the cornfields, the poplar trees, even your father.' 'What?' I gasped. 'But *how?*' Babatunde smiled gently at my amazement. 'The trick is to learn how to make that contact consistently and with intention. Like with mastery of any skill, it takes hours, days, months and years of practice to learn to harness the universal energy at will. But that's not the most important part.'

Babatunde paused to navigate the elephant around a fallen tree trunk. Once we were back on the path, he resumed the lesson. 'The ultimate test is to understand the concept of energy so that you will be ready when your spirit returns into the incorruptible homogeneity of the one true universal source, a process humans erroneously refer to as "dying". The proper way to "die" is to accept that your energetic force is not dispersed but is instead becoming a part of everything—a moment of total communion with all that exists. During this process, you will recognize the various energy forces with which you have communed throughout your life.'

'Start practising now,' Babatunde advised me as we rode through the jungle. 'You should begin now so that the transition will be less difficult. Commune with everything around you—the trees, the seas, even the breeze—on a daily basis. The Antahkarana is a symbol of the bridge we can all cross to go over to the next phase prior to death. It is the Eagle's Gift of awareness, real to those who learn to use energy properly. Learn to harness energy consistently and your life will become very interesting.' At this, I laughed. 'Babatunde, I really don't know if I can *handle* a life more interesting than this.' He chuckled back at me. 'Ah, but if it is to be, what a glorious life that would be!'

49

Home Redux

The final days before we arrived in Mumbai with the Antahkarana were a blur. We were in a state of heightened awareness induced by Aijeba's magic, so all our abilities were enhanced. We moved quickly and efficiently as we negotiated the final leg of our trip. There were no more tales, no more traipsing leisurely through the jungle, no more dalliances with Aanya. We knew we were prey and acted accordingly, so that we would make it back to the Kings safely with our prize. By day nine, things began to look and smell familiar. We were nearing the city; I had never thought I would welcome the stench, but it had become my home, my stench, my city. It smelled like aspiration and achievement, sordid power and sublime holiness, a masala unique to Mumbai. I was glad it was still there, and I wondered if any of the denizens of the city had any idea how close they had come to complete annihilation. I now understood the sensibilities of generals, presidents, viceroys, policemen, doctors... All those who perform the thankless task of keeping others safe. Today, I could proudly claim my place among their ranks; I too had saved lives. Unfortunately, my efforts, like many of my brethren before me, would go unrecognized and unheralded.

We finally arrived in Mumbai close to midnight on the fourteenth day. But there was no time for pleasantries; our task must be completed before the deadline. Bereft of the hard-won friendship and intimacy we had become used to, the Tutsis acted like strangers and led us to the Council in stiff military-like fashion. Our journey was complete; they were first and foremost the Kings' guards and must thereby adhere to the proper protocol. As we entered the serpentine catacomb of halls that led back to the Council's chambers, the path this time seemed familiar. I could smell the fragrant pines and oaks burning as we neared the hearth.

We were guided to the antechamber to rest and await the Kings' presence the next morning. Despite the Tutsis' assurances, we kept the Antahkarana near us overnight to ensure its safety and so we could personally present it to the Kings. Babatunde gracefully allowed us that privilege.

The next morning dawned with much excitement. Well rested and elated about saving the ashram, we were looking forward to fulfilling the terms of our agreement by presenting the Antahkarana to the nine Kings. Aanya was also uncharacteristically excited, smiling and speaking only in superlatives, which was definitely not her norm. But, despite her usual pragmatism, I guess even she could not help but rejoice after our successful journey. A sumptuous breakfast awaited us upon awakening, with a fruit salad filled with karonda, carambolas, pomegranates, guava and sweet purple jamuns, pancakes served with blackberry syrup and sliced ham—although I declined the latter as being a little too close to cannibalism for comfort. Aanya laughed. 'Go ahead, *nol gahori*, you know you want to.' But, after having been one, of course I couldn't.

After we had eaten our fill, Babatunde accompanied us to the Council chambers and struck the gong to bring the proceedings to order. 'I present the Kings of Kings, Leaders of the Nine Tribes. The Council of the Ancients shall hereby commence.' *Bong*...in walked the Yadav King, a tall man with hair liberally peppered with grey, dressed in a dark-brown long coat and a violet jewel-encrusted turban. Like Maha, he could have been either forty or seventy years old, depending on the light, although unlike her usual serene look, he had an air of intense seriousness about him. *Bong*...next came the Bishnois King, a much younger gentleman of the new breed, dressed neatly in a dark rose-coloured three-piece suit. *Bong*...a portly man in his late sixties strutted in, his appetite for life apparent in his swagger. The Meghwal King had the look of someone battle-tested and worldly. This was a man who lived in the moment, enjoying each second. He smiled at me as he walked in and I swore he gave me a wink as if to say *'Job well done, half breed.' Bong, bong, bong*...the Rajpurohit, Bhils and Meena Kings walked in as a group. Their attire was traditional with ornate tunics befitting their royal status, each adorned with peafowl feathers and other plumage from those of the shikra, the colourful Impeyan pheasant and even Aanya's other form, the serpent eagle. *Bong, bong, bong*... Finally, the Jat, Gurjar and Rajput Kings completed the nine, each receiving their clash of the gong from Babatunde as they entered the circle. An impressive group, all and all; I recognized my inquisitor, King Matsya, among them. I still could not tell if they were all physical human beings or some heavenly facsimile. They all seemed to pulse rhythmically as if they were composed of spirit rather than matter, but I could not tell if this was merely a trick of the firelight.

After they had settled around the hearth, King Matsya spoke first. 'We have conferred with the Tutsis; they have told us of your quest. According to their testimony, you all acquitted yourselves admirably during your journey. While some of you had a steeper learning curve than others...' *Was that directed at me*, I wondered. 'You succeeded as a group. Although I was concerned about you...' Here, the King paused and looked directly at me. *Ah, yes, I was right*, I thought sardonically, *he's talking about me*. 'You have outdone yourselves, communed with your true self and the universe. Your ancestors are elated.' We all smiled and bowed our heads in gratitude.

Turning his head, the King addressed me specifically. 'Good job, young man, and welcome home. I hope you will stay and continue to serve mother India as well as you have done thus far.' I rose to my feet. 'Your majesty, I very much intend to stay... especially if my lovely companion here, Aanya, will do me the honour of being my wife.' Pleasantly surprised, Matsya and the other Kings began to chuckle. 'You are indeed a bold man, John Yogacara Asanga. A public proposal is a strong move, but not necessarily the best one if your chosen love is not in agreement.' He turned to Aanya. 'What say you, Aanya Devi Ghosa, to this proposition?' Nonplussed, Aanya stared at her hands for a few seconds before lifting her face proudly to face the Council. 'Your Highness, John is a brave but impetuous man. While I do appreciate him and all that he has done for me and for my country, I am not sure he is right for me or for Mumbai. So, while I am flattered by his proposal, my focus lies on the ashram and its survival.'

The King looked thoughtfully at Aanya for almost half a minute. All were silent during his focused gaze; Aanya reddened under the scrutiny but did not avert her gaze 'My dear,' he finally declared, 'I see far more in you than you know or are aware of. I see a woman who has been sufficient for herself and for those around her for a very long time and is not used to the idea of others wishing to provide for her. I see a woman who says the time is not right, but does not deny her love for this man. I see... well, I will not tell you what else I see. I will let it unfold. Love is a strong and powerful force that survives time; it is eternal and cannot be denied or deferred.' He smiled and sat down.

The interlude over, one by one the Kings stood and praised us for our efforts. In honour of our agreement, the money to purchase the ashram was brought forward. It was clearly a moment to celebrate, but I barely heard their words, nor did I appreciate their praise. *King Matsya was right*, I thought bitterly, *a bold move can either succeed wildly or fall flat on its face.* I was flat on my face; I had done everything I could to save the ashram, risking my very life, pouring my blood, sweat and heart into this journey. What's more, I had poured my heart out to Aanya, only to have her demur as if my marriage proposal was a choice of tea or coffee that she had simply passed up.

My love, my heart, it was all I that had, and I had given it to her willingly only to have her throw it away as if it were worthless. *Father*, I lamented in my head, *I thought I made it through the storms.* I thought everything I had done had led me to this moment, of becoming one with the woman I loved. All those lonely nights in Indiana, the chicanery in Chicago and my bravery in Mumbai and Kaziranga, they suddenly all made sense. It was for her—Aanya was the reason I was brought here and tested.

Yet, she didn't care. Although I knew I'd told her I would ask her three times, I was done. I couldn't face a third rejection. I would go back to the ashram, gather my things and head back to the US After all, I was nothing if not resilient. I would find my way to a rich and fulfilling life, one far away from this stench that was no longer my stench, a city that was no longer my home. I gathered myself, thanked the Kings appropriately according to the customs and prepared to say my goodbyes.

50

Eternity Beckons

As a small token of the Kings' gratitude for having successfully completely our mission, Maha, Aanya and I were given a jitney to make our way back to the ashram. It was a rather large horse-drawn carriage with a compartment in the back for the many other gifts bestowed on us by the Nine Tribes. Thus, we arrived at the ashram with great pomp and fanfare. Although they did not understand the precise nature of what we had done, all the women and the other workers who lived there nonetheless understood that we were instrumental in saving the ashram and were appropriately grateful.

The entire community partied and feasted well into the night. We danced, we sang, we howled at the moon. I enjoyed seeing my fellow janitors one last time; they were a kind, decent group of men, living a humble yet honourable life of service. They were fulfilled. I slipped away as the moon was low in the sky, having said my goodbyes to most of them. I needed to pack and was dreading the next morning where I would have to say so long to Maha and Aanya. As much as I was devastated by Aanya's decision, I owed her a proper goodbye and I could not bear to leave without seeing her for one last time.

The next morning, I met with Maha first. I took her hands and looked deep into her eyes. She smiled sadly as if she knew what I had come for but did not speak. 'My dearest Maha,' I began, 'I cannot thank you enough for all you've done for me.

You opened my eyes and helped me come to terms with myself, my ancestors, and to finally act on behalf of others as opposed to just myself. On our journey, I felt I was truly alive for the first time in a long time, probably since I lost my father. Before our mission, I was merely a façade faking my way through life; you helped me become a real person.' Swallowing hard, I attempted to lift the sombre mood which had descended. 'Although even now, I don't understand all of the shape-shifting and wizardry! Sometimes I find it hard to believe it even happened. Years from now, as the memories fade and blur, I will probably doubt that it did.'

Maha smiled. 'Now, John, you know that it *did* happen. You know that because you believe in the universal connection, in Yoga. I want you to promise me that you will continue to hone that union between you and the One. Keep working on harnessing universal energy at will. It will serve you well until we meet again.' I felt moved to tears at the idea that I would no longer benefit from this wisdom of this wise, wonderful woman in front of me. 'Don't be sad,' she said as she patted my cheek in motherly fashion. 'We will meet again, in this life or the next.'

At that moment, her eyes looked past me to something behind me. I knew it meant that Aanya had entered the room. This was the moment I had been dreading. There was a hard, dense, thorny knot in the pit of my stomach. I could not imagine that it would ever undo itself. Turning, I walked up to the woman I loved with all my heart. So far, I had managed to look everyone in the eye during my farewells and give them a strong 'Goodbye, until we meet again', which is as close to Namaste as I could get. But this was Aanya—I simply couldn't look her in the eye and say goodbye. I knew my eyes would betray the irrepressible pain I felt at the thought that we would never be together.

I had thought I knew heartbreak. I had honestly believed that I'd had my heart broken before, first with Lucy and then, more intensely, with Nicole…but neither of those emotions were anything in comparison to how I felt now. This was the real deal. The aching in my chest was as heavy and insistent as the stomping of my loquacious elephant friend. It reverberated throughout my entire being and decimated all my thoughts. I could not think of how to begin to say goodbye to her. Thankfully, Aanya, in her inimitable fashion, was not willing to wait for me to find the words. Funnily enough, she had decided that *she* was upset with *me*. 'Listen up, you insufferable fool,' she ranted, poking her finger indignantly into my chest. 'You've barely spoken two words to me since your *ridiculous* proposal the other day in front of all those people in the Kings' chambers. How dare you! How could you do that to me?'

I was flummoxed. Slowly, my confusion turned to anger. 'How *I* could do that to *you*? What are you talking about? *You* humiliated *me* in front of Maha, the Nine Kings and our Tutsi guides!' Glaring at her, I began pacing backwards and forward. 'Oh, don't worry, princess,' I shot sardonically, 'I'm sure the story of my epic failed proposal will be one they can share forever. You can all laugh at the proud, confident American shot down by the true Indian.' At this, Aanya crossed her arms and shook her hair angrily over her shoulders. 'That's unfair. I had good reason to turn down your proposal. I turned you down because I can't trust you. I know that you're a liar.'

'What are you talking about?' I retorted. 'I had to hide my identity from everyone, not just you! Otherwise, I have *always* told you the truth. Any wrong that I may have done you can be attributed to the temporary insanity which befalls me every time I am near you, you crazy woman.' Aanya shook her head stubbornly. 'No, you're a liar, John.' Frustrated, I ran my hands through my hair and finally looked her in the eyes. 'Tell me! How have I lied to you?' In her brown eyes, I saw anger and sadness, desire and pain, and a whole myriad of emotions. I felt like it would take me a lifetime to parse the look in those beautiful eyes for meaning. 'You promised me three proposals, John. You lied.'

Silence fell between us as we stared at each other. I could not deny that I had failed to do as I had promised. But did she really expect me to go through the charade a third time, just to appease her ego? Stunned, I could not think of a way to respond. Finally, she sighed, and her shoulders loosened. There was no more anger in her voice when she next spoke. 'Listen, I'm a very private person. I don't go along with the crowd; I don't trust the things that everyone else wants to do. If I had said yes in that moment, at the height of those feelings of reverie and giddiness and adrenaline, high off of having survived and completed our mission...would you have been happy? Would it have been the answer you wanted?' I nodded wordlessly. She shook her head. 'But, John, neither you nor I nor anyone else would be able to say if that answer was given out of love or just from the excitement of being swept up in our situation.'

I considered her words. It had never occurred to me that my proposal might be taken for a spur-of-the moment decision, one based on shallow desire and the endorphins that flood the system after a near-death experience. Despite myself, I could see the sense in what she was saying. 'When I give my heart to the next man, it will be forever,' Aanya continued gravely. I swallowed and nodded. 'I understand, Aanya, and I respect your decision. I understand what you are saying.' I bowed to her and began to leave the room.

'No!' Aanya shouted, stopping me in my tracks. 'You clearly

don't understand, John.' I looked at her in pure confusion. What more could she possibly want from me? 'John, if you are a man of your word, then prove it. Ask me again.' I could not believe my ears. I looked at her, this beautiful, intelligent, wonderful, firecracker of a woman. Could this really be happening? Aanya swept her arm around, indicating our surroundings. 'This time, it's just you and me...and, of course, Maha because we're in her office. And, this time, make it a *good* proposal. Say what you really feel. I won't have any more of this "I'll stay if she'll have me" nonsense.'

At that, I smiled quickly before sobering up. Stepping close, I looked deep into Aanya's warm brown eyes, gazing directly into her soul. 'Aanya,' I confided, gently tracing the curve of her cheek with my thumb. 'You are the love of my life, the light of my light, the dawn to my sunset. I have loved you for every one of my past lives. Seeing your face, your eyes, touching your hair, smelling your fragrance—these physical impressions only refresh past recollections of the bond you and I share on a spiritual level.' I felt a small hitch in her breath as the raw sincerity in my words sunk in.

'Now, after realizing what true love is, after feeling its resonating vibrations in my heart, in every nucleus of every cell of my being, I know that I can never live without you again. I have waited too long to find you; now that I have, I cannot let you go. I know deep within your soul that you remember too. Our love is more than physical, it is spiritual. It always has been and will always be. It simply is.

'Aanya... Be my wife, here and now. Let us love each other now and forever more.' Her eyes beseeched me to ask the question. I could not wait any longer. 'Aanya, will you marry me?' I asked, every fibre of my being screaming for her response.

Aanya sighed happily, returning my hopeful gaze with a look that went past my eyes and deep within, striking the very core of my being. Finally, just as I thought my nerves would give out from the tension, she whispered gently, soulfully in my ear, 'Yes.'

We embraced, my arms wrapped tightly just under her shoulders and hers around my waist. Our lips parted and we kissed the kiss of a thousand years. At that moment, we became one. One heart, one mind, one soul. At that moment, we ceased to exist separately. We returned to forever, to each other... I was finally home.

Acknowledgements

I thank all those people I have met throughout my journey for inspiring me to write and to keep telling stories. A special thanks to Natasha Savoy Smith for her invaluable assistance with this story. She helped me organize my initial thoughts into an actual story. Thanks, Beverly Kelly, for the referral. Thank you, Pamela Painter, writer and teacher extraordinaire, for showing me the way. Brian Doyle, thank you for inspiring me to be great. I aspire to reach your level of nonchalant yet incisive communication. I know I will never get there, but it is fun trying. Cedering Fox, thank you for introducing me to Pamela and the works of Brian Doyle. Thanks to my in-laws, Floyd and Claudette, all my brothers and sister (Kimmi), friends and even enemies, as Tennyson said best, 'I am a part of all that I have met...'